Love Like Water,
Love Like Fire

Love Like Water, Love Like Fire

MIKHAIL IOSSEL

Bellevue Literary Press
New York

First published in the United States in 2021
by Bellevue Literary Press, New York

For information, contact:
Bellevue Literary Press
90 Broad Street
Suite 2100
New York, NY 10004
www.blpress.org

A list of publications where certain stories in this collection first appeared is on
page 301 and constitutes an extension of this copyright page.

Library of Congress Cataloging-in-Publication Data
Names: Iossel, Mikhail, author.
Title: Love like water, love like fire / Mikhail Iossel.
Description: First edition. | New York : Bellevue Literary Press, 2021. |
    Includes bibliographical references.
Identifiers: LCCN 2020027687 | ISBN 9781942658566 (paperback) |
    ISBN 9781942658573 (epub)
Subjects: LCSH: Soviet Union—Social life and customs—Fiction. |
    LCGFT: Short stories. | Fiction. | Autobiographical fiction.
Classification: LCC PS3559.O88 A6 2021 | DDC 813/.54—dc23
LC record available at https://lccn.loc.gov/2020027687

Bellevue Literary Press would like to thank all its generous
donors—individuals and foundations—for their support.

 This publication is made possible by the New York
State Council on the Arts with the support of Governor
Andrew M. Cuomo and the New York State Legislature.

Book design and composition by Mulberry Tree Press, Inc.

Bellevue Literary Press is committed to ecological stewardship in our book
production practices, working to reduce our impact on the natural environment.

♾ This book is printed on acid-free paper.

Manufactured in the United States of America

First Edition

1 3 5 7 9 8 6 4 2

paperback ISBN: 978-1-942658-56-6
ebook ISBN: 978-1-942658-57-3

For my daughter

Contents

Love Like Water,
Love Like Fire

The Night Andropov Died

I T WAS AN EVENING like many others. The dedicated drunks Lyokha and Olezhek, two of my fellow security guards at the Krestovsky Island Amusement Sector of the Leningrad Central Park of Culture and Leisure, were sitting at the large plywood-topped table in the main room of the Amusement Sector's administration cabin, finishing the last of the three bottles of toxic ersatz port, purchased, with money I had given them earlier in the afternoon, at the nearest liquor store—the one on Bolshaya Zelenina Street, some ten bus stops away—in exchange for their agreeing to take my shift at some unspecified point in the foreseeable future. The two could not have looked more dissimilar—Lyoukha, who was in his thirties, was flaxen-haired, flat-nosed, pale-eyed, void of any hint of muscle tone, while Olezhek, pushing sixty, presented to the world a cue ball–bald, sharp-featured countenance—yet trumping all the superficial differences between them was the simple, hard fact that they both belonged to the timeless, ageless, million-strong army of eternal Russian alcoholics.

For the past couple of hours, they had been complaining bitterly to each other about their lives. They effectively had none—no families of their own, no money, no worldly possessions to speak of, just the acrid smell of their tiny rooms in decrepit, overcrowded, communal flats—and no realistic expectations of any kind for a better, more dignified future. While they talked, I was reclining, with my eyes half-closed, in a half-broken armchair by the window, beyond which, in the dark, in the meager moonlight, covered in snow, loomed the hulking diplodocus of the city's only—and the country's oldest—roller coaster. It was enormous, ominous, and comforting at the same time. The Russian for *roller coaster* means "American Hills."

"You could always simply kill yourself," Lyokha suggested to Olezhek in a solicitous tone. "As long as there's death, there's hope. That's something always to look forward to. Don't lose heart—there's tunnel at the end of the light." Pouring out into two chipped, cheap faience cups the remains of the swill in the bottle, Olezhek shook his head, with a heavy sigh.

"Too fucking late, Lyokha. Too late. I missed my opportunity to kill myself when the time was right, and now it's too fucking late. Now I'll just have to fucking wait until it fucking happens naturally, in due course of my growing decrepitude. There is nothing to be fucking done about it now. . . . Okay, here's to merciful death." He raised his cup, with his pinkie held apart from the rest of his dirty, hirsute fingers delicately, high society–style.

"To death," Lyokha echoed, and they clinked their cups and drank greedily.

"You two should go home," I told them, yawning. "It's

late, and it's been my shift for three hours now, and I just want to lock up and go to sleep."

They turned their wistful, wet faces toward me. "Ah, traitor, traitor," Olezhek said with feeling. That's what he and several other fellow security guards there, at the Amusement Sector, called me, affectionately—"traitor to the motherland," or, simply, "traitor"—in reference to my having applied, unsuccessfully, for an émigré exit visa from the Soviet Union two and a half years earlier, right after quitting my job as an electromagnetic engineer and shortly before, in a bid to heighten my uselessness quotient, joining the shiftless pool of the shift security guards at the Amusement Sector. It was a time of bad people in power, and the worst time to be a Soviet citizen like me: a Jew, an underground writer. It was essential for me, and for people like me, to keep as low a profile as possible—and no one's profile could possibly be lower than that of a nighttime security guard at the Central Park of Culture and Leisure, charged with the duty of keeping an eye on the roller coaster.

"You, my dear traitor, you lucky bastard! You will yet see diamonds in the sky—and, maybe, in the end, manage indeed to get the hell out of here and go see Paris and Rio de Janeiro and . . . and New York and . . . oh, who the fuck knows what other wonderful places. And, even if not, if push comes to shove, you're still young, and it's not too late for you just to up and kill yourself, calmly and optimistically. You have your whole death still ahead of you, you bastard! How I fucking envy you, traitor!"

"That's so true," Lyokha piped up, mumbling, his head lolling on his chest.

"Out, Olezhek, Lyokha, out!" I told them. "I'm tired, and the American Hills and I need some privacy. We want to be left alone. Out, out. You can take the empties with you—that'll be enough for a couple of beers, come morning. You'll miss this bus. There won't be another one until midnight."

When, finally, laughing like mad children and cursing, tripping, and falling all over themselves on their way down the steep flight of stairs and out the front door, they had gone, I locked up after them and wandered aimlessly around the cabin space for a while, not quite certain what to do with myself. I didn't feel like plowing my way, with an English-language dictionary, through the book of contemporary American short stories that had been left behind, a couple of weeks earlier, by some rare wayward foreign visitor to the underground literary club to which I belonged. Sometimes, during my night shifts, one or two friends would come to the amusement park to keep me company, bearing bottles of wine, and we would while the night away drinking and talking about everything and nothing, about the humdrum lives we'd lived thus far and the imaginary ones that we hoped still lay ahead for us. This evening, however, the night air was downright frigid, and the hour was already too late for visitors.

I went back to the main room, and, with a spare key that I was not supposed to have, I unlocked the

Amusement Sector administrator's office. It was pitch-dark in there, and the stale air smelled thickly of ersatz port. It didn't take long to find what I was looking for in the desk's cluttered bottom drawer: an old portable VEF Spidola, the compact yellow plastic box with black trim and an intensely green cat's eye of a dial, the exact replica of one that I, and millions of other Soviet citizens, had at home.

Back in the main room, I turned the radio on. The air filled instantly with a forest's worth of joyous sounds. Here, in this remote, wooded, scarcely populated part of Leningrad, you could actually get a few foreign stations on the radio. The routine beastlike howling of the KGB jamming frequencies—which suppressed the shortwave radio broadcasts in Russian by "enemy voices" in larger residential areas along the giant city's irregularly shaped perimeter—was muted, depleted of energy, and disinterested in itself, as though unwilling to carry out its patriotic duties.

I had three "enemy voices" in Russian to choose from: the Voice of America, the BBC, and the German Wave. (Radio Liberty, deemed the most perniciously and openly anti-Soviet by the Soviet counterpropaganda officials, was unintelligible everywhere in Leningrad.) They were playing moody jazz on the German Wave. The BBC, disappointingly, offered an in-depth overview of the contemporary London art scene. The Voice of America, however, was a different matter. As soon as I tuned it up, I heard the broadcaster saying, in a baritone too melodious and a

Russian too correct to belong to someone living in the chaotic midst of it, "The official sources in Moscow are unofficially reporting the death of General Secretary Yuri Andropov, after a long . . ." Yuri Vladimirovich Andropov: the refined, bespoke suit–wearing, tennis-loving, single-malt scotch–sipping, terrible poetry–writing head of the KGB; Brezhnev's successor at the helm of power in the Soviet Union; "the butcher of Budapest," who crushed the 1956 Hungarian uprising.

At that point, as though suddenly realizing that there were dramatic circumstances at hand, the local jamming installations swung into action, commencing to howl and ululate with a doubled fury. I gave the dial a few quick nudges and heard nothing but the same enraged howling everywhere, as though the world had suddenly been taken over by a giant pack of wounded wolves caught in a blizzard.

I went back into the administrator's office and returned the Spidola to the desk drawer. In the dark, I lifted the receiver of the massive black beetle of a telephone and, bringing it to my ear, heard nothing but silence. The line, as usual at night, was dead. I was alone in this tiny world of mine, holed up in my cabin. As far as the rest of the world was concerned, I did not exist. And anyway, there was no one with whom I could share and discuss the news of Andropov's death—not any of my friends, who likely had gone to bed already; and not with my girlfriend, who lived clear across town, at least forty minutes and five rubles away by cab, and had no phone in her one-room apartment.

Restless, I returned to the main room, switched off the unshaded yellow light there, and stood by the window for some time, with my forehead pressed against the frosty windowpane, contemplating the roller coaster's hulking, snow-covered mass, placidly mysterious in the pale moonlight. There was nothing for me to think or feel. Something was happening; something was going to happen—that much I knew. I couldn't wait for the morning to come.

I winked at the roller coaster, feeling a protective warmth toward it. "You stupid thing, you be well," I said. It just sat there.

"*Andropov est mort*," I said aloud—in French, for some reason. My voice sounded hoarse, wild in the night's solitude.

If someone—some lost, ersatz port–begotten ghost—materializing before me at that moment had told me that, thirty years later, I would be writing about Andropov's death in English, in America, on the week when post–Soviet Russia's ruling class—made up, to a considerable extent, of the old KGB cadre—would be celebrating the hundredth anniversary of his birth with a large exhibit dedicated to his life, at whose opening a glowing telegram from his spiritual successor, President Vladimir Putin, would be read—well, I would have known for certain that I had finally and irrevocably, once and for all, lost my mind.

I went along the hall and into the room where the security guards slept while on duty—which, of course, they were not supposed to do—on the long, narrow leatherette couch with uneven, cracked skin. Taking off my sweater, I rolled it into a semblance of a pillow, lay down on the couch, with my head propped on it, and then picked up from the floor by the couch and covered myself with the stinking ancient communal goatskin that my Amusement Sector colleagues used as a makeshift blanket.

I thought that I would have difficulty falling asleep, given the state that I was in, but this was not the case. I was out like a light the instant I closed my eyes.

Some of the World Transactions My Father Has Missed Due to His Death on September 14, 1999

T HE ELECTION of former KGB operative Vladimir Putin as president of Russia. Boris Yeltsin's peaceful retirement. The second war in Chechnya. George W. Bush's dubious electoral victory over Al Gore. War with Iraq. His widow's wearing all black for more than a year. *"Death is something that happens to other people," wrote the late, great Joseph Brodsky.* The death, at sixty-five, of Judith Campbell Exner, the reputed mistress of both Mafia leader Sam Giancana and President John F. Kennedy. *Cecil Rhodes's last words: "So little done, so much to do."* The sentencing to death, in Bryan, Texas, of Lawrence Russell Brewer, one of the murderers of James Byrd, Jr., of Jasper. His older son's purchase of an oxblood red Subaru SUV. Céline Dion's becoming the recipient of a star on Canada's Walk of Fame in Toronto, Ontario. *"When a man dies, you see, along with him dies his whole century," wrote the objectionable Soviet poet Yevgeny Yevtushenko. The words* man *and* century *rhyme in Russian.* The terrorist attack on New York's World Trade Center. *William Saroyan's last words: "Everybody has got to die, but I have always believed an exception would be made in my case. Now what?"* War with the Taliban government in Afghanistan. His family's perpetual regret over their inability to recall his last words. *Cotton Mather's last words: "Is this dying? Is this all? Is this what I feared when I prayed against a hard death? Oh, I can bear this! I can bear this!"* Remnants of Hurricane Floyd's bringing of torrential rains to the eastern seaboard, resulting in rainfall records being broken throughout the Mid-Atlantic and the Northeast and the declaration of the state of emergency in Pennsylvania, New Jersey, Maryland, and Delaware. *James Thurber's last words: "God bless ... God damn."* His three-year-old grandaughter's signing off after a telephone conversation with his widow: "Lotsa love." *John Quincy Adams's last words: "This is the last of earth! I am content."* The Love and Hope Ball at the Fountainebleau Hilton Hotel, at which Barry Gibb, of the Bee Gees, performed a "Night of Sinatra." *Archimedes' last words: "Wait till I have finished my problem!"* The population of planet Earth reaching six billion. His older son's purchase of an amazingly inexpensive three-story oxblood redbrick house in upstate New York. *Yukio Mishima's last words: "Human life is limited, but I would like to live forever."* The premiere of *Saturday Night Fever* on Broadway, with the Bee Gees donating one hundred opening-night tickets and one hundred invitations to a celebrity party after the premiere to MusiCares. *Pancho Villa's last words: "Don't let it end like this. Tell them I said something."* Van Halen's announcement that Gary Cherone was no longer the band's lead singer. The great American writer Eudora Welty's death. His older son's apparent inability to come to terms with the ineluctable reality of his getting older. *Beethoven's last words: "Friends, applaud, the comedy is over!"* East Timor gaining independence. His twenty-year-old granddaughter's staunch refusal to relocate to the United States, despite the fact of her being legally entitled to the status of a green card holder, owing to her father's recently acquired U.S. citizenship; her superficial claim that "life is more fun in Russia these days than it is in America." *Leonard Bernstein's last words: "What's this?"* The stock-market roller coaster. The sensational success of the quasi-lesbian Russian pop duo t.A.T.u. in the West; its participants' lengthy kiss on *The Tonight Show with Jay Leno*, both women wearing white T-shirts emblazoned with an extremely crude expression in Russian, meant to register their antiwar stance. *Anne Boleyn's last words: "Oh God, have pity on my soul!"* His younger son's persistent stomachaches, ultimately revealed to be the result of stress. The deaths, in fairly rapid succession, of three of his old friends, also one-time prominent Soviet scientists in the field of submarine electromagnetism, as well as those of several hundred million other human beings; trillions upon trillions of unregistered, undocumented, unnoticed deaths among the mosquito, dung beetle, fish, dog, cat, goat, etc., population of the planet Earth. His younger son's growing vinegariness. The Russian *Kursk* submarine tragedy. His mother's heartfelt statement: "When am I going to die already? What's wrong with me?" Rhode Island Senator John

Chaffee's death, at seventy-seven. *Lenny Bruce's last words: "Do you know where I can get any shit?"* The hostage crisis in Moscow. The death, at sixty-one, of the singer and songwriter Hoyt Axton ("Joy to the World"). *Cassanova's last words: "I have lived as a philosopher and die as a Christian."* Shania Twain's purchase of a magnificent chalet in Switzerland. His older son's four trips to Russia, four to Africa. His older son's intermittent drinking. *Picasso's last words: "Drink to me!"* His widow's two trips to Canada and three to Russia. His younger son's three trips to Russia, two to Europe. The death, at seventy-one, of Lonnie Donegan, Britain's first pop superstar. The crash of American Airlines Flight 587. *Chekhov's last words: "It's been a long time since I've had champagne."* The whole Harry Potter thing. The sale of his house in Boston. Hasim Rahman's beating of Lennox Lewis. His younger son's apparent inability to live up to his parents' expectations of him. Lennox Lewis's subsequent brutal beating of Hasim Rahman. The discovery of two supermassive black holes, each with the mass of at least a million suns, circling each other in a single butterfly-shaped galaxy. *Hart Crane's last words: "Good-bye, everybody."* The sinking of the oil tanker *Prestige,* 150 miles off the coast of Spain. *Georges Danton's last words: "Show my head to the people. It is worth seeing."* The anthrax scare. Lennox Lewis's seemingly effortless knocking out of Mike Tyson. *Darwin's last words: "I am not the least afraid to die."* Two—or is it three?—new James Bond movies. *Emily Dickinson's last words: ". . . the fog is rising."* Slobodan

Milošević's standing trial before the UN war crimes tribunal in The Hague. *Dylan Thomas's last words: "Eighteen straight whiskies—I think that's a record."* John "the Teflon Don" Gotti's death, at sixty-one. Fifty-six-year-old Scotsman David McCrae's death from rabies, the first such occurrence in a century in Britain. *Theodore Dreiser's last words: "Shakespeare, I come!"* The Enron debacle. His older son's considering himself an abject failure, during a bout of depression. *Huey P. "the Kingfish" Long's last words: "I wonder why he shot me."* The *Columbia* shuttle disaster. *Isadora Duncan's last words: "Farewell, my friends. I go to glory!"* George Harrison's death. The great saxophonist Grover Washington's death. The great punk rocker Joe Strummer's death. Dozens of suicide bombings in Israel and in Chechnya. *Thomas Alva Edison's last words: "It's very beautiful over there."* The euro becoming the legal currency of twelve European countries. *Douglas S. Fairbanks's last words: "Never felt better."* The Bee Gee Maurice Gibb's death. *Archduke Franz Ferdinand's last words: "It is nothing. It is nothing."* The AOL–Time Warner merger. The AOL–Time Warner merger dissolution. The ban on foxhunting in Britain. *Genghis Khan's last words: "Let not my end disarm you, and on no account weep or keen for me, lest the enemy be warned of my death."* The whole Eminem thing. The Kmart bankruptcy. *Goethe's last words: "More light! More light!"* The whole human-cloning thing. *Theodore Roosevelt's last words: "Please put out the light."* His being buried in San Francisco—on the other end of the planet from the only city he ever loved in his life—Leningrad. *Lord Byron's last words: "Good night."* The great Swedish children's writer Astrid Lindgren's death. *Che Guevara's last words: "I know you have come to kill me. Shoot, coward. You are only going to kill a man."* Her Royal Highness the Princess Margaret's peaceful death in her sleep. *Heine's last words: "Write . . . write . . . pencil . . . paper!"* The great British comedian Spike Milligan's death. The great Borscht Belt comedian Milton Berle's death. The great film comedian Dudley Moore's death. The great tragic actor Rod Steiger's death. The great Shakespearean actor Sir Alec Guinness's death. The ever-virginal Peggy Lee's death. *O. Henry's last words: "Don't turn down the light. I'm afraid to go home in the dark."* The disappearance of both of those names—Leningrad and the USSR—from every up-to-date map of the world. *Franz Kafka's last words: "Kill me, or else you are a murderer!"* The death of Her Majesty Queen Elizabeth the Queen Mother, at 101. *Karl Marx's last words: "Go on, get out! Last words are for fools who haven't said enough!"* The world's general propensity for going to hell in a handbasket. His youngest granddaughter's unaccountable utter lack of interest in unicorns. *Nostradamus's last words: "Tomorrow, I shall no longer be here."* *Peter Abelard's last words: "I don't know."*

I don't know.
Everything—and nothing.

Necessary Evil

"SON," THEY SAID, "sit down. We have something important to tell you."

I sat down.

Intensely yellow and warm was the light in the kitchen. The irrepressibly upbeat song "Fourteen Minutes to Lift-off"—an unofficial anthem of the Soviet cosmonaut squad, all nine of those great Soviet heroes to date—was playing distantly on the wall-mounted radio, a ship-shaped off-white plastic box of futuristic proportions.

The radio, turned to low, was always on in the kitchen.

"Son," they said, "you're a big boy now. Before too long, your age will be expressed in double digits. The world will not keep on hiding the unkind side of its face from you forever. It's time for you to know the bitter truth: Unfortunately, you're a Jew."

"Oh wow," I said. "Are you sure?" It was as though someone evil—it would have to be an elf, given the smallness of my size—creeping up on me from behind had smacked me on the back of the head with a small burlap sack full of rotten potatoes.

For a short while, I just sat there in silence, at a loss for words.

"Caravans of rockets, my friends, will shuttle us from star to star, I believe!" Mark Bernes, my old Bolshevik grandfather's favorite performer and his fellow Great Patriotic War veteran, soulfully recitative, continued to rejoice mutedly on the radio, in his soft, raspy baritone. I wondered momentarily what it must feel like—to be able not to understand the words of that or any other of the songs played on a daily basis on the radio. It had to feel weird, but good.

A small black ant, entirely improbable at this time of year and seemingly stunned into deep grogginess by the very fact of its own sole survival, materializing out of nowhere, was making its laborious way diagonally across the crimson oilcloth covering the Formica-topped kitchen table. The little creature's fate was hanging in the balance of my benevolence. I decided to let it live on.

According to the calendar, it was spring already in our hemisphere, if a very early one still; but in Leningrad—the world's northernmost city with a population of over one million, after all—winter still reigned supreme. Outside, beyond the frostbitten double-paned kitchen window, sealed shut until late April by multiple layers of homemade starch glue and cotton-padded isolation tape, lay, in impenetrable darkness, the desolate Cosmonauts Avenue—our fast-growing Upper Kupchino microdistrict's main street—along with all the rest of the vast snow-blanketed wasteland of the giant city's far-flung southwestern outskirts.

"I so wish I could go back in time right now, just to a minute or two ago, so that I could unhear what you just said," I said finally, clearing my throat. "But I guess that would be impossible. Well, at least now I know, I suppose, why my nose is bigger and crookeder than those of almost all of my friends. Everybody knows Jews have big noses. . . . Let me understand, though," I went on, feeling strangely distant from myself, as though lost in the middle of a desert. "When everybody—well, *almost* everybody— talks about how Jews are these unbelievably bad, horrible, disgusting, evil people, just the worst of the worst, the lowest of the low, vicious and traitorous and deceitful and arrogant and altogether despicable, rotten baby-blood drinkers, ratlike in their grubby greediness, constantly plotting and conspiring to dupe and swindle and otherwise cause as much harm as possible to the poor, naïve, and too kindhearted Russian people—well, that would be me they talk about, right?"

They exchanged quick glances. "Us," they said, correcting me softly. "All of us. You and us. We're all in the same boat on this, together. It's important to keep that in mind. You only are a Jew because of us. And we are Jews because of our parents. We're all Jews, you know: you, us, our parents, our parents' parents, our parents' parents' parents, our parents' parents' parents' pa—"

"I get it," I said.

On the radio, someone shrill and stuttering from too much happiness was carrying on about how last year had been additionally meaningful and special because it had marked the forty-seventh anniversary of our Great October Socialist Revolution of November 7, 1917, the most momentous event in the world's history—and in 1917, how old was Lenin? That's right: also forty-seven! What a fateful coincidence! Then, with barely a second's pause, the husky-voiced, French-speaking young Leningrader of Polish descent, the beautiful Edita Piekha, and her supporting vocal-instrumental ensemble, Friendship, launched into their popular new song, in which she repeatedly kept telling the nameless man of her dreams that, due to him, her world had become a narrow cone of white light, with him at the top of it.

"Jews!" they said insistently, leaning into me closely. "Jews! Jews-Jews! Jews! Go ahead, wince away! It is an unlovely, grating word, we know—a hungry crow of a word: *evrey*—but you must keep repeating it inside your head, over and over again, until you get used to it completely and accept and embrace it unreservedly, because it defines by far the most important part of you! Later, when the natural shock you're in right now subsides, you will have to learn to be proud of it, too—this unfortunate congenital detriment of your being a Jew—if you want to spend the rest of your life walking with your head held high through the unremitting rain of hate and vicious ridicule. Be proud of being a Jew, bizarre as that may sound now! Jew! Jew-Jew! Say it! Repeat after us! Jew! Jew-Jew!"

"Jew! Jew-Jew!" I said quietly. "Jew-Jew-Jew."

"Jew-Jew-Jew! Say it louder!" they commanded. "We can't hear you! Louder!"

"Jew! Jew-Jew! Jew!" I yelled. "Jew-Jew-Jew!"

"Okay, maybe not quite that loud. Tone it down," they said, smiling. "You'll wake up your little brother, and someone might hear you out on the landing, too."

"Jew-Jew-Jew!" I hollered. "Jew-Jew!"

"Keep it quiet, you silly little Jew!" they said, laughing. "Shut your mouth, Jew!"

"Dying won't do you any good," said the radio, chuckling.

"Are you sure, though?" I said, lowering my voice. "Can you actually guarantee me we are not, in fact, those very bad, evil people everybody says we are? Can we even know ourselves what kind of people we are, if we are bad and evil people from birth, and as such have no other choice but to be evil and bad? Are we not always just who we are? The snake has no other choice but to be a snake, or the wolf a wolf—or the hyena a hyena. Those animals have no idea that lots of people fear and loathe them. If everybody around us says we are bad and evil people, then who are we to say that isn't so? We all know that Soviet people can be wrong separately, but never jointly, as a group. A group of Soviet people is always smarter than just one person, no matter how smart. The larger the group, the smarter it is, obviously—the greater its collective rightness. Everybody knows that. Well, then . . . What if the overall number of Soviet people convinced that Jews are bad and evil creatures is greater than the total number of us, Jews, and those non-Jews who don't hate us? What if we simply are deluding . . . well, lying to ourselves? I'm just trying to understand. It's like this: Most Soviet people are convinced, it looks like, that Jews are never to be trusted, not under any circumstances, because they—us, Jews—are born traitors, who lie constantly and as naturally as they breathe. Well. If what they, all those Soviet people, believe about us is true—which it must be, because the numbers probably are on their side—and we, Jews, do indeed lie about everything to everybody, all the time, without even knowing it, simply because lying is our way of telling the truth, well, then we also, just as easily and unknowingly, must be lying to ourselves, right? That would only make sense. And if we, Jews, are in fact constantly lying to ourselves, just as a matter of being who we are, then we simply cannot ever believe anything we may believe we believe! That's just logical. I, for instance, after what you've told me, don't know if I can continue holding on to my belief that, even as a mere harmless little boy, I am not, nevertheless, a horribly bad, evil person. I am a—"

"Nonsense!" they burst in angrily, looking at me with a mix of indignation and dismay. "Hogwash! Don't you ever give in to this defeatist mode of thinking! You're the best goddamn little boy in the whole world! It's those who hate us, separately and jointly, sight unseen, who are bad, evil people! Ignorant, miserable, hateful! Disgusting, vicious losers! Unfortunately, between us, there still are quite a few bad, ignorant, evil, hateful people—many millions of them in this goddamn great country of ours! Presumably, they'll all just die out, like the dinosaurs, before we're supposed to enter the era of communism. What a joke—don't tell anybody we said this." They gave a little chuckle and looked at themselves with meaningful reproach, shrugging their shoulders guiltily and shaking their heads.

"Let's cut to the chase," they continued in a business-like tone. "Here is the truth of the situation: In terms purely practical, your being a Jew means, in essence, that in order merely to stay on a par with your peers, all the Soviet non-Jews, gradeswise and otherwise, all through the rest of your life, you will have to work twice as hard, be twice as conscientious and diligent, constantly applying yourself to the best of your ability, jaws clenched, proverbial bullet bitten, belt tightened, shoulder against the old grindstone—unless, that is, you are some kind of genius, an Einstein or Landau, which, frankly, you are not, because no one is. You just have a very good, hungry memory and are a quick learner, in addition to possessing this odd, random capacity for spelling correctly even the words the meaning of which you don't know, but that's a whole separate story. . . ."

They chewed their lips thoughtfully. "Of course, you could instead take the opposite path, an easier one," they went on, frowning and waving contemptuously, "and spend your life wallowing in self-pity, wailing in despair, flailing your arms, beating your chest, and tearing at your hair mentally, while calling out to the empty sky, 'Why me? Why? Why, the sky? Why not someone else? Why did it have to be me? Why such cruel unfairness?' Well, big man—it's your life to live, you know. It will be entirely up to you to decide which . . ."

". . . In the heady atmosphere of steadily mounting historical optimism, the Soviet people are preparing to celebrate the year's most romantic and feminine holiday: the International Day of Working Women!" the radio exclaimed breathily. "The eyes of the entire progressive humankind are focused on Moscow! Today, in the Kremlin, the world's first woman cosmonaut, Valentina Nikolayeva Tereshkova, our heroic Soviet white-winged seagull, met with the delegation of young women partisans from brotherly North Vietnam, whose indomitable freedom-loving people, on behalf of the entire progressive humankind, are waging their historic heroic battle against the dark forces of planetary evil, epitomized by the egregiously pernicious United States of America: that quickly disintegrating outpost of international imperialism, with its giant sproutlike military-industrial complex and its Pentagon and Wall Street. . . ."

"But—yes, why? Why, though? Why, indeed? Why me? Why?" I wailed in despair, mentally tearing at my hair. "Why did it have to be us? That's so . . . unfair!"

"Because!" they snapped, fuming—and causing me to withdraw my hand quickly from the tabletop, as I'd had a fleeting feeling they were going to slap it. "The answer to your silly, pointless question is—because! We are Jews because Jews we are! How's that for an answer? If Jews must exist in the world—and exist they do, which means that exist they must—then there also have to be people in the world, chosen from among all other people, who would be them—Jews. And it's us. It's as simple as that. You understand? It just happened so. Somebody has to be them—Jews—and that means anybody. Anybody could be them! Why not us? If not us, who? And if somebody has to be us, it makes sense additionally for that somebody to be us, right? No, wait. . . . Well, whatever. It just fell upon us to be Jews. Just your typical Jewish bad luck. Just joking. Bad luck, after all, is the same as good luck, only it's bad instead of good. Right? We just have been negatively lucky. Negatively lucky. Yes, that's it. That's no big deal, though. Life is unfair, you say? On the contrary, it is perfectly fair—once the basic fact of its essential unfairness has been accepted and internalized. Some people are born tall and beautiful, while others, short and ugly. That's life for you—a mere chaotic interplay of random chances and probabilities. Some people are gifted from birth with an angelic singing voice or extraordinary athletic ability, or a brilliant scholarly mind, while many others, sadly, emerge into the world with a cleft palate, or an incomplete set of fingers, or a clubfoot. Think of your being a Jew in terms of having been born with a clubfoot—unfortunate, of course, but not the end of the world. On the contrary, as we just suggested, it could even end up working to your long-term advantage, as the single most powerful motivating factor in your life. *Per aspera ad astra,* clubfooted champ, whatever that expression means. Just keep plowing your way through the onion field of life, steadily and single-mindedly—and don't concern yourself with the extraneous circumstances over which you have zero control. Why are we Jews? Because. Because Jews we are. Because we are not not-Jews. That's all you need to know. We were born as Jews, all of us, unbeknownst to ourselves, without having been asked first for our opinion on the matter—and at some point in the course of our respective childhoods, in one way or another, we, too, were made aware of our being Jews. One could say—if one were a philosopher or writer or some such—that we are the involuntary, accidental Jews ... the designated ones. ... Yes, that's it: the designated Jews—ones having been identified and entered as such, by the rulers of our destinies or whatever, on the old ethnicity line, fifth from the top, in our Soviet hammers and sickles, as you will be also, when the time comes for you to be issued your own Soviet passport, in a little over six years. ... Only six! How time flies! Then only—when you see that little word, *Jew,* glaring at you, with mocking jauntiness, from your hammer and sickle's front page—will you, too, become the real, genuine, no-nonsense, true-blue, irreversible Soviet Jew: one who only is a Jew because he knows he's a Jew, and also because he knows in his bones that he is a Jew solely for the reason of having been chosen at random, designated to be one, a Soviet Jew. That's how it happens. Strange, isn't it? Well, not really strange, but . . . strange, isn't it? Knowing is tantamount to being. Knowing is being, in our case. We could not be what and who we are without having been told first we are it. You are told you are something, someone—and then you are it. Yes. That's how it works. You become it. You just have no other choice. That's us in a nutshell. Think about it: We, Soviet Jews, are no different from anybody else in the Soviet Union, in any meaningful way—well, maybe, indeed, as you mentioned earlier, our noses are bigger than most other people's, and we tend to speak Russian a little better and excel at sciences more—and yet, at the very same time, we are very different, and how, because we know we are different, we have been told so! Had we not known we were different— well, any different we would not have been. But knowing that we are—we are. . . . Moreover, it just occurred to us—and this feels like an important thought, actually— we are substantively different, at this point, too, because in the process of absorbing and internalizing the knowledge of our being different, and as a result of that process, we have, willy-nilly, become different. Wondering about the ways in which you are supposed to be different from other people makes you different, see? In other words—okay, all right, we're going to shut up now, promise—one's having been informed, by the ultimate rulers-shmulers of one's destiny and in the most categorical of manners, of one's having been designated randomly as something inevitably leads to one's becoming just that, indeed, sooner or later.

Yes. It's as simple as that. Mind you, that does not mean we actually know just how, exactly, in what specific way we are different; we just know we are. We are . . ."

It was very warm in the kitchen. My head was swimming pleasantly. "Jew-Jew-Jew," said the radio sweetly, in the voice of our elementary school homeroom teacher, Ninel Vilenovna. "Jew-Jew. You people. You . . . You people. I just don't get you, I swear. Cross my heart. So stuck-up. Always putting yourselves ahead and above everyone else. Like you're smarter than everybody or something. You people. You make me sick. Don't get me wrong, I like you personally very much, and some of my best friends are . . . But—oh my. Seriously. Sometimes you people, you . . . you just repulse me." Then Tamara Miansarova, known to everybody throughout the Soviet land, and possibly throughout the whole world also, as the original performer of the most famous and beloved children's song ever—one about the little boy who drew the sun in the sky on a piece of paper and then wrote in the corner additionally that he really wished the sun and the sky and his mom and he himself were to exist forever and *blah, blah, blah*—launched into her second-most-popular number, one of the radio's current top favorites, characterized by a nauseatingly infectious tune and presented in the form of a one-sided conversation with a forest mushroom, of the humble *ryzhik* variety, which she inexplicably kept inviting us to come closer to so it all the sooner could be picked and end up in an appropriately pickled state. Mid-song—after yet another round of the rowdy "rudy-rudy-rudy-rudy-rits," and in Russian, "*ryzhik!*" roulade—she suddenly stopped and said matter-of-factly yet in a distinctly accusatory tone, "By the way, Mark Bernes also is a Jew."

"Look, he's crying," they said, sounding worried. "Crying without tears, Chekhov-like, although . . . well, that would be the other way around, wouldn't it. Whatever. Is he falling asleep? Strange—it's not even that late, and they'll start showing the figure skating world championship on television in a half hour, from America, and tonight it's the pairs night, and he would never want to miss Belousova and Protopopov. . . . He probably is just overwhelmed by . . . all this, you know. He's just a little boy. Maybe we shouldn't have . . . Maybe it wasn't such a good idea after all. . . . Maybe we've gone too . . . Hey, big man, are you falling asleep or what? Or are you crying or something?"

"I'm awake, and I'm not a little boy, and I'm not crying," I said, crying a little, without tears and without really feeling sad. "And it's not the pairs. . . ."

"Of course you're not!" they exclaimed, slapping me lightly, cautiously on the shoulder. "We never would've thought such a thing! We know you better than that! You're the champ! You're our future Yuri Gagarin! You . . . Well, we're proud of you! Okay, but . . . You know what? Listen! Can we tell you something? There is much more, as it happens, to the . . . Well, there's another side to the story, in short, to everything we've just told you! To this whole thing, you know. Yes, and it's a good thing, too! Really, really good! You'll like it! We guarantee! We . . . Well, we're going to share with you, big man, the only true, secret, extremely important and top secret information about why—well, why in fact we are Jews. Yes. Are you interested? Ooh, you bet you are! We can tell! Why would we even ask, right? . . . You know what, though? First you'll have to promise, to swear, you know, to keep mum about it, that great secret, on pain of—let us think—having Americans drop their atomic bomb, that's right, right on top of Lenin's tomb in Red Square? Ha ha, just joking. On pain of not being able to play soccer with your friends for a week— how's that? Would you promise to keep mum like . . . like a fish smacked headfirst on lake ice, that's right, about what we're about to divulge to you? You must never, ever tell anybody, because, as we've just told you, this happens to be one of the world's most important and secret secrets when it comes to the eternal worldwide struggle between the forces of good and evil, and so . . . well, you know, if someone even remotely or unknowingly affiliated with the forces of evil were to get wind of it and then just as accidentally pass it on along the chain of command or what have you, straight up to the evil forces' top leadership . . . That would be so incredibly bad, we don't even know how to express it adequately in words. . . . You promise, then?"

Leaning back against the cool ridge of the kitchen wall, painted salad green, with my eyes closed, I nodded weakly.

"We knew we could rely on you! Good boy! Listen, then!" They switched to a whisper. Hot on my face was their hasty breath. "We are Jews because such was the extremely secret and covert and top secret assignment that we, Jews, or only future Jews back then, received many thousands of years ago, maybe ten or more or who knows how many, at the time of the human race's just coming into existence, yes, from the secret, underground, omnipotent, worldwide, cosmic organization with no known name tasked with the responsibility of oversee-ing and supporting in any way possible the multifaceted force for good on our planet. Being Jews, in other words, is the extremely important and secret quest and whatnot we have been on ever since: tirelessly to serve . . . tirelessly . . . tirelessly to serve the eternal cause of humanity and so on, as the covert agents of that cosmic force for good we just mentioned, only—and there's the rub, so to speak—disguised as the collective embodiment of, you guessed it, human evil, deep inside the enemy territory, yes, of humankind's dark side. Pretty neat, huh? Thus, simply put, throughout history we Jews have been performing the crucially important function of being, you know, this universally agreed-upon, by all the peoples, object of hatred: the animate bull's-eye, if you will, for the aggre-gate human animus, the singularly towering lightning rod for humankind's free-floating and constantly overflowing vicious anger . . . the latter of which, if left unchecked and allowed, you know, to spread uncontrollably in every direction, like some noxious primordial black ooze, would destroy our civilization, and all of us along with it, in no time flat. We, collectively, are humankind's punching bag, unique safety valve for the surfeit of human evil, invisible giant vacuum cleaner, or else this humongous, you know, million-strong perambulatory bipedal magnet for the excess of darkness in human hearts, or . . . well, whatever other similar metaphors you can come up with: human-kind's secret blood cleanser in the form of a giant Jewish canary in a coal mine? No matter . . . In any event, there you have it! Now you know! Such is the totally amaz-ing nature of our extremely secret mission! We, of course, would be remiss not to let you know that it is a plenty dangerous cross to bear, too. There is no need to sugar-coat it, leaving you potentially with the wrongful impres-sion this is all just some sort of inspirational make-believe historic costume drama. Now and then, periodically, and regularly, the united forces of evil overtake us, along with the rest of the human race, prevailing for some unpredict-able length of time completely over the entire world—and that leads to truly terrible, catastrophic consequences, for us as a whole. Unspeakably tragic. We're being serious now. Suffice it to say that if our history, the history of Jews as a people, were to be summed up in just one word, that word would be *Tragedy*, with a capital *T*. Yes. But—well, not to sound pompous or anything—there is just no other path for us in life. Seriously. We are who we are. We are . . . But you already know who we are. We are . . . Okay, listen: As far as the world at large is concerned, you know, in terms of balancing what on the whole it thinks about us against what we Jews understand about ourselves, it could be said that we are, well, you know—one could say we are the necessary evil. Yes, that's it. Necessary evil. That's right. The opposite of evil, but perceived by many, if not most, as evil. The secretly good evil, which . . . which actually is quite a concept, huh? We don't expect you to understand right away, at this point, because we don't quite understand it ourselves, either, but . . . Necessary evil—that means goodness, only a victimized, like, martyred one. The secret, hidden, misunderstood good, perennially hated and vilified: That's us. Yup. No bull. We are the ultimate, if involuntary, martyrs for the cause of good. Think about it! What calling could possibly be nobler? Not one, let us tell you—not even close! Feeling better now? Beginning to feel proud yet of your specialness, and of how unbelievably lucky, too, you and all of us are, really, even despite and in full recognition and acceptance of our obvious inescapable deep misfortune? By the way, do we still have a piece of that boiled tongue left in the fridge? For some reason it . . ."

Their words were the shining, lightning-quick little black snakes flitting and darting to and fro on the inner side of my eyelids before shooting upward to burrow without a trace into my brain.

"Well, big boy who doesn't cry," they said with forced cheeriness, "what say you we just put a lid on all this talking for now—enough talking, we say!—and instead go watch some world-championship figure skating from America? With our favorite magicians of ice, Belousova and Protopopov? Aren't you glad we have a television set? Aren't you glad we had this little conversation, too? Knowing is always better than not knowing, except in the cases when it isn't. Aren't you glad to be alive? Just joking . . . well, not really. In the meantime, some of us will try to finish already that pesky little article that should've been . . ."

"It's the dancing night there tonight," I muttered under my breath, feeling unconquerably sleepy. "It will, of course, be the Czechs, brother and sister Eva Romanová and Pavel Roman, winning the gold, which is pretty funny, because . . ."

Shining, lightning-quick little black snakes, darting to and fro on the inner side of my eyelids, then burrowing in the dirty-gray ugly mound of my brain.

"Oh! Dear boy! We love you so much!" they cried quietly, sniffling. "We're so sorry we overdid it! We can be such fools sometimes. Such fools! We just got carried away. We are so sorry!"

"In our Soviet reality, life invariably outpaces even the most daring of Soviet people's dreams!" the radio enunciated sternly.

"I want to go back," I said from afar.

Then everything went dark, disappeared before my eyes.

In impenetrable darkness, I awoke with a start, damp with sweat. I was engulfed by unaccountable strong fear. I could tell, somehow, that the hour was very late—as late as it possibly could be without beginning to bleed into the same pitch-blackness of meager dawn. It crossed my mind then that I had never been awake this late before, or this early. Everyone was asleep in the world—or at least the small part of the world of which I was a tiny particle: the desolate Cosmonauts Avenue, our far-flung Upper Kupchino microdistrict, plus the roiling, overcrowded, anger-filled midtown neighborhood of my very first years.

My heart was beating rapidly. I could hear its urgent rabbitlike thumping in my ears. In my dream, for reasons I no longer could recall, I had jumped off the St. Isaac Cathedral's upper colonnade—where my old Bolshevik grandfather, on one of his and my grandmother's visits from Moscow, had taken me when I was little, three years earlier, for a bird's-eye view of the world's most beautiful city (too overwhelmingly beautiful for the little me to appreciate or remember that breathtaking view with any clarity)—but instead of being smashed into pancake lace upon impact with the cracked gray asphalt, erupting into a festive fountain of blood mist, I had virtually sailed down and landed softly and smoothly on all fours, like a cat on the bottom of the sea, with a scratched knee proving to be the only injury sustained, when I had gotten up and looked myself over: none too deep a gash, to be sure, but, much to my horror, oozing some viscous tar black substance, foul-smelling black tar, instead of the normal human bloodred blood.

Ugh! This was too terrible and ugly for me to take, even in a dream!

I got out of bed and tiptoed out of my room (my younger brother was snoring quietly in the opposite corner) and back into the kitchen. I was stepping carefully along the way, trying not to let the bumpy linoleum covering the floor in the narrow hall and in the kitchen squeak under my feet. I was shivering all over.

I turned on the light in the kitchen because all of a sudden, oddly, like years ago, I found myself being afraid of the dark.

After swallowing, in several painfully greedy gulps, half of the stale boiled water in the dented aluminum kettle on the stove, I stood in the middle of the kitchen for some time, shuddering with fear and self-revulsion in the cone of intensely yellow light from the shaded lamp directly overhead. I was feeling disgusted with myself to the point of . . . to a near-unbearable degree.

My black, viscous, tar-thick, foul-smelling blood! My ugly black heart pumping ceaselessly that disgusting ugly primordial ooze through my disgusting resinous aorta! All that disgusting, ugly black swamp sloshing and circulating in spasmodic spurts inside of me, all those slippery black inner organs of mine, my black spongelike liver, my blood-filled lungs, all those different, disgusting snake-like intestines of various sizes, all that disgusting stuff moving and shifting heavily and sloshing around slowly in that ugly primordial black ooze inside of me—oh, the unbearable ugliness and disgust! And that brain inside my skull? Double, triple disgust! That ugly gelatinous dirty-gray mass, trembling and shuddering minutely, I imagined, like a large toad-shaped mound of sambuca Jell-O from the old Nord confectionary over on the Nevsky, where grandfather had taken me once, too, the same day we'd gone up the St. Isaac's colonnade. Was it still dirty gray with dark red speckles, inside my skull—or had it also, just like my blood in my dream, turned black? Ugh! What ugliness and disgust!

The next instant, the fear gripping me became a roiling black wave of pure panic. It was all I could do, for some strange reason I wouldn't be able to explain, not to bolt into the night, screaming. I stayed still, shivering, inside that shimmering cone of harsh yellow light in the kitchen. After however long a time, one minute or maybe ten, that roaring black wave of panic begin to ebb and recede.

Breathing deeply and freely, I came close to the frost-bitten double-paned kitchen window. Leaning ever farther into it, until I almost touched it with my forehead, I saw in it an unfamiliar, sad, and blurry face of an old man with deep-set lifeless black eyes who—as I knew somehow right away, even while being aware I was just seeing things in my night-dreaming state—was me, only an infinitely older me; so old, he might even have been dead already, that old me, and only seemed alive in the window, in the same way as the light of long-dead stars could be considered real. I regarded it—that infinitely old, dead face—with some strange grim satisfaction for a few seconds.

It was, according to the calendar, spring already, yet winter still maintained the full firmness of its icy grip on Leningrad. Snow covered the ugly, barren terrain of the giant city's distant southwestern outskirts for as far as the eye could see, or imagine itself seeing.

Necessary evil. I was the necessary evil. That's what I was. I liked that.

From the kitchen counter, I took the long bread knife with the sharp serrated edge and chipped black handle. Quickly, lightly yet resolutely, biting my lower lip hard, I drew the blade across the pale narrowness of my wrist. There was no real pain—just the quick pinch of startled skin being cut. I gazed intently at the white-ridged welt on my wrist. In a small fraction of a second, blood welled up from it. It was red.

"I am a magnet for evil," I said, winking at the blurry face of the dead old me in the windowpane. "I am the necessary evil. How about that."

A small droplet of blood slid toward the edge of my wrist. It was too light and insubstantial to develop enough independent momentum to fall off onto the floor.

From the window, the black void of the night gazed back at me without blinking.

"Necessary evil," I said, licking the blood off the wrist.

Klodt's Horses

ONE DAY, MANY YEARS AGO, in another lifetime, a friend told me that the sculptor Peter Klodt, creator of the famed four-part *Horse Tamers* composition gracing the Anichkov Bridge in the heart of Leningrad/Saint Petersburg and serving perhaps as the city's most iconic image, had etched into the scrotum of one of those majestic four horses the facial features of the politically powerful man who had cuckolded him with his wife. I was quite impressed by that bit of information—the sheer impotent ingenuity of the purported artistic gesture in question.

A few days later, strolling along the Nevsky in the company of another friend—both of us being in a somewhat inebriated disposition and, consequently, the most inquisitive of spirits—I recalled it and suggested we walk over to the Anichkov Bridge and check out the horses' private parts.

So we did, without a second's delay.

There we stood, then, swaying slightly in thoughtful silence, at the edge of the ceaseless human flow, in front of the first man-horse duo we'd come upon in our southbound progress, peering up into the giant horse's scrotum from as close a distance from it as the front of its massive granite pedestal afforded us. Staring intently and for a pro-tracted length of time at the horse's scrotum with my head thrown aback eventually made me feel dizzy.

"I don't see any face in there—do you?" I said to my friend. He shook his head in the negative. "Nope. Nothing. No face."

"Let's check another one," I suggested.

We moved over to the second of the four sculptures, on the other side of the bridge.

There we stood again, swaying and rocking to and fro, and hiccupping under our breath, as we stared with utmost intensity, feeling vaguely nauseous, into the second horse's crotch area.

"I think I'm beginning to see something," my friend said uncertainly, at length. "Yes, definitely . . . There, see? The nose, the mustache, the curved chin . . ."

"Yes, me, too," I concurred. "Oh man, that's exciting!"

Indeed, all of a sudden, I was looking at the small rodentlike features of a mustachioed man with tiny eyes and a broad, flat nose and . . .

At that instant, our reverie was interrupted by the local militiaman, who, apparently, had been watching the two of us for some time.

"Young men, what exactly do you think you're doing here?" he addressed us, approaching from behind and tapping me on the shoulder.

"Oh, not much," I stammered. "Just, you know, enjoying the timeless artistic genius of the . . ."

"I'll tell you what you're doing," he went on, with a dismissive wave of a pudgy hand. "I've seen the likes of you here too many times to count. You're trying to find in the horse's gonads the face of that guy who supposedly slept with Klodt's wife. Ha! Such foolishness! Who ever starts these idiotic rumors! There's no face, young men! Unless, that is, you want to convince yourself something's there that isn't, in which case, that'd be your own mental problem: your overactive imagination and proneness to hallucinations. All right, let's move on, young men. I can see you've had quite a bit to drink. Just go home, if you want my advice, or you'll get yourself in some sort of trouble before too long."

For some reason, I felt bitterly disappointed and upset by his words. It was as though a beautiful white pigeon had just died right before my eyes. Such lovely apocryphal tales of transforming the essentially base emotion of jealousy into a hidden symbol of inherently ennobling and love-driven art don't come along too often. "Are you sure, comrade militiaman?" I said in a tremulous voice. "Do you know this for certain—that, for instance, his wife never cheated on him?"

"For certain, I don't even know whether my own wife's cheating on me or not," the militiaman replied with a wistful smile of quiet wisdom. "As far as I'm concerned, Klodt's wife might've been cheating on him with the entire cavalry regiment of the Winter Palace guards. What I'm telling you, though, is that these here horse's gonads have been inspected numerously and over a long period of time by the most authoritative Tsarist Russian and later Soviet historians and other arts specialists, as well as the high-level Party officials, specifically on the subject of dispelling those very pernicious rumors—because you know this is a goddamn slippery slope: Today you're looking for some random and long-dead horny dude's mug up in there, the obscene secret place of this particular sculpture, and tomorrow, before you know it, someone will be searching for some other person's face, a much more important person's—I don't even want to speculate on who that might be—and looking for it in some other secret hidden place, up in the folds of some other horse's gonads, because there're thousands of horse sculptures in this city, as you know, and lots of deranged individuals just waiting for the opportunity to make fun of our, not to mince words, political leadership—and guess what. Long story short: no face. No face. In the case of these here horses. No face . . . Which stands to reason, too, in terms of being the way it should be." He chewed his lip, lost in thought momentarily, twirling lightly the makeshift iron truncheon in his hands. "If you're a man, a real man, and your wife has gone astray with someone you know, or don't know personally but know how to locate him, maybe because you can't get it up, you know, or don't make enough money or something like that, or for some other reason or without a one—well, you know how this can come about; we've all been there— well, instead of hiding the bastard's face up in the folds of a bronze horse's gonads, like a goddamn coward and pathetic loser, you should just be a man and up and beat the hell out of him. Just beat him to a bloody pulp . . . To a bloody pulp!" he repeated with pleasure, clearly relishing the taste of that energetic phrase on his tongue. He slapped the flat of his palm with the hefty truncheon in his other hand, with a juicy, meaty sound. "Or else you just jump him from behind, unexpectedly, and start strangling him, and keep on strangling while maybe simultaneously gnawing at his throat, his main artery, with your teeth, until he's completely dead, the worthless piece of shit, and falls sagging to the floor like a sack of flour! Yes! That's what you do! . . . And if—well, if you can't beat him to a bloody pulp or strangle and chew him up to death by yourself, because you're too weak or too cowardly or something, you pathetic little worm, then you just pay someone to do that for you! That's what you do, you son of a bitch! It takes but five minutes to find someone to do it for you, and for a very reasonable sum, believe you me, if you know where to look for the right person! Bastards! Bastards! That's what a real, manly man would do!"

He seemed quite angry now, all of a sudden. His face had acquired the unhealthy hue of an undercooked beetroot. His breathing was like a storm in a bathtub! He was gazing off into the distance, at something indeterminate yet located high above our heads. He looked more than a bit crazy, in other words—and for a moment I thought he might not have been a militiaman at all, but, rather, some deranged individual dressed up as one. But then I swept away my doubts on his account. He was, of course, the real deal, the genuine article: the state-sanctioned defender and guarantor of our safety and security.

Quietly, with as little visual fanfare as possible, my friend and I had removed ourselves from his immediate presence, resuming our unsteady walk in the general direction of the coffee and cognac place, nicknamed "Café Saigon," at the corner of the Nevsky and Vladimirsky Prospects—our original destination—where the city's artistic-underground types congregated in large numbers on a daily basis. There we were going to find all the love and understanding we needed, not to mention coffee and cognac and cheap red wine.

"Hey, listen," I said to my friend after a minute or so of walking in silence. "I've just thought of a good opening sentence for a short story: 'Life is both simpler and more complicated than it is.' What do you think?"

"I think it sucks," he told me bluntly—and after a moment's consideration, I had to admit he was right.

Why? Why?? Why???

CUSTOMS OFFICIALS AT THE I-87 checkpoint strike one at times as touchingly childlike. Especially—with all due respect!—on the U.S. side of the border. Their curiosity can be refreshingly insatiable.

Just two days ago, for instance, a stern-looking female officer, in the course of our brief interview, kept following up on most of my answers, in the fashion of a four-year-old, with an earnest "Why?"

Why? Why?? Why???

This, more or less, is how the exchange unfolded:

—Where are you going today?

—New York City.

—Why?

—To see some old friends.

—Why?

—Because they're old friends, some even going all the way back to my Russian days, you know, and I love them, and I feel I don't get to see them enough.

—Why?

—Because they live in New York and I live in Montreal, and—

—Why?

—Why? Why . . . Hmm . . . Well, because I have a full-time job at a university there, in Montreal, and it's a good job, a professor's job, and so I—

—Why?

—Well, because I was hired to do that job by the university I just mentioned.

—Why?

—Because they needed to hire a professor of English to teach creative writing in their, you know, creative-writing program, and so they conducted a job search for that purpose, and they ended up hiring me.

—Why?

—Probably because they liked me.

—Why?

—Well, because. You know. They just liked me.

—Why?

—Because I'm painfully handsome.

—Why?

—Because I come from a long line of painfully handsome Eastern European Jews.

—Why?

—Because Eastern European Jews are notoriously, you know, painfully handsome.

—Why?

—I have no idea, Officer.

—Why?

—Because there're things—lots of them, in fact—that

I have no idea why they are the way they are and not some other way, or the other way around!

—Why?

—Because, Officer! Because! Because life, in case you haven't noticed, is a sad affair! Because it's winter already, Officer, once again—and, in the end, we're all going to die! Yes, Officer, die! Because on the way here, I saw a long triangle of, you know, ducks, low in the sky, headed south . . . or maybe it wasn't ducks but, like, mini-cranes, headed by a mini-Putin or something. . . . Never mind. Because—see, look what's become of us, Officer! Look around! The leaves are brown! And the sky—oh, the sky is a hazy shade of winter!

—Okay, sir. Good enough. Welcome home.

Sentence

To the memory of Arkadii Dragomoshchenko

REMEMBER WHEN ... remember ... remember how, thirty years ago, yes—after the requisite sum of money had been collected, in half handfuls of small change and occasional crumpled rubles, for however many bottles could be afforded of whatever toxic domestic ersatz port or esophagus-singeing Bulgarian dry red might be available that night at the basement liquor store diagonally across the darkly illuminated *prospekt,* five tall floors below; and then, after the eager young person dispatched to fetch the booze had returned to the loft, however many long minutes later, laden with bottles, winded but happy and greeted with discordant cheers; and then, after we all, all of us, wasting no time, had gathered around the massive and incongruously sturdy table in the middle of the otherwise desolate and unlivable mansard building where we had our nightly gatherings, and the first two bottles had been opened, quickly and expertly and without the use of a corkscrew, and their fetid contents had been poured out into the dense assemblage of thick-faceted railroad tea glasses and dainty mayonnaise jars and cheap china teacups with chipped edges, amid the flowering of dentally

challenged Leningrad smiles and the animated rubbing
of hands, whereupon all of us would claim for ourselves
one of those mongrel drinking vessels and take our seats
on the motley assortment of rickety throwaway chairs and
milk crates around that inexplicably elephantine table in
the middle of the empty, dusty, decrepit loft space, and
then, as if on cue, pause for a few beats, fall silent for a
protracted instant or two, lifting our heads or turning or
half-turning to face the dark window, all at once, for no
clear reason, strictly because of some unspoken and almost
unpremeditated ritual, putting ourselves wholly into that
moment, with nothing preceding and nothing following,
as it were—well, do you remember how, just then, as we
were sitting there, in that sprawling, empty, dusty, unlivable mansard loft with the scuffed, uneven floors and the
cracked stucco walls and the exposed electrical wiring and
all manner of disagreeable smells, inside that odd moment
or two of hushed silence, not even dragging on the hard-
bitten lighted Belomors in our mouths, before commencing to drink the night away, there, on the rooftop level
of that uninhabited, condemned five-floor building on
Chernyshevsky Prospect, a stone's throw away from the
vigilantly guarded U.S. consulate, to say nothing of the
distance to the eponymous upscale metro station, partially
visible from the loft's window at a sharp angle during the
light time of day, which is to say never, since we never
went there before dark or in the light time of year, and
it was always very dark when it was dark in Leningrad

back then, yes, how we, a small gathering of momentarily silent, semiunderground young people seated around a massive rectangular table in the middle of a sprawling, empty, dusty loft up at the top of a condemned and otherwise unpeopled Dostoyevskian building, in the stark yellow light from a couple of bare lightbulbs suspended from the concave cracked ceiling on twisted lengths of black cord, yes, how we all, all of us, momentarily silent and not even dragging on the lighted Belomors in our mouths, peering intently out of the dusty and forever winterized yet still drafty cracked old window and into the immense pitch-dark outside, the unconquerable, boreal Leningrad wintry darkness, made darker still by the tiny yellow dots of thousands of windows in apartment buildings near and far, just a small gathering of ten or twenty of us, semi-underground and altogether inconsequential, prematurely young and childlike people between the ages of twenty and forty, peering in silence into that great and boundless yellow-dotted darkness that enveloped our part of the vast and great and terrible country to which we solely belonged, the largest and darkest and strongest and strangest and most terrible country in the world, which we likely knew would never let go of us, never release its mortal grip on us, because it owned us by birthright, chapter and verse, body and soul, though mainly body, and in the end it probably would kill us, too, just have us suffocate to death on its immense darkness and the unimaginable gravity of the black hole that it was, even if it was populated by hundreds of millions of people, our fellow citizens, whom we didn't really know or understand, even though we spoke the very same language and knew and understood anything and everything that there was to know and understand about them, which was both not much and an awful lot, the realization of which made us feel all cold and dark inside, though at the same time oddly comforted, frightened and petrified and awed and oddly comforted, still and silent in that yellow fish tank of the empty rooftop loft space, floating above the giant, dark city, at the top of a condemned, uninhabited Dostoyevskian building, peering out intently into that immense darkness, all of us at once, silhouetted darkly and sharply in the harsh yellowness enveloping us, awed and frightened and oddly comforted, until one of us finally shook his head, horselike, shaking himself out of the sheer catatonic strangeness of that momentary silence and immobility, and raised his drinking vessel, dragged on the Belomor in his mouth, and said, loudly and hoarsely, "Gentlemen! We're surrounded by a sea of darkness!" thus signaling the end of that strange, ritualistic intermission; and then, with much relief, we turned or took our gazes away from the dark window and, talking animatedly all at once, commenced to drink the night away.

A Soviet Twelve Days of Christmas

AT MY FIRST POSTCOLLEGE JOB, as an entry-level engineer in the Department of Submarine Screening/Demagnetization, at Leningrad's Central Naval Electrotechnics Research Institute, I was paid 120 rubles a month. In 1979–1981, to the best of my sporadic recollections, and with the aid of some perfunctory and doubtless imprecise online research, with 120 rubles in a large Soviet city one could afford:

12,000 boxes of matches (50 matches per box), 12,000 glasses of carbonated water (no fruit syrup) from a street vending machine, 12,000 standard pencils, 12,000 slices of bread at a public cafeteria

6,000 pay-phone calls

4,000 glasses of carbonated water with fruit syrup (flavor indeterminable) from a street vending machine, 4,000 small (.25-liter) mugs of *kvas* (a popular drink) from a street vendor, 4,000 copies of most Soviet daily newspapers (*Pravda, Leningradskaya Pravda, Izvestiya, Soviet Sports,* etc.), 4,000 streetcar rides, 4,000 glasses of tea (no sugar) at a cafeteria, 4,000 eraser-tipped standard pencils

3,000 trolleybus rides, 3,000 hot meat/cabbage/liver/
potato/fish *pirozhki* from a street vendor

2,400 metro/bus/Ferris wheel rides, 2,400 sprigs of dill/
parsley from a street vendor, 2,400 *bubliks* (a fresh-
fried Russian bagel of sorts), 2,400 table-tennis balls,
2,400 tins of mint tooth powder, 2,400 glassfuls of
sunflower seeds from a street vendor

2,000 large (.5-liter) mugs of *kvas*, 2,000 regular post-
cards, 2,000 meat patties (*kotlety*) at a cafeteria, 2,000
small tins of vitamin C

1,710 paper cups of fruit ice cream, 1,710 buzz cuts at a
barbershop, 1,710 portions of generic vegetable salad
at a cafeteria, 1,710 standard-strength lightbulbs

1,500 *pryaniki* (hard honey cakes), 1,500 standard pocket-
size notebooks, 1,500 glasses of birch-tree juice at a
grocery-store counter

1,333 paper cups of milk ice cream

1,200 glasses of tomato juice at a grocery store, 1,200
kilos of salt, 1,200 boiled-sausage sandwiches at a
cafeteria, 1,200 kilos of potatoes, 1,200 boxes of
mustard plaster

1,091 hot, large, open-faced meat *pirozhki* (*belyashi*) at a
cafeteria, 1,091 copies of *Literary Newspaper*, 1,091
portions of chocolate ice cream on a stick (Eskimo)

1,000 kilos of carrots

923 chicken eggs, 923 standard loaves of wheat (or white)
bread

857 packs of cheap unfiltered Prima cigarettes

800 kilos of watermelon (in season; availability uncertain)

750 kilos of wheat flour, 750 triangular .5-liter milk
packages, 750 large round loaves of rye (or black)
bread

600 kilometers' worth of cab rides within city limits

545 packs of unfiltered Belomorkanal cigarettes (*papirosy*)

500 small (.25-liter) mugs of beer at a street beer stand,
500 .5-liter bottles of vinegar

480 loaves of high-grade white bread, 480 movie tickets,
480 packs of margarine, 480 .5-liter bottles of milk

430 .33-liter bottles of Pepsi, 430 bars of imported soap

400 soft packs of filtered cigarettes, Yava or Laika

360 cans of anchovies in tomato sauce

343 large (.5-liter) mugs of beer at a beer stand, 343
plastic hair combs, 343 packs of mid-level Bulgarian
cigarettes, Rodopi or Aeroflot

320 preset-menu three-course dinners at a cafeteria

250 tulips at Kolkhoz market, 250 state lottery tickets,
250 packs of high-end Bulgarian cigarettes, TU-154
or Opal

219 cans of condensed milk

170 pairs of scissors, 170 standard ballpoint pens

167 3-liter jars of apple juice

160 metal hair combs

150 cast-iron frying pans, 150 packs of high-end BT cigarettes

133 pairs of socks, 133 hand towels, 133 kilos of granulated sugar

120 quality cafeteria dinners, 120 days of shared-room accommodations at Black Sea resorts (peak season)

118 bottles of Cabernet wine

114 bottles of dessert red wine

109 bottles of table white wine, 109 kilos of bananas (in theory; rarely available)

92 copies of either the first or the second part of the most popular Soviet English-language textbook (edited by N. A. Bonk)

86 kilos of oranges (in theory)

80 small (.25-liter) *chekushka* bottles of Moskovskaya vodka, 80 bottles of white vermouth, 80 months of home-phone bills (in theory; rarely paid)

73 bottles of sunflower oil

71 kilos of Chainaya boiled sausage

63 kilos of low-grade meat or chicken (so-called blue bird), 63 standard music records in paper sleeves from the state-run music company Melody

50 bottles of Rkatsiteli white wine

48 pairs of domestically manufactured swimsuits

45 Fairytale cream cakes

42 .5-liter bottles of Moskovskaya vodka (green label)

41 kilos of high-quality Doktorskaya boiled sausage

40 kilos of quality cheese (Rossiisky, Dutch), 40 standard dinners at a restaurant, 40 pairs of made-in-China Keds, 40 new books, 40 pairs of imported underwear, 40 months' worth of electricity bills (largely in theory), 40 leather soccer balls

38 pairs of tracksuit pants, 38 bottles of domestic ersatz port 777

33 bottles of Soviet champagne, 38 .5-liter bottles of Pshenichnaya vodka

30 wooden chess sets

29 bottles of three-star Soviet "cognac," 29 bottles of Extra vodka

28 aluminum frying pans

24 irons

18 feather-stuffed pillows, 18 bedsheets

17 wooden chairs

14 pairs of made-in-China summer sandals

12 kilos of chocolate truffles, 12 Leningrad–Moscow train rides

11 half-linen tablecloths

10 wooden tennis rackets, 10 rabbit-fur winter hats, 10 months' worth of apartment fees (in theory)

9 folding cots

7 regular shirts

6–7 Leningrad–Moscow flights

6 inexpensive photo cameras (Smena)

5 flights to the Black Sea (Odessa, Simferopol)

4 pairs of Soviet-made dress shoes

3 vacuum cleaners

2 cheap bicycles

1.8 Soviet-made suits

0.8 Soviet fall coats

0.67 flights to other end of the country (Vladivostok),
    .67 pairs of black-market jeans (if lucky)

0.6 cheap black-and-white TV sets

0.4 cheap bicycles

0.35 Vega record players

0.3 Minsk, or comparable class, refrigerators

0.27 portable Elektronika mini-TVs

0.17 color TVs

0.024 Moskvich-412 automobiles

0.01–.0001 most other automobiles

Being young and carefree—well, obviously, priceless

The Night We Were Told
Brezhnev Was Dead

I T WAS A CHARACTERISTICALLY DAMP and cold November morning, the third after the sixty-fifth anniversary of the October Revolution. I was nearing the end of my fourth semiweekly twenty-four-hour shift as a security guard at the Roller Coaster Unit of the Krestovsky Island Amusement Sector of the Leningrad Central Park of Culture and Leisure (TsPKiO). At seven forty, I was still fast asleep on the long and narrow leatherette couch on the second floor of the Amusement Sector's administration cabin—the uneven, cracked black plastic-coated fabric under me; a stinking, ancient communal goatskin over me; my head propped on the pillowy lump of my rolled-up sweater—when my replacement arrived, twenty minutes ahead of schedule, and started banging on the bolted and latched cabin door downstairs. His name was Victor: a big, beefy, mean-looking fellow with a bumpy russet face, constantly chewing on a chunk of gristly raw meat and followed everywhere by a mangy black dog with spindly legs, a runny nose, and dolorous eyes. He smelled just awful. I knew from other security guards that the year before he'd spent a few months in prison for killing—by lunging on, wringing the neck of, plucking, and then cooking over an open fire and devouring—one of the several old, people-friendly swans that swam from April through October in the narrow moat between the Amusement Sector and the rest of the park territory. The man was a piece of work.

"I couldn't sleep," he said hoarsely. "Too many fucking thoughts. I hope you don't mind I woke you up." Clearly, he was not the type of man to be rebuked about anything, no matter how mildly.

"Happens to me all the time, too," I told him, my head spinning with the previous night's hangover (two bottles of ersatz port with a fellow security guard from another part of the park), and then I signed off in the shift ledger without saying another word, whistling quietly under my breath the French composer Camille Saint-Saëns's timeless opus known to every Soviet child as the world's greatest ballerina Maya Plisetskaya's timeless performance piece "The Dying Swan."

On the way from the Amusement Sector's administration cabin to the bus stop, I cast a quick, fond glance at the gloomy diplodocuslike silhouette of the city's only, and the country's oldest, roller coaster, American Hills, as translated from the Russian, looming forlornly in the mist on my right. It looked perfectly unharmed, with all its faculties intact. As always in such unsettled morning moments of leaving it behind, for an instant my heart was flooded with tenderness for that stupid thing, so manifestly out of place and out of time here. I felt a strong sense of spiritual kinship with it. "You be well while I'm gone, okay?" I whispered, gazing at it moist-eyed. Like me, it was all about merely existing, subsisting, just being there, stuck in one place in this unlikely remote locale and going nowhere, immobile, rooted inescapably through no will of its own. To be sure, I reminded myself with drunken pride, there were some significant differences between us, too: In addition to being its unnecessary guard, I was also a Jew, a repeated unsuccessful applicant for an exit visa from the Soviet Union—a refusenik—and a college graduate and, until recently, a young (admittedly indifferent and mediocre) engineer at a secret research institute of submarine electromagnetism; and I happened, as well, in my own modest way, to be a samizdat writer and translator and a newly minted member of the Club, the Soviet Union's first officially registered organization of unofficial writers and poets; while that inanimate creature, the sad Leningrad roller coaster, was none of those things. It was nothing more than itself: an antiquated amusement ride, the old American Hills, closed for the season and possessed of no desire to be anything or anywhere else. . . . *Life, life,* I thought abstractly, just so as to think something in words.

Some fifteen minutes later, on a bus to the Petrogradskaya metro station—a half-hour ride—I was thinking about the reading I was going to give that night at the Club. It was to be my first there, and I felt excited, but also a little nervous. Days earlier, I had decided I would

read a short excerpt from the vaguely surrealist and somewhat anti-Soviet dystopian novella I'd written on an
impulse in three heady days the summer before, one nar-
rating an entirely random, abstruse, and fanciful tale of a
small crew of herpetologists, or snake milkers, gradually
and irrevocably losing their minds in the mind-boggling
vastness of an imaginary Central Asian desert, and one,
too, that, importantly, two months prior, had earned me
the invitation to join the Club from its venerable chair-
man, veteran of the city's literary underground movement
and founder and coeditor of the country's preeminent
samizdat journal. Then, for some fifteen or twenty minutes, I planned to read my translations of several young
American poets (Charles Simic, Robert Hass, Sharon
Olds, Deborah Digges, and Michael Palmer, among others) from the thick paperback collection of new American poetry I'd found lying uselessly around on the Club's
premises, apparently left behind by some wayward member of American cultural intelligentsia, along with the
much slimmer anthology of avant-garde (if that was the
right term to use) American prose, called *Superfiction, or
The American Story Transformed,* edited by Joe David Bel-
lamy, which contained another text whose translation I
also intended to read—the heartbreakingly beautiful story
by Gilbert Sorrentino, "The Moon in Its Flight," with its
devastating final line, "Art cannot rescue anybody from
anything" (*Iskusstvo nikogo ni ot chego ne mozhet spasti*).
Finally, time permitting, I would round out the one hour

and fifteen minutes or so at my disposal with the short story I wrote a while back, while still in college, about one day in the life of a puny little Jewish kid from the outskirts of Leningrad, a third grader inexplicably endowed with a rare and, admittedly, useless capacity for correctly spelling every word in the Russian language—all the sheer infinity of them, including the countless and indeed prevalent words whose meaning he couldn't begin to guess, such as the fearsomely multisyllabic, foreign-rooted words culled from the thickest of Russian thesauruses. It was, to a considerable extent, an autobiographical story.

As the bus, sighing and rumbling along, wended its melancholy way through the grayness of yet another joyless, misty November morning, I also, and not for the first time, tried to sort out my thoughts and feelings concerning the unfortunate fact that, obviously, the Club owed its existence primarily to the Leningrad KGB's seemingly counterintuitive, but in reality coolly pragmatic, benevolence: Such an essentially "un-Soviet" structure, an official club of unofficial people, would not have been allowed to be founded and properly registered, let alone continue receiving a steady measure of logistical support from the Leningrad branch of the Union of Soviet Writers (the de facto literary subsidiary of the "organs"), had the Leningrad KGB's Fifth Directorate, one charged with overseeing the whole gamut of internal dissent-related issues, not concluded, in a sudden display of thinking outside the old box, that having all or the majority of them pesky samizdatchiks gathering under the same roof on a constant basis, in order to get drunk out of their minds and talk their crazy, impotently subversive talk, blabbing their mouths like there was no tomorrow, offered a much easier, more time- and energy-saving opportunity to keep tabs on their permanently evolving illicit little schemes—of having the manuscripts of their novels or sonnets or whatever smuggled abroad, usually by some idealistic, softhearted foreign exchange student of Russian or else some ambitious and diplomatically immunized third assistant to the fourth attaché on something very important at some capitalist-enemy consulate—than the daily hassle of having to run all over the giant city in efforts to obtain the same information on each one of those underground geniuses individually. It was not all that complicated, really—and it did, of course, bother me that I was part of something facilitated by and ultimately benefiting the KGB. They were aliens to me, the evil creatures from another planet—the organs, the KGB people, onetime-ordinary human beings who for some reason had voluntarily decided to sign their hypothetical immortal souls over to the eternal forces of infinite diabolical darkness, or some such thing. They were . . . well, the undead among us? Sure, why not. But then, realistically speaking, without unnecessary melodrama, all of us Soviet people existed largely at the mercy of the KGB, with its tacit permission or perhaps even by virtue of its disdainful oversight, with our boring little Soviet lives held aloft since birth in its monstrous paw to wax descriptive about it—so who was I to . . . to . . . I didn't know how to finish that thought.

Before diving into the slow whirl at the entrance of the Petrogradskaya metro station, I stopped by the beer stand some fifty meters away for a small cup of warmed-up Zhigulyovskoye. Uncharacteristically—or, perhaps, so it seems to me now, through the haze of remote hindsight—there was no line in front of it. I glanced about, searching for an explanation for that oddity (if that's what it was): Everything and everyone appeared to be the same as usual—which, given the state I was in, I found to be a little strange in and of itself.

While counting out the shallow jangle of small brass coins in my cupped palm, under the beer-stand woman's habitually hostile gaze, I felt someone's hand tapping me lightly on the shoulder from behind. A high-pitched nasal voice then said accusingly into my back, "Young man, why are you drinking beer first thing in the morning, instead of being at work or going to work in a sober state? Don't you have a job, or are you maybe a social parasite?"

Startled, I spun around and saw a pint-size rodent of an old guy with a tattered and stained red satin band tied around the dirty sleeve of his ratty oversize over-coat: a *druzhinnik,* voluntary militia assistant, nettlesome botherer of ordinary Soviet people going about the mundane business of their lives, sometimes including that of drinking a morning cup of beer before going home after a night of sleeping in the tenebrous shadow of the city's only American Hills. What a waste of human energy! He was staring at me with the exaggerated, almost comical severity of a self-righteous fool. I knew he wouldn't leave me alone now, not even if I were to explain the exact nature of my so-called job to him ten times over, because in his previous life he was a goddamn bloodsucking tick and none of my words would make the slightest difference to him; and I knew, too, that if I were to try ignoring him altogether and concentrate on enjoying my beer, he'd make an ugly scene and summon, with the dirty gray plastic whistle hanging around his scrawny neck on a dirty ropy lanyard, his partner, an equally obnoxious pest—*druzhinniki* never walked alone—doubtless hanging around somewhere in the immediate vicinity.

"What's it to you, old man? Screw you! Art cannot rescue anybody from anything!" I said to him, and took off briskly for the metro entry, feeling a bit displeased with myself for wasting such a beautiful line on him. The poor fool, having recovered from the initial shock, trilled his stupid, helpless little whistle into the emptiness left by my departure.

Thirty-five minutes later, I emerged on the surface at my metro station—Park of Victory. In twelve more minutes, I was back home, in my cozy, densely cluttered one-room apartment. My late maternal grandparents had lived in it only very recently, too, it seemed. Taking off my shoes and my street clothes, I plopped down on the bed, facedown, and fell asleep. It was about a quarter to ten in the morning.

———————

Insistent phone ringing woke me up. I opened one eye and squinted at the alarm clock on the nightstand by the bed. One-thirty in the afternoon. I could've slept a good while longer. My reading at the Club was not until seven. I got up, feeling groggy, unsteady on my feet, and picked up the phone, deciding for once to disregard the fact of the caller's failure to use the admittedly childish little code— one that the KGB eavesdroppers, whether imaginary or real, certainly would have had a good imaginary or real laugh at—known to all my friends and relatives: two long rings, then hang up the phone, count to ten, and redial, thus letting me know this was not someone undesirable on the other end of the line, such as the district military commandant, for instance, with an urgent inquiry about my lapsed young army officer's registration, or a point- lessly aggressive clerk from the Housing and Maintenance office, ZhEK, wondering when I might be kind enough to pay my phone/gas/electricity bills. Oh, but what the hell. At that instant, with my head full of fog, I felt unusually fearless. "Who is it?" I said hoarsely into the receiver. "If you're someone wanting to speak with the person living in this apartment, he's not here at the moment, and I have no idea when he'll be back. I am just an acquaintance of his,

visiting from Moscow, doing him a favor as his cat-sitter."
As if on cue, my cat, a Siamese named Maya, meowed
loudly in the kitchen, letting me know that in her opinion,
it was high time for a feeding.

"Turn on the TV, now," my friend SK, also a Club
member and the publisher and editor of the city's only
samizdat journal of foreign literary modernism and post-
modernism in translation, said in a voice fairly vibrating
with excitement. "And the radio, too."

"Why? What's happening there?" I said, yawning.
"You could just tell me, no?"

"Just do it," he said impatiently.

"Okay, fine."

Rubbing my face, I went over to the wall-mounted
radio on the other side of the room and turned it on. The
familiar sounds of lovely classical music filled the space—
Tchaikovsky. I shuffled over to the TV, the old black-and-
white Ladoga, in the opposite corner, and switched it on.
Two little swans, cute as buttons, were dancing there. I
flipped to the second channel, then the third. Same thing
there—little swans . . . My heart skipped a beat. Somehow, I knew right away what this meant.

"Really?" I said, returning to the phone. "Seriously?
For real? Is this what I think it is?"

"Yup. Yup," SK replied in a giddy voice. "That's
what it is. Finally. Yes, man! There already has been an
official announcement, at ten, plus many people heard
about this last night, on 'enemy voices,' outside the city,

or wherever else there's no jamming; plus, they canceled the Militia Day concert from the Kremlin last night, which of course was unprecedented and a surefire sign of something extraordinarily serious, so lots of people had already put two and two together. But I figured that you in your American Hills wilderness were still in the dark. This is huge, man! Immense! But wait. Wait." He coughed into the phone a few times, indicating he was about to launch into the derisive "the organs are listening" mode. "Oh, but just listen to me! What am I even *talking* about? What enemy voices? Am I out of my goddamn mind? Everyone knows no decent, self-respecting, patriotic Soviet person would ever listen to those contemptible paid capitalist liars! If I may have sounded less than crushed a minute ago, that was because of my being shocked, shell-shocked, shocked out of my mind, totally devastated, and having had a glass or two of something to soothe my nerves and unbreak my heart a little, as a result. I am de . . . deva . . . stated! My friend! We've been, like, befallen, um, by a great tragedy, as the saying goes. We've been orphaned, as a nation. . . . Yeah, that's right: orphaned. Like goddamn motherless children."

"Terrible, terrible!" I agreed, playing along, speaking loudly and distinctly, as if addressing a house pet or a small child. "I couldn't even begin to tell you just how heartbroken I am. I'm like an arid desert inside right now. A desert full of venomous snakes. Yeah, that's it. Snakes. We've been defanged, as a nation, so to speak."

"Awful, just awful," SK chimed in. "I also am extremely heartbroken. That was the right word you found. Thank you. Heartbroken. Who wouldn't be?"

"No one wouldn't be," I said emphatically. "What are we going to do now? How are we going to live without . . . without . . . No, I can't go on. Too damn heartbroken. Too hard. Tears, hot, bitter tears, are constricting my throat!"

"I know, I know," SK echoed mournfully. "You're right: better not talk about this anymore—way too painful. Let's change the subject. You're reading tonight at the Club, right? Nervous?"

"A little," I admitted. "But then, in light of . . . these new developments, maybe there won't even be a reading tonight."

"That's a possible scenario," SK agreed. "Well, we'll see. I'll see you there."

I went back to the bed and lay on it, facing the wall, for a long time.

Eighteen years! Eighteen years spent under that nonentity's rule. Most of my life—almost all of it. My childhood. My youth. And now that he was gone, I felt neither jubilation nor even a fleeting twinge of condescending sadness. I'd been waiting for this day too long. I felt nothing.

November days are short in mad Tsar Peter's dream city. By four o'clock, it was already pitch-dark outside, and inside my apartment. Somber classical music kept playing mutedly on the radio. By six, as I walked out of my apartment building, it was darker still, it seemed: The blackness of the air was accentuated, deepened by the dimmed yellow of scattered street lanterns. There were no stars in the sky, and no moon—and there was nothing out of the ordinary about that. Everything was the same as usual. All the stores and eateries along the stretch of the Moskovsky leading to the metro were closed, but that also was par for the course. The neon slogans up on rooftops of tall buildings—THE PEOPLE AND THE PARTY ARE ONE! GLORY BE TO THE KPSU! FLY AEROFLOT!—all functioned properly, more or less, with their subdued wasplike buzzing, and only a few were unlit, missing letters here and there.

On the metro, too, all the passengers were their normal selves: gloomy, concerned, angry, drunk, insane-looking, lost in thought, engrossed in reading garish weekly magazines and cheap detective novels. The ruler of their and all of our lives for eighteen years, even if only half-cognizant toward the end, was dead, but one could detect neither sorrow nor excitement on people's faces. He was dead because he no longer was alive, and that's all there was to it.

The car was full, though not overflowing; there were no free seats—and there was nothing at all remarkable or even mildly unusual about that, either. Two middle-aged women sitting in front of the spot where I stood holding on to the overhead handrail were talking to each other, neither too loudly nor very quietly.

"He looked downright terrible, like a corpse, three days ago, on November seventh, on top of the tomb, barely able to wave his hand or nod his head," one of them was saying. "It was clear as day he was out of it, completely, and didn't really know where he was. I think they brought him a chair or something in the end, so he could sit down, and then they just led him away. When I saw him in that condition, I told my Nikolay he sure as hell was not long for this world. Everyone and their mother could tell where this was going."

"Sad, I'm telling you, that they wouldn't have let him retire years ago, when people say he was downright pleading with them, the Politburo, almost on his knees, sick old man like him, with a couple of strokes," the other woman replied, shaking her head. "It's cruel, that's what it is—but then, on the other hand, they probably just wouldn't know what to do without him, even if they were kind of tired of him, too. I feel sorry for him, though not really, in truth, although it sure is all the same to him now. I feel sorry for his wife, that's who. But his daughter—she just downright raises my ire, with her . . . her, you know . . . well, you know."

"Lovers and diamonds, diamonds and lovers and booze," the first woman said, cutting in angrily.

"Disgusting! Don't even get me started on her!" Then, suddenly noticing me as I leaned in toward them, a tad too close for her comfort, she gave me a baleful look and said off into space, enunciating every word, "Too great for words is the tragedy that has visited us all today."

Two routinely drunk, unkempt old geezers of indeterminate age—angled toward each other on steps directly below me on the Chernyshevskaya metro station's upward-moving escalator—were continuing a conversation begun, apparently, some time before.

". . . but what really saddens me is that women don't smile at me anymore," one of them said, hiccupping. "Although, to be honest, they never smiled at me in the first place."

"Well, if I was a normal, regular-minded woman, I wouldn't be smiling at you, either," the other one replied. "Not while you're still alive, at any rate. Speaking of which . . . Fucking death, man. Huh? Well, good for him, though. That's where he belongs—nowhere. In the earth. In the dust. In the open fucking cosmos. He doesn't matter no more. Who do you think's going to be next? Andropov? Or maybe that semidead fucker Chernenko?"

"Who cares," the first man said with a sigh. "We have our own deaths to worry about. Let's face it, our lives are practically over, and we haven't even fucking started living yet, if we look truth in the eye. Oh life! Were you just a cruel joke played upon me by the universe? Oh death, don't take me yet. My life has been one big mistake; give me another chance!" There was a second's pause, and then the two burst out in a fit of drunken, cackling, coughing laughter.

Five minutes later, I was at the entrance to the Club—an unadorned scuffed door leading into a long semibasement flat with many rooms in a half-occupied building two doors down from the U.S. consulate. As always, approaching it, I had a mixed feeling of fear, knowing my every move was being watched, and a timid thrill caused by the notion that I was someone consequential enough to be worthy of the organs' observation, even if only a stationary and automatic, strictly impersonal one. Two burly, bulky, heftily clad armed militiamen of forbidding disposition—that is, the crack KGB operatives dressed up as ones—were always stationed in front of the consulate: one inside a large steel booth, painted white, with an almost certainly bulletproof window in its side; and the other standing still or walking to and fro a few steps away, at times speaking quietly into the massive walkie-talkie strapped to his shoulder. No regular, ordinary Soviet citizen was allowed to get past that booth, let alone attempt to enter the consulate, that single spot of American territory in Leningrad, without a previously scheduled appointment with one of its relevant U.S. personnel. It was, of course, bugged to the hilt inside and surveilled around the clock from the outside. Late at night, so others told me, the tiny glowing dots of the KGB's infrared cameras in the apparently unpopulated building directly across the street produced a hauntingly lovely sight; and I seemed to have witnessed as much myself on one occasion, albeit while seriously inebriated. And so, automatically, simply by dint of the Club's sheer proximity to the consulate, along with the latter's staff and all of its visitors, into the organs' field of ceaseless vigilance fell also the near-always drunk and often borderline-derelict unofficial writers and poets ambling in and literally falling out of the Club's always-open doors—those asocial, narcissistic samizdatchiks, in the surveillants' view, with their insane anti-Soviet talk and constant illegal determination, by a seemingly inexhaustible succession of ever-new inventive stratagems, to have their doubtless timeless, Nobel-caliber masterpieces smuggled abroad—a nice little bonus for the organs, if perhaps a somewhat superfluous one, since the latter had their informants on the inside, in addition to their official representatives, the Club's KGB "curators": two reasonably young and moderately sophisticated men with cute birdlike noms de plume, who would be regularly visiting the premises and engaging in soulful conversations about literature and life in general with the loose-lipped habitués of the place.

The Club's door, surprisingly, was locked. I'd only seen it open before. Some twenty or so people, by my quick count, were milling about outside—SK and two of my other close friends among them. It was a more modest turnout than I'd expected, perhaps overoptimistically so; but then, this was not an ordinary evening—and still, its strangeness notwithstanding, several well-known underground writers, whose work had appeared virtually in every samizdat magazine of note in the country, had shown up. One of them, RK—he of the large Assyrian beard and fierce stare of a wild mare of the night—nodded at me encouragingly. A little off to the side, three young women were speaking among themselves in rapid Lithuanian: a friend of a Vilnius friend, named Vita, a philologist in Leningrad for a month of research for her Ph.D. ("candidate's dissertation") at the State Public Library, and two of her colleagues, or friends, presumably. I liked Vita; she was smart and pretty, and she hailed from the remote and mysterious land of Ciurlionis and the best basketball players in the Soviet Union. Lithuania, where I'd only been once before—some twelve hours by train from Leningrad—had long fascinated me, and not just because it represented both the literal and figurative end of any ordinary Soviet citizen's journey in a westerly direction, the metaphorical anteroom of the unimaginable and forbidden Western world I was unlikely ever to see, realistically speaking, but, rather crucially, too, because it had been the ground zero of the Holocaust, what with all but a tiny percent of Lithuanian Jews murdered during the first years of World War II—something I and many other Soviet Jews did know, if without quite knowing how we knew it, even though they never wrote about this in newspapers or magazines, needless to say, and the school history textbooks made no mention of it whatsoever, or of that very word, *Holocaust,* unfamiliar to the absolute majority of

Soviet people. (And the very word *Jew*, incidentally, was one that anyone, and especially the Jews themselves, was supposed to be embarrassed by a little, ashamed of a bit, sort of, as if having been born a Jew in the USSR was a sin . . . which it was, actually, in the eyes of the country's rulers and many millions of its people—even though we were nominal Jews, strictly speaking—Jews in designation only, so to speak, since hardly any one of us knew the first thing about Jewish history or a single word of the Jewish language, which was called Hebrew and was banned from private study, under penalty of law, and . . . But enough. This is a needless digression.)

Plus, again, Vita was lovely and smart and fun to talk to. She had a charming accent in Russian. I liked her.

I waved at her, and she saw me and waved back, with a cute conspiratorial smile.

"The door is locked!" SK shouted merrily, throwing his rumpled fedora up in the air and then almost catching it. It was clear he had been coping with the tragic news of the day by drowning it in alcohol. "That's weird! Who's got the keys?"

"I've got the keys," said one of the Club's two primary KGB curators quietly and authoritatively, materializing out of the darkness around the guard's booth in front of the U.S. consulate and coming over to where I stood. He was an artistic-looking, subtle-featured man in his mid-thirties, whose nom de plume, as mentioned earlier, was derived from the name of Russia's favorite bird of prey.

He liked to visit the Club unannounced now and then, in order to discuss the latest literary developments abroad with finely cultured, if often wasted off their asses, people in the know of such developments. Frequently he would complain about the uncouthness of his Fifth Directorate colleagues, and especially those from the parallel Second KGB Directorate, one in charge of counterintelligence and internal political control: bruisers, hoodlums, low-brow individuals, completely uninterested in literature and incapable of telling Philip Roth from Mark Rothko; no one to discourse with about things of intellectual nature among them! Just about the only fully sober person on the Club's premises, he would talk little, preferring to listen to what his interlocutors had to say. He liked it when people told him stuff. He was a very good, close, sympathetic listener. Of course, being a lover of literature and on friendly terms with many of the Club members did not in any way preclude him from occasionally having some of the latter beaten up, purely for pedagogical or prophylactic purposes, by the *organs*-employed former boxers gone to seed and other such skilled scumbags—but it was understood by everyone to be part of his job, so there were no hard feelings. He just knew how to compartmentalize work and pleasure.

"I took the keys," he said, "given the special, unprecedented tragic national circumstances of the day." And he peered at me with exaggerated intensity, suppressing a sardonic smile.

"I see," I said, just to say something.

"I haven't received any concrete directives to cancel the reading," he continued, "even though our entire nation is in spontaneous deep mourning, but it hasn't been pronounced an official nationwide situation just yet, so it would have to be my call, for the time being. Of course, it's a bit unfortunate that it's you, of all people, scheduled to read tonight: a refusenik, would-be traitor to the motherland and all that. You know what I mean, as an object of attention of two directorates at once, which actually is an unfortunate situation, because everyone would have preferred if you just made up your damn mind as to whether you're leaving the country or participating in samizdat literature. Well, but that's beside the point now. Topic for another conversation. The point is, you should be the last person reading tonight. . . . But then, come to think of it, there could also be a nice, cool, counterintuitive and rebellious, in-your-face quality to that, too—some subversive Freemasonic-like frisson, rather in keeping with the Club's nonconformist spirit. So—fine, let's do it, until further notice. But there'll be some ground rules, still, in view of the reality we're facing today. First off, who are those foreigners over there? What are they doing here?" He pointed with his chin at Vita and her friends, who kept on chatting animatedly among themselves. "There shouldn't be any foreigners from capitalist countries tonight. Not tonight. Out of the question. Nonnegotiable." He paused, listening. "What language is that anyway? Portuguese?"

"They are from Lithuania," I said. "Lithuanians they are. Our, Soviet, people."

He chortled, cocking his head to one shoulder. "You, of all people, should be the last one making this determination—who is or isn't a true Soviet citizen. And if you think they, Lithuanians, like us or being part of us, in spite of all their basketball glory and their great film stars, then I have a bridge across the Neva to sell you. They hate our guts, deep down. They fought us tooth and nail, for many years, after we liberated them from the fascists. Haven't you seen *Nobody Wanted to Die*? . . . But fine. That, too, is beside the point now." He waved his gloved hand dismissively. "Lithuanians will be fine. Unimportant. What's more important is, what are you going to read tonight? I must warn you: no Americans. I know you love them, translate them, love your precious America, which you may or may not ever see with your own eyes, but tonight is not the night for them. My superiors would be unhappy if they found out that this tragic night was sullied by dirty Americanness. It's just not . . . Well, you understand." He cut himself off with a lopsided grin pointedly belying the humdrum severity of his words.

We stood in silence for a few seconds, gazing at each other. "What's the matter?" he said ironically after a bit. "That throws you for a loop, my friend? You have nothing to read if you can't read your American stuff? Without

America, you're nothing? No offense, comrade, but that's pathetic. In any event, you were also going to read your own old story, weren't you, about that wondrous little Jewish speller? You can still read it. Your anti-Soviet nonsense snake novella won't do, but that story will. It's a little silly, of course, but . . . At least there is no mention of America in it."

I stared at him wordlessly. He winked at me. "You want to know how I know all that? Well, I have my own little ways. God didn't grant me talent for fiction writing, but he did give me instead the ability to read those writers' minds. It's not much, but it's something." He patted me on the shoulder. Involuntarily, I recoiled.

"But how would they know?" I said.

"Who?" He frowned at me. "What?"

"Your superiors. How will they know what I read tonight?"

"Ah!" He threw his head back and let out a hearty laugh. Everyone turned to look at him in cheerful incomprehension. "Oh, they'll know, don't you worry about them," he said, chuckling. "They'll know. They, too, have their mysterious little ways about them. Let's just say art cannot rescue anybody from anything. Right? Am I right or . . ."

At that precise moment, suddenly and all at once, the lanterns went out all along the street, as well as on the observable part of Chernyshevsky Prospect, a stone's throw away—and everywhere else within one's field of vision, in every direction. Darkness enveloped the great city. It was as if a giant unseen hand had covered it, like a cage full of parakeets and cockatiels, with thick black cloth, though one still punctured by a myriad of tiny, intensely yellow window lights. A hush fell over the city. Everyone among our minute gathering stopped talking, too. Silence engulfed us.

"Well, then, that settles it," the curator said, in a tone of palpable relief, from the newly condensed darkness next to me. "The decision has been made for us—and, as always, it's the only right one. I was half-expecting this to happen. A mourning is a mourning. There can be no half mournings. So then, no literary readings tonight by strange, asocial elements, by refuseniks and enemies of the people—not any such foolishness. Now all of us— the bad and the very bad—will go home and mourn." He chuckled. "We'll go and mourn the hell out of this night. In darkness. In solitude. In heartbreak. Disperse, disperse, unbeautiful losers."

———————

The metro was still working, though its entrance no lon-ger was illuminated. Dim figures were moving around in the dark, silently. Somehow, inexplicably, even in the moonless, starless night, the as-yet-unfrozen ink black puddles dotting the pavement still managed to hold star-light and reflect the ephemera of moonglow, and one could still see—if not know, exactly—where one was going. We—six or seven of us, SK and others, including Vita and her friends—were headed to my place. SK had three bottles of Bulgarian red in his decrepit shoulder satchel, and someone else said he had something else along the same lines; plus, we could count also on buying a bottle or two of vodka from night-shift cabdrivers. This had, of late, become a thing with them, their risky side business, in the absence of any legal outlets for a thirst-addled Soviet citizen to purchase bottled alcohol at any time past seven in the evening. "Tonight, they might be more cautious than usual," SK mused aloud, walking toward the metro station next to me. "There could be an extra number of cops and *druzhinniki* out. But, then again, maybe not. How can any decent national mourning be conducted without vodka? There is no way, what with there being nothing on TV, and that it's dark and cold outside. What else is there to do but drink? Cops and *druzhinniki* are people, too."

"I wouldn't be so sure about that," I replied.

"You know what?" SK said after a pensive pause. "I think I'm going to miss the old bastard. Seriously. Just a little. Funny, isn't it? For years you just can't wait for him to croak, because—well, obviously . . . and when he finally does, it kind of hits you out of nowhere, the fact that we'll never see the poor, crazy, half-dead buzzard again. You know? Like Edgar Poe's raven: never-friggin'-more. After eighteen years. *Never.* That's a scary word."

We walked into the deep dusk of the Chernyshevskaya metro station in silence, passed through the turnstiles, and proceeded on to a downward-moving escalator. It was clear to every one of us that things would be different now, that this was the beginning of something large, whose implications for our little Soviet lives we could not yet foresee or fully appreciate.

"I don't know," I said, more to myself, just in order to hear the sound of my own voice, than in delayed response to him. "I don't feel much of anything right now. It's strange. I wish I did, but I don't. I wonder why that is. I'll figure it out later. I guess I'm feeling happy. I don't know. I feel nothing."

But then, I don't remember what I said then.

I looked at my watch, its face gleaming dully in the dark. It was exactly twelve hours since I'd been awakened that morning.

Moscow Windows

I WAS FIFTEEN AND IN MOSCOW over the winter break from high school, staying with my mother's cousin and her family. Those three—the cousin, a neuropathologist; her husband, a nuclear physicist; and their son, Marat, one year older than I—had been among my most favorite people in the world for as long as I could remember.

One night, a sinewy old man of a stealthy, vaguely animalistic bearing, with faded icy-blue eyes, a bushy gray beard, and a tight-skinned, tanned, bald head materialized on the threshold of their cozy new three-room apartment on the tenth floor of a modern midtown high-rise near the Prospect of Peace metro station, bearing across his shoulder a voluminous rugged burlap bundle, inside of which, as soon as he had put it down and untied its frayed leather straps, there presented itself to view a giant, headless, humpbacked smoked red fish, as rigid as a rolled-up wall carpet—*gorbusha*, or Kamchatka salmon, as Marat told me in a whispered aside. "A little personal souvenir for you, good people," the old man—whose name turned out to be Lev Konstantinovich—said in a strange, uncertain, lowing voice, smiling mirthlessly, showing a mouthful of uneven dark metallic teeth, while his eyes remained sharply vigilant.

Judging by the warmth with which Marat and his parents had greeted his—clearly unanticipated—appearance in their apartment, he was someone they'd known and liked for years—and because of that, I couldn't help feeling drawn to him also.

Amid all the good cheer and gladsome commotion and *oohing* and *aahing* over the glorious fish in the cramped hall, Marat's father quickly explained to me that Lev Konstantinovich was his uncle—his late father's brother—who for the past many years had been living in the remote corner of the vast Kamchatka Peninsula eleven time zones away, out in prehistoric wilderness, hunting and fishing in total isolation—and only rarely serving as a guide to groups of visiting volcanologists from across the Soviet Union and generally being self-sufficient and taking the fast-flowing river of life one unbroken instant at a time— except for the few days out of every year when he would come to Moscow, always on the spur of the moment, to pay visits to his grown son and some of his old friends there—and also to stop by his late wife's grave.

"And this," he added, half-turning to Lev Konstantinovich and pointing at me, "is our relative from Leningrad. My wife's kinfolk's son. We have relatives in Leningrad, as you may know."

The old man fixed his unblinking gaze on me, for a fleeting second investing my insignificant being with a greater intensity of enigmatic scrutiny than it possibly could merit, when a shadow of wistful recognition seemed to pass over his harsh, unyielding features. "Ah, Leningrad!" he said dreamily, in the same strange, distant, discordant voice, haltingly unsure of itself. "The most beautiful city in the world, or so they say—and the most terrible one, too, according to other people. I'm told I used to go there myself on occasion, in my life as another person, but I certainly haven't been there once since my death, so I have no basis for any independent judgment on the matter."

After those words, unsurprisingly, a momentary silence fell over the hall.

"Well!" Marat's father exclaimed at length with a short laugh, bringing his hands together and rubbing them animatedly. "Enough standing around, I say! Let's go have you settled—in Marat's room, this time. The boys will sleep in the living room, which will be fine by them, since they like talking late into the night anyway. How long are you here for, Uncle Lev?"

"Just one night," Lev Konstantinovich replied in a distracted manner, staring off into space. "Tomorrow, I will no longer be here."

"Oh, nonsense!" Marat's mother said, mock-frowning. "You'll stay for as long as you need to stay. Our house . . . well, it is not our house, strictly speaking, of course, but it is just as much yours as it is ours, and I've told you so before. You're safe here. We're your friends. The most loving and reliable friends you have! ... Well, but really—enough talking! Let's get you something to eat first. When was the last time you had a morsel of food in your mouth—yesterday? You must be famished, hungry like a wolf."

"A wolf!" Leonid Konstantinovich repeated with a crooked grin. "Wolves are fine people. They have lots of inner resources."

When the three of them went into Marat's room, which was adjacent to the kitchen, he and I bugged our eyes out at each other in pretend horror and, our palms tight on our mouths, burst with suppressed laughter. "What was that? Who is this old guy?" I asked, giggling. "He seems nice enough, sure, but—what the hell was he carrying on about not going to Leningrad since his death? That was creepy."

Pressing a finger to his lips, Marat motioned toward the living room with his head. We tiptoed out of the hall.

"Lev Konstantinovich—well, he's an interesting case," Marat said once we were seated on the large gray leatherette living room couch on which I slept. "He is my grandfather's—Dad's father's—older brother, like Dad just said. You've never met my dad's father, and I don't really remember him, either, because he died, of a heart attack, when I was too little to retain any memories. He also was a physicist, like my dad—and so, too, was his brother, Leonid Konstantinovich. Apparently, however, while my grandfather was only a moderately talented physicist, his older brother was quite remarkably gifted—a brilliant mind, practically a genius, one of the brightest young stars of Soviet science back at the time, Pyotr Kapitsa's favorite mentee. Surely you've heard or read about Pyotr Kapitsa? Leonid Konstantinovich followed Kapitsa—I just like repeating that name—Kapitsa!—to England, and he also worked with Rutherford, the famous inventor, alongside Kapitsa; yes, and he even married an English woman there and had a son with her. In other words, by all indications, he seemed intent on staying in England for the duration, especially after he failed to follow Kapitsa back to Moscow in the mid-thirties. But then—and this is where the story gets murky—in the end, he did decide to return, despite definitely having forebodings about it, closer to the forties, after receiving a cablegram from his younger brother, apparently—Dad's dad, right?—to the effect that their father was in rapidly declining health and wanted to see his older son one last time, which might or might not have been the truth of the situation, if you know what I mean . . . and, well, just as he had feared, he was arrested almost immediately upon his arrival in Moscow, as a supposed British spy, and a few days later sentenced to twenty-five years of hard labor in a prison camp, somewhere in the Magadan or Kolyma region—and that was a relatively lucky outcome for him, too, according to my dad, given the severity of his alleged crime, for which the standard punishment was a bullet in the back of the head—but was returned to freedom, *re–ha–bil–i–tat–ed*, in the parlance of the era, after serving out only eighteen years of that quarter-century sentence of his, due to Khrushchev's amnesty or something like that. . . . A fairly tragic destiny, objectively speaking. But then, on the other hand—" Cutting himself off, he gave me a serious, probing sidelong look.

"I've heard a little about similar stories," I told him cautiously. "A few times, well, on the *enemy voices* on my parents' VEF-Spidola radio, when they were listening to it late at night in their bedroom, as they often do, and thought no one else could hear it and, for some inexplicable reason, there was no usual howling background noise from those frequency-suppressing KGB jamming installations, you know, that particular night. They were talking about Solzhenitsyn, of course. But I only could catch a few scattered phrases. Some of my father's friends, too, said certain things about Stalin, sort of obliquely, at Dad's birthday party last year, in low voices—mentioning prison camps, the word *Gulag,* mass executions, again in connection with Solzhenitsyn. Of course, none of them had read whatever it was he wrote, which kind of makes one wonder. But whatever. But then again, my grandfather, whom you know well, he still believes Stalin was a great man—although, of course, he's an Old Bolshevik, who always adored Stalin, throughout his entire life, so his words on this subject should be taken with a serious grain of salt—and so, too, does our high school history teacher, Ninel Sidorovna. She also claims Stalin was a great man and heroic leader, the best ruler we ever had, who took over the levers of power when Russia was a land of horse-drawn wooden plows and left it as one of the world's two nuclear superpowers, even though she does admit that some certain unfortunate accidental mistakes had been made indeed during Stalin's rule, in terms of the limited number of unjustified imprisonments and executions Khrushchev spoke about in his secret speech at that Party congress all those years ago. But frankly, I don't know whether to believe her or not, either. I have my doubts. I don't like it when innocent people get thrown in prison or killed by mistake. That doesn't sit right with me. If Stalin was such a great leader, how did he allow for that terrible stuff to happen? I don't know, Marat. To be honest, I think he might've been a bad man. Stalin, that is. I do. What if Solzhenitsyn wrote the truth? I—"

"Our history teacher says the same thing," Marat said, interrupting me with alacrity. "She also tells us Stalin was a great man—and I believe her. Why shouldn't I? Seriously, why shouldn't I? This is our country, the Soviet Union, we're talking about here—the society of ultimate justice, one based on our common shared faith in the essential goodness of human nature, to put it perhaps a bit loftily! I don't mean to sound, you know, like . . . like . . . the *Pravda* newspaper. But you know what I'm saying. I'm being sincere now! We're not a gloomy, backward-bound place like America, thankfully! We are the good guys of the world, even if not everyone in the world realizes this yet. But everyone in the world respects, or at the very least fears, us! So yes, absolutely, I do believe Stalin was a great man, all those unfortunate excesses everyone knows about notwithstanding, because our present superpower status ultimately, to a giant degree, is due to him! And I'll tell you more, while we're at it: I, for one, have a bit of a hard time believing one hundred percent that with some rare exceptions, anyone in our country, even during the understandably severe Stalin era, could be arrested, much less executed, totally and completely without a reason, for having done absolutely nothing wrong at all! I find it difficult to accept that notion! Regardless of what Khrushchev—who probably had his own personal ulterior motives for tarnishing Stalin's reputation—said in that vaunted secret speech. Regardless, all the more so, of what that traitor Solzhenitsyn may have written! No, no! I won't! There had to have been something, some shadow of a reason, however possibly unintentional or tangential, in the absolute majority of instances! There is always something! Always! Inevitably! Some small line of wobble, some minor area of mental rot! Cannot *not* be!" Marat was speaking in a fierce, shouting whisper now, his eyes aglow, nostrils flared.

"Don't get me wrong," he continued in a more placid tone after a short pause to catch his breath. "I'm not suggesting Lev Konstantinovich necessarily was an actual British spy or anything. But . . . All I'm saying is . . . Oh, who the hell knows! Why are we even talking about all this difficult, confusing stuff?" He chuckled, shaking his head. "What are we even arguing about?"

"Well, I suppose one could say that at this point, the main difference between us is that you believe your history teacher, while I don't think I believe mine," I said, also forcing a smile.

"It would seem that way, yes," Marat agreed, "But that's neither here nor there, really. I was telling you about Lev Konstantinovich. Like I said, he is a curious character. Obviously, he never talks about any parts of his life at all—at least not in my presence—so the little I know comes from my parents, who, as you can imagine, don't like talking about him in my presence, either. This, then, is the condensed version of what I've been able to piece together: His English wife, knowing, or sensing to the point of certainty, that she was about to be arrested next, as his probable accomplice, committed suicide soon after he'd been taken in, by slashing her wrists in a bathtub. His son—still very small at the time—was placed in a special orphanage for children of the enemies of the people, where he almost immediately started experiencing an array of psychological problems, and as a result was subsequently transferred to a mental institution, his permanent residence ever since. He doesn't know his father, nor does he even care to find out whether or not he ever had one—and Lev Konstantinovich, because he has no memories whatsoever of his life prior to his arrest, which memory loss occurred presumably due to some sort of mental trauma–related syndrome, does not remember his son, either, although he makes believe he does, so as not to upset the people who keep telling him he has a son. As you saw in a glimpse tonight, he's convinced that his real, original self, the one he was born with, has been dead for many years, and he's been existing ever since as someone else, with some other man's wiped-clean brain having been transplanted into his skull. Sounds insane, I know. But—there you have it. Here's what I believe he believes happened to him: One day, at the logging site in the taiga outside his prison camp, he received a massive blow to his head from a falling treetop and went into a coma, turning as good as dead. However, instead of finishing him off on the spot, right then and there, amid the taiga permafrost, with the frozen butts of their rifles, as they normally would do in such cases, the camp guards—presumably, on their superiors' latest directive—had his immobile and insensate body brought back to the camp's medical ward, whence without delay it was transferred, by lorry and then by an NKVD airplane, to some supersecret medical-research facility, as part of some supersecret experiment; his permanently concussed brain was then removed from his head and fed to the dogs, and the new one, harvested from some other unfortunate comatose prisoner, was put instead into the echoing chamber of his cranium: a brand-new preowned brain, and a completely empty one, with all of its previous contents having been expunged by a superpowerful electromagnetic field . . . or some such thing—and that's when he believes he was born again, this time as a perfectly blank slate of a human being, with a brain infinitely more vacant than that of a newborn

child, containing no past memories whatsoever. And that's
it, you know. That's his story, to the best of my understanding. That's his predicament, in a nutshell: a man with
no past. Sounds like an Alexander Dumas novel or something, right? He doesn't recognize anyone he used to know
before going into a coma that ill-starred day in the taiga—
literally, no one. Not a person, not a soul. Crazy, huh? He
feels zero affinity with anyone, cares for no one. He simply
is incapable of that. He just pretends, puts on a show—and
does that rather halfheartedly, indifferently, too—of actually recognizing those he is told by a small number of other
people that he must recognize when meeting them for the
first time or even the second or the third one. The only live
creature he trusts for real, imaginably, would have to be
his dog, or maybe a few dogs, up there in Kamchatka—the
beautiful and almost unpopulated, enormous prehistoric
land of wild bears and volcanoes, the land of my dreams,
where he'd moved immediately after his release from
that prison camp, or wherever it was he ended up being
released from, a dozen or so years ago. There, as my dad
mentioned to you, he stays as far away as possible from any
human presence, and for as long as possible. But as you've
heard also, once a year, without fail—but also without any
advance warning—he travels, somehow, to Petropavlovsk-
Kamchatsky, the peninsula's only real city, and gets on a
plane to Moscow there. Once here, he always comes to
our apartment first, for some reason, and spends one night
with us, after which he just disappears, vanishes without

a trace—until the next year, that is. What exactly he does here, in Moscow, is not fully clear. He probably goes to see some people whom he doesn't remember to a lesser degree than others, and he likely makes quick, perfunctory stops at the psychiatric clinic where his son is kept, and at the grave of the woman who, according to other people, those claiming to know his dead self's past, used to be his wife. Poor old guy . . . Well, now you know almost as much as I do about him. Insane, huh? Just imagine—or maybe don't, actually—what it must feel like, to be him. Damn unimaginable, I'd say."

"Unimaginable," I echoed.

We sat in silence for a while, in the dark. The ceaseless flow of trucks and automobiles along the Prospect of Peace ten floors below manifested itself in a number of muted multicolored splashes of light shifting slowly, languorously on the dusky low-slung stucco ceiling in random, kaleidoscopic patterns. It was a comforting sight to behold.

I loved being in Moscow! I loved being in my relatives' cozy new apartment! As a child, I'd used to love their old apartment, too—the one they and our other Moscow relatives had occupied until several years ago. Long and narrow, but also as wide in places as the delta of some medium-size seasonal river and consisting of a seemingly variable number of variously shaped old rooms and a plethora of little nooks and crannies and other potential hideouts, it was full of heavy, creaky oaken furniture and it was suffused with quiet dusky brown air, situated in a looming century-old gray stone building a few hundred meters away, amid the dense maze of the ancient Sretenka area's crooked side streets. Some of the happiest, warmest memories of my early childhood, sweetly imprecise yet also starkly vivid, were connected to that beautiful old apartment.

Moscow! I loved the sprawl and the self-assured power of its broad avenues, always thronged with purposeful-looking, historically optimistic Soviet people; and the small, homey old wooden houses with ornately carved window shutters lining its snowbound downtown alleyways! I loved the sheer bold sweep of its panoramic vistas, and the heady sense I always had in Moscow of belonging to the most important and hopeful place in the entire world! I loved the smell of Moscow snow in the morning—much crisper, more redolent of cold Russian apples than the damp gray seabound exhaust of Leningrad's endless wintriness.

Once, when I was little, no more than five or six years of age, my grandfather, an Old Bolshevik, who still lived in Moscow at the time, took me to a place called the Bird Market, not far, seemingly, from the city center, where all kinds of animals were sold, not just birds: kittens and chickens, puppies and lizards, grass snakes and goldfish, piglets and baby goats, bear and wolf cubs, ponies and butterflies, beetles and dragonflies, miniature wolverines, Siberian saber-toothed cows and carnivorous lambs from the Urals, amphibious squirrels and tree-dwelling

sturgeons, mice-size lice and taiga crawfish! Noticing that
I was on the verge of passing out from too much emotional
overstimulation and wishing to calm me down, Grandfather bought me a little black baby chicken then, whom,
inexplicably, I named Edouard, and we proudly took it, in
a Skorokhod shoe box it came with, to my grandparents'
apartment in the Moscow suburbs—in a small, quiet little
town called Moose Island. Grandmother, the local school's
principal and biology teacher, got angry when she saw the
chicken in the apartment, because she knew it would bite
the dust in no time flat—as indeed it did wind up doing,
sadly, despite all the love I showered it with over those two
days it was with us, leaving me feeling bad, heartsick at the
thought that my love had not been enough of a reason for
Edouard to keep on living. Memories . . .

I liked the slightly pharmaceutical, musty odor of my
grandparents' two-room Moose Island apartment. It put
me in mind of something I knew I'd never known yet still
knew intimately. It was a poignant feeling. On the man-
telpiece in their living room, a marble owl sat, blinking its
burning red electric eyes. It was a night-light.

On another occasion, Grandfather took me to the
VDNKh—the Exhibition of Achievements of the People's
Economy—where I soon became hopelessly confused by
the boundless crowds of Soviet citizenry from every corner
of our one-sixth of the world's landmass, and by the sheer
majestic, cosmic scope of the Soviet economy's relentless
invincibility, as well as by the vertiginous height and sweep

and the implacable steely resolve of that iconic *Worker and Kolkhoz Woman* sculpture, by the famous sculptor Vera Mukhina; I started to cry, disconsolate, fairly dissolving into tears; to soothe and comfort me, to make me stop my embarrassing and inappropriate behavior in that most pointedly optimistic of Soviet locales, Grandfather bought me a memorably delicious pork *shashlik* on a stick from a wooden kiosk just outside the spacious pavilion with the largest and heaviest sow in the world—just an immensely, mind-blowingly humongous, world's largest Soviet sow, gloriously resplendent and mountainlike in her dirty pinkness, luxuriating on her side, since she had long ceased being able to stand on her feet, in a mess of straw and mud beneath a giant hammer-and-sickled Soviet banner.

I loved the pungent aroma of Marat's father's expensive filterless Kazbek *papirosy*, which came in a beautiful cardboard pack featuring on its cover the dark silhouette of a horseman in a large disheveled *papakha* hat galloping across a mountain ridge, with the white-topped Kazbek rising majestically into boundless cobalt blue sky in the background; Marat's father stuffed the hollow air shaft of each *papirosa* with a wad of cotton, to diminish the amount of smoke's potentially pernicious components entering his lungs. I couldn't wait to grow up and be old enough to start smoking those sophisticated *papirosy* myself. Sometimes he also smoked Herzegovina Flor, which happened to be made with Stalin's favorite sort of pipe tobacco. Marat's father sat in an old, plush grandfather's armchair in the living room, next to a set of bookcases, and, puffing away contentedly, read one of the many detective novels collected on those shelves: Georges Simenon and Agatha Christie, Arkady Adamov, the Vayner Brothers, Lev Ovalov, Yulian Semyonov, Stanislav Rodionov, Nikolai Leonov, and scores of others.

Oh, I loved everything about Moscow! The solemn grandeur of Red Square at sunset hour, the Kremlin's stern blood-tinged beauty, the ominously melodious Kremlin Courants, the never-dormant little illumined square window of Stalin's onetime study, according to rumor, up at the top of the darkly menacing Spasskaya Tower; Lenin's tomb and the surprisingly small wax-skinned, black-clad Lenin, supine inside a large bulletproof glass cube—I loved it all! I loved the merry New Year's Tree children's gala at the recently opened Kremlin Palace of Congresses I went to with my Old Bolshevik grandfather, and the world-famous Moscow Circus, with *the sunny clown* and world's most lovable man, Oleg Popov . . . Everything!

I loved, too—already as an adolescent, with my heart full of romantic stirrings and a painfully keen premonition of love—the beautifully sad, suffering, wistfully light and tender, softly velveteen, ironically pensive voice of the great Bulat Okudzhava, the idol of the Soviet intelligentsia, Vladimir Vysotsky's only near equal as the Soviet Union's preeminent guitar-strumming balladeer, on Marat's parents' *magnitofon,* or on the one in our family's apartment back in Leningrad, the bulky and extra-heavy *Dnieper.*

Specifically, with regard to Bulat Okudzhava, I loved his Moscow-themed songs: one about the little Moscow ant who needed someone to idolize and pray to; and also one about the last trolleybus coursing slowly and tirelessly through the gentle velveteen Moscow night, to make sure all the lovelorn souls stranded in the city after hours would get home safely in the end; and the one about Lyonka Korolyov, the "king" of the old Arbat city area, a street-smart noble-hearted boy felled by a Nazi bullet, like millions of his peers, young boys like him, before his life had even had a chance properly to begin. Okudzhava's floating, flowing, ironically sad, weightless voice was, to me, the very audial exhalation of Moscow. Tears of joy and longing rose in my eyes, blurring my vision, and my heart raced anxiously in the hollow of my chest when I listened to him in the dark—always in the dark, late in the evening, in the soft, kind night alive with yellow and blue lighted windows, either in Leningrad or in Moscow, but especially in Moscow, the movable feast of my childhood and adolescence.

Oh, those lovely, warm, cozy Moscow windows, memorialized unto all-USSR collective awareness, by the celebrated composer Tikhon Khrennikov and the famed lyrical poet Mikhail Matusovsky in their eponymous song, "Moscow Nights," performed on the radio typically by the beautifully voiceless yet soulful Vladimir Troshin, who sounded, somehow, like an old friend of all the Soviet people at once: How I loved them, in my imagination—those yellow- and blue-lighted Moscow windows in the dark, in the tender, gentle, teeming Moscow night! There, beyond those windows, lived and loved and suffered and rejoiced and moved about aimlessly and dreamed abstractly and held hands for hours and stared off into space blankly the regular Muscovites: the ordinary Soviet people just like me, those very little working ants of Soviet life—except, of course, I was from Leningrad.

O Leningrad, my hometown, the Soviet Union's self-styled cultural capital and the heroic site of the 1917 Bolshevik Revolution! How I loved you also, world's most beautiful city! . . . But then, enough exclaiming.

As kids, Marat and I sometimes would argue ferociously and at length about which city, Moscow or Leningrad, was better, mightier, lovelier, and offered its citizens more of an abiding reason to count themselves lucky by calling it home. We would be hurling the most ridiculously overblown insults at each other's wonderful cities during those spats. On a few occasions, we even came to blows! How silly we were then!

"You are told a lot about your education, but some beautiful, sacred memory, preserved since childhood, is perhaps the best education of all," Dostoyevsky writes in *Notes from the Underground*. "If a man carries many such memories into life with him, he is saved for the rest of his days. And even if only one good memory is left in our hearts, it may also be the instrument of our salvation one day."

O the soft, comforting glow of Moscow windows in the night! O Moscow, the warrantor of my well-being, the unwitting guarantor of my eternal salvation!

O this! O that!

"But why, Marat—why in the world did he decide to come back to the Soviet Union?" I asked, unexpectedly even to myself, puncturing the comfortable silence between us.

"Who? Where? What do you mean?" Marat asked distantly, still submerged, apparently, in his own private thoughts.

"Lev Konstantinovich!" I said quietly. "I can't understand it: Why did he agree to return to the Soviet Union from England? Didn't he know what would or very likely might happen to him there . . . here, that is? Especially with a wife from a capitalist country? I mean . . . It almost sounds as though he were deliberately committing suicide, along with his whole family—which is *not* cool, if you ask me. He shouldn't have ruined the lives of his wife and child, too, while wilfully demolishing his own. That was not a manly thing to do."

"Why, what a question!" Marat replied in an astonished voice. "Are you serious? Are you not the true son of our motherland? Well, I know you are, obviously, but really . . . How could he not have come back? Think about it! Even if he did know, or suspect—let's just posit that, for argument's sake—that he might be arrested upon arrival, because he might have sensed this was a ruse of some sort, this urgent request for him to return, a trap laid for him against their will by his heavyhearted relatives, presumably on the organs' orders, in the form of the fake sad news about his father's supposed grave illness, which actually might have been real, too—still, even with all that in mind, this was his beloved motherland . . . his sternly loving fatherland! Sometimes you really surprise me. There is no choice in such matters, even when technically there would seem to be one—no choice as to where you are going to be born; and once you're born somewhere, you belong to that place forever . . . if that place happens to be the Soviet Union, that is, of course, rather than somewhere in the capitalist world, for which latter one can have no loyalty, feel no fealty, because it clearly doesn't give much of a damn about one, either. But in our case—we, the Soviet people . . . We are Soviet people! You cannot not come back to the Soviet Union, ever, no matter what. It's as simple as that. It's just the way things are! No matter the consequences! What is meant to happen to you is going to happen, regardless. Let the falls chip where they may, or . . . what have you. That's life for you. Our Soviet life. Deal with it! Bite the old bullet! Accept it! Born in the USSR—USSR's forever. Born in the USSR—you will die in the USSR, too. Period. End of discussion."

In the silence, I could hear his breathing, and the beating of my own heart.

"I hear you, and that makes me feel scared," I told him.

Late at night, lying quietly on my back with my hands

behind my head on the living room couch, under a soft cotton blanket, in friendly, festive darkness, and feeling strangely unsettled, to the point of being unable to sleep, I gazed at the milky swirls of stucco in the dusky screen of the low-slung living room ceiling, with its random pattern of slow-moving, shape-shifting, muted multicolored refracted shadows of automobile lights from far below, down on the never-dormant Prospect of Peace. No outside sound reached my ears.

"Marat!" I called cautiously, in a hissing whisper. "Are you asleep, Marat?"

He shifted on his screechy, flimsy foldout cot a couple of meters away, in the impenetrable dark. "Mmm . . . What?" he said in a hoarse, faraway voice. "Sleeping, yes. Asleep . . ."

"Marat, do you remember how, five years ago maybe, all of us, my family and yours, in two cars, drove out to see first Tolstoy's estate, Yasnaya Polyana, near Tula, and then Turgenev's Spasskoye-Lutovinovo, near Orel?" I kept on whispering. "Wasn't that an amazing trip? It took us three days to make our way to those places from Moscow and back, remember? It was summer, and it was hot. My parents and my little brother and I were in my dad's research institute assistant's Pobeda, and the assistant was driving it himself; his name was Edouard, like that chicken's. And you were in your dad's Moskvich, of course, with him driving. Remember? And one of those nights we stayed at a roadside inn, not far from Yasnaya Polyana, and it felt really strange to be staying at that place. You must remember. It was my first time spending the night in an inn, and yours also. We were sharing a room."

"*Mmm-hmm,*" Marat mumbled again. "Well, yeah . . . I do. Why? What the . . . Let me sleep."

"We couldn't sleep, you and I, we were so excited, and so wired," I went on quickly. "So we started talking about all kinds of scary things, just for the hell of it, including what would be the most awful, torturously painful way to die, right? And you brought up Giordano Bruno and Jan Hus, who were both burned—burned!—at the stake. Burned! God! Remember? And Joan of Arc, too! Oh! And you told me then also how, when his death sentence was read out to Giordano Bruno, for his refusal to renounce his conviction that the Earth revolved around the Sun, he said to his judges, 'Perhaps you pronounce this sentence against me with greater fear than I receive it.' Those words, I was completely bowled over by them. Such composure! Me, I would've just collapsed on the floor, in his place, in a weeping heap of flesh . . . had I been told I'd be burned alive at the stake. I'd have died on the spot, of the sheer excess of horror—well, hopefully. And when an old woman, in medieval Prague, added an extra handful of straw to the pyre upon which Jan Hus was about to be burned, he said, rolling his eyes heavenward, almost ironically and in Latin, the dead language of his God, 'O holy simplicity!' Remember? I imagined all that just then, that whole thing—my own being tied to a pole, naked, and probably gagged, so that my piercing screams would not upset too much, instead of entertain, the assembled audience of random voyeurs of a sadistic bent; and then all that straw and other flammable materials being piled high all around me and then getting lighted, yes, set on fire, and everything starting to burn all at once, with great vengeance and terrible roaring, crackling deafeningly, columns of acrid, unbearably hot smoke rising to the sky in a tightening circle, with me at its dead center, and ... well, and my only hope at that point would be to die, cease to exist as quickly as possible, of smoke poisoning or pure psychological megashock, maybe even of a fortuitous heart attack, like I said—just to pass out and die on the spot right then and there, before those infernal tongues of flame started lapping at my naked flesh. ... Marat! Marat! Remember? How intensely horrifying those images were in my mind, how utterly and completely ... how ... fire ... Fire! All of a sudden, I started crying and screaming at the top of my lungs then, and ran out into the hall, which was dark and empty and smelled of shit and urine and stale tobacco smoke, and there I proceeded to run up and down its length, flailing my arms like a crazed bird, tripping and falling over myself and getting back up to my feet and continuing to run and scream, completely out of my mind with horror, until my parents and yours rushed out of their rooms, terrified. ... Remember?"

"Ummm ... What? What is it?" Marat grumbled,

sounding vaguely annoyed. "Yeah, I remember, but what does it . . . What . . . What's wrong with you tonight?"

"I don't know," I said guiltily. "I have no idea why I remembered this now."

"*Mmm* . . . Well . . . It happens," he said, turning over on his cot, his back to me. "That's fine. Let's just sleep now."

I lay silently in the dark, listening to Marat's quiet snoring and gazing at the muted, warm, live splashes of light across the ceiling. I wondered what it must feel like—at some point in your life, just out of nowhere—to forget everything about your past, lose all memories of yourself as a child, as a young man. How could it even be possible—living as a hostile stranger to yourself and your own past, carrying your own enemy within at all times, that permanent eraser of all your previous memories? How it must feel—to die and be brought back to life with no recollections preceding the moment of your death, no memories to rely on for your eternal salvation—how odd, how terrible! Why would one even choose to go on living, I wondered, under such hopeless circumstances, as a man with no past, when the past is all we have and all there is?

Well, but then, I thought, what choice is there for someone with no past but to just keep on living? What would be resolved by one's killing oneself? How would nonexistence improve one's terrible predicament? When you are someone with no memories, no past, your present may not mean all that much to you, either, because of its essential nonexistence, so it's not all that terribly tragic in the end. It was easier just to keep going with the old flow. ... There was a measure of comfort in the thought that life always, under all circumstances, had some independent value of its own, making it always preferable to death, even if that was only by the narrowest of margins.

Could, I wondered briefly, something like that ever happen to me? Could I, too, unimaginably, lose all traces of my past in my mind, completely out of the blue and for no interpretable reason, at some point in the impenetrable future? Well, of course it could. As a matter of fact, I thought, how could it not happen to me, or anyone, at least to some partial extent, at one point or another in our lives, given how limited memory's storage space must be, relatively speaking. It had to be quite limited indeed. Memories came and went. Would I, for instance, be able to remember this very night in Moscow, I asked myself, this warm cocoon of a perfectly uneventful moment in the night, a whole bunch of years later, on the threshold of the twenty-first century, still more than three decades away, unimaginably? I rather doubted it—but by the same token, I could not possibly conceive of ever managing to forget it, either. How could I ever forget that which I was remembering at any given moment? It was inconceivable! And yet, I knew, somehow, that forget most of my past up to now I ineluctably would have to.

Forgetting was inconceivable to the one who remembered, as death made no sense to one still alive. ... That,

I knew, was too advanced and abstract a thought for me to mull over so late at night. Still and all, I wondered whether or not I would remember my present, fifteen-year-old self, many eons into the future—just a sleepless little Jewish Soviet kid from Leningrad lying quietly flat on my back late at night in Moscow and thinking of whether or not he would be able to remember that very precise moment. . . . Oh well. Finally I was starting to feel heavy-lidded, and no longer capable of carrying on a thoughtful internal conversation with myself. What was the point or even the exact nature of my wondering? Life? Yeah, great. Life was one of those things . . . with too many unknown variables.

I yawned and stretched, feeling cozy and happy.

An unimaginably endless life lay ahead of me, almost frighteningly so. Sometimes, when I thought about it, I became so agitated that I found it difficult to breathe. Everything and anything could happen at any point in the course of my hazy future's pure vastness. By the time the year 2000 rolled around, I'd already be a very old man, living—if still living and if one could even call that life— well, where? On Mars, maybe? Maybe on Mars. Sure, why not? Or perhaps even in America, if it still existed—if, that is, by the year 2000, the whole world wouldn't have long become one giant Soviet Union. That was possible. Who could foretell such things, peering so insanely far into the chimera of the future? Or maybe—but that was a dangerous line of thinking, and I told myself to cut it out at once—maybe it would be the Soviet Union, conversely, that would cease to ... you know. Too many unknowable variables. It was possible, too, that by the time I got old, medical science would have progressed to the point of making it easily feasible for people's old and tired, slow, worn-out brains to be replaced on a routine basis with everlasting synthetic brains. Maybe by the year 2000, anyone and everyone who wanted to be immortal, to live forever, would have that option at their disposal. Again, sure, why not? And maybe, too, as a result of that ready availability of quick, routine brain replacement on demand for everyone, remembering nothing of one's past would become a new social norm in that future world, with people actually being proud of how perfectly complete their nonremembrance of things past was. Again, sure, why not?

It might be interesting, mildly curious, I thought distantly, from afar, if one night in my old age, pushing fifty maybe, all of a sudden, completely out of the blue, finding nothing better to occupy my newly installed synthetic brain with in the middle of my futuristic nocturnal nondormancy, on Mars somewhere or in Soviet America, I were to attempt remembering myself as a boy, a fifteen-year-old, say—and then, after drawing predictably nothing but a big fat blank and remembering instead that, of course, remembering my previous selves no longer was an option for me and that the fifteen-year-old boy who'd used to be me therefore had been dead for a veritable eternity, poor little thing, maybe for a fleeting instant I would feel uncharacteristically sad, in a long-forgotten and indeed impossible kind of way, but then I, or that very old me with a new brain, would shake his head self-ironically, engulfed by night's gentle darkness, on his futuristic invisible pillow made of pure ionized air and solar energy or whatever, and he would smile wistfully in the dark and say to himself, very quietly, under his breath, just so as to hear someone's voice in the night, "I bet he was a reasonably good kid—that boy I used to be once. I wish part of me still could be him."

Sure, why not? I thought, drifting off. Old people often were tearfully sentimental for no good reason. A wave of quiet ardor passed over me in the dark, and I closed my eyes, breathing deeply and evenly, falling into the night, remembering everything and nothing.

Our Entire Nation

W HEN I WOKE UP EARLY that sunny and nice early-
September morning, my parents had already left
for work. My father, a promising young scientist in the
field of submarine electromagnetism, was always the first
to leave. His secret research institute, guarded by a bunch
of hungry Caucasus-mountain shepherd dogs, was situated on the far end of the city, in a well-known (though
not to me) but undisclosed location.

On her way to her rubber-goods factory (the second
largest in the country), where she worked as a junior tech-
nologist, my mother dropped my screaming and kicking
little brother off at the nursery school around the corner
from us. We lived in a large communal apartment on
the sixth floor of a sturdy nineteenth-century apartment
building on Egorova Street (named apparently after some
prominent Bolshevik), in a small enclave of quietness amid
the constant frenetic activity in the roiling blue-collar Len-
insky District neighborhood in a more Dostoyevskian area
of midtown Leningrad, a mere five-minute walk from the
giant new Frunzensky Department Store (the second largest in the city) and the bustling Varshavsky and Baltiisky
train stations. In the shallow niche in the wall that went

around the former train station's perimeter, overlooking the odoriferous Obvodny Canal (the city's main open-air sewage artery), a life-size bronze Lenin stood on a stumpy little pedestal. Every time, accompanied by my nanny, Lyuba, I drew level with him on our daily morning walks around the neighborhood, I saluted him smartly. Lyuba—an awkward, ungainly, too-tall, myopic peasant girl of nineteen, originally from Cheboksary (capital of the Volga-bound Chuvash Autonomous Soviet Socialist Republic)—lived with us, in our single room, taking care of me almost since the day I came into the world. She had no legal right to live in Leningrad, lacking as she did the requisite permit (*propiska*) to reside in the city permanently. She lived with us *illicitly*. I was in love with her—and she, in turn, was in love with, or at least had a powerful crush on, Yuri Vlasov, the greatest Soviet weight lifter of all time: the bespectacled, thoughtful, erudite hero of the 1960 Olympic Games in Rome, Italy. Vlasov, however, already had a wife, according to Lyuba—and besides, he didn't even know she existed in the first place—and so instead she was now about to marry someone else—a firefighter named Nikolay. Nikolay, though not the sharpest knife in the drawer (by Lyuba's own lighthearted admission), had two crucial advantages over the little me: He was a grown man and, even more important, had a room of his own, which he shared with his mother, in a communal apartment not too far away from us. Marrying him would provide Lyuba with that coveted, precious, and elusive Leningrad *propiska*. She dreaded and abhorred the very thought of being found out and forced to go back to Cheboksary someday. Such, in brief, was her situation, in my understanding.

Lyuba's upcoming wedding—about which I'd only been told, by her, the day before—and her subsequently imminent and permanent departure from my life, was the primary reason I was in an unusually surly, grumpy mood that morning. I barely touched my breakfast—a plateful of steaming buckwheat kasha (which, under ordinary circumstances, I rather liked), with an uneven cube of yellow Cuban lump sugar and a dollop of Bulgarian butter, in addition to a white-bread sandwich (*buterbrod*) with a slice of half-smoked Polish sausage (*krakovskaya*) and Finnish soft processed cheese, Viola, plus a poppy-seed *bulochka* (cake). I was, ordinarily, a healthy eater!

As soon as Lyuba, muttering disapprovingly under her breath, excused me from the table, I ran over to the discordant old Red October piano in the corner of our room, clambered onto the black swivel stool in front of it, and started pecking out on it, with one finger, my current favorite song: "The Bearded Men's March." Dedicated by the freedom-loving people of brotherly Cuba to their indomitable leader, Comrade Fidel, it had a very catchy tune, beautiful in its sheer simplicity. "Our entire nation / Is fighting on our side! / We know / We're going to win this fight!" It was played day and night on the radio that early fall—the sixth one of my life.

While I was busy extracting this melody from our discordant piano, Lyuba—across the room from me, by the door, kneeling alongside the lumpy roll of striped straw-filled mattress she slept on at night—was performing her morning ritual of praying to the crudely painted paper portrait of the Virgin of Voronezh, her personal female saint, unfurled on the buckling, unvarnished parquet floor.

I had no clear notion as to what exactly she was doing in those moments and what kinds of strange thoughts passed through her inclined head just then, nor who that supposedly saintly painted woman with an inordinately long neck and big haunted eyes was; nowadays, I might be tempted to suspect Lyuba unwittingly was using a magazine reproduction of a Modigliani painting as an object of her moist-eyed devotion, had I not known that, of course, there were no reproductions of any Modigliani or any other such bourgeois-deviant, decadent paintings allowed to circulate back then in the Soviet Union. However, I *was* aware, even at the tender age, that the general thrust of what she was doing—making believe that God, despite Yuri Gagarin's having proved his nonexistence during his first-ever orbital flight when I was a little younger still, actually did exist, incredibly, incomprehensibly, shamefully, and improperly in the extreme, to the point of being downright forbidden—could land her in a world of trouble, were I to decide to rat her out, so to speak and not to mince words, to my parents . . . let alone someone else, a priori less lenient and forgiving. In that sense, she was in my power, totally. That morning, overcome with sadness and resentment, I was actually contemplating doing just that—yes, ratting her out—in a desperate attempt to prevent her from marrying Nikolay and abandoning us, and especially me. I thought—and I knew, too, that this was a pretty advanced consideration for a six-year-old—that I could keep her all to myself by making her too, well, dangerous, untouchable, so to speak, for Nikolay the firefighter, most certainly a Komsomol member, to marry. I was not proud of myself for thinking of betraying her and having her sent back to Cheboksary, or worse, but . . . desperate times called for desperate measures.

Our . . . entire nation . . . is . . . fighting . . . on our . . . side. . . . We know . . . we . . . we . . . we . . . are going . . . to . . . win . . . win . . . win . . .

"You're just like your father when he's peck-peck-pecking away at his typewriter," Lyuba said, smiling, and got back up to her feet to hide the rolled-up icon (for that's what that odd painting was called, as she'd told me once) under a loose parquet block near the base of the blue-tiled floor-to-ceiling wood-burning oven (*pechka*) that dominated our room's meager horizontality. "Only the sounds he makes are maybe a little pleasanter," she added, turning back to face me with a jolly wink, "because at least they're not supposed to make any kind of sense to one's ears!"

"Just joking, my love," she added quickly, before I could register the insult in my mind and start pouting.

My father's old, impossibly heavy black German

typewriter, a little scary to look at, sat on the window-sill. He used it only rarely, preferring to work in longhand at his small desk by the windowsill, cluttered with books and sheets of paper. Sometimes he stayed up, writing away, until as late as three or four o'clock in the morning. (Occasionally, unaccountably, I would wake up at that dead-of-night hour and watch him silently for a while from my bed, his face severe and yet also soft in the glow of the green-shaded desk lamp.) When, infrequently, he needed to have some of his writings typed up, he would lift that heavy cast-iron German machine off the windowsill and, walking on tiptoes, carry it over to the communal kitchen, which was situated at sufficient remove from all other tenants' rooms for him not to run the risk of disturbing anyone's fitful sleep or sleeplessness in the apartment. He was, at the time, busy putting the finishing touches, as he was wont to say, on his first full-scale monograph dedicated to the exploration of the corrosive properties of various types of metals in the immediate presence of submarine electromagnetic fields. (Many years later, I would also own a typewriter—and also one of German make, but mine would be a much lighter, sleeker, less ominous-looking one: a portable Erika, made largely of plastic. On it, among reams of other, perfectly forgettable stuff, I would one day compose a story about one day in the life of a little . . . Oh well, never mind. It's a different story. Some other time.)

It was, I could tell, already pretty late in the morning. While Lyuba washed the dishes in the communal kitchen, I immersed myself, as I often did, in my father's amazing stamp collection. It was contained in four special beige philatelic albums, which he kept in the upper-right-hand drawer of his desk. In his child-hood and youth, he had been an avid stamp collector. (Even as a child, I am quite willing to concede, he was a more interesting, multifaceted person than I ever would become. . . . Or maybe that'd be overstating it a little.) Contemplating all those variably beautiful (and invari-ably fascinating) stamps, many thousands of them, always made me feel good, warm inside, comfortable and safe, additionally protected. It was like a soft embrace, that feel-ing. My favorite Soviet stamp in the entire collection was the one commemorating Lenin's death back in 1924: deep crimson, bloodred, with stark black trimming—extremely tragic and dramatic! There were stamps from all over the world in that amazing, voluminous, and precious collec-tion, and most of them were really old and therefore rare and valuable, some even hailing from countries that no longer existed in the world, such as Mesopotamia, Trip-olitania, Prussia, Zanzibar, and the Austro-Hungarian Empire. Some American stamps also were present in the collection, but their visual appeal left much to be desired. Americans, it seemed, did not place too much emphasis on the aesthetic aspect of their stamps . . . or anything else, for that matter, since, as it was known to me and all the rest of us, the Soviet people, that it was a country of coldly pragmatic, materialistic, money-crazed, profit-oriented, soulless, spiritless, uninspired and uninspiring people, which, in fairness, wasn't all their fault, but, rather, that of international imperialism, also known to the world as the military-industrial complex or else the Pentagon.

(I have just thought about my grandfather, my mother's father and my only grandfather, for no clear reason. Maybe because he was an Old Bolshevik, having joined the Party at the very young age of fourteen, according to him. The Revolution liberated him from something called the Pale of Settlement, so no wonder he loved it so much. Whatever the Pale of Settlement might have been. He and my grandmother lived in a sleepy, leafy, snowy, quaint little suburb of Moscow called Moose Island. The year before, I had spent many months there, living with them, because . . . Oh well, some other time. It's a different story.)

One American stamp in the collection featured a big, fat, beefy, mustachioed man with a cold, arrogant face. His name was Theodore Roosevelt. Roosevelt. Some important imperialist. It was perfectly well known to everyone, of course, that America would never allow putting on one of its stamps the face of a good, decent, nonimperialist, proletarian man, rather than a capitalist exploiter of proletarian labor or an unabashed representative of the military-industrial complex, or the Pentagon. That much was clear, of course.

America, America. A dark, dangerous, ominously rumbling, potentially deadly word. It was important, as I'd been warned by my grandfather—and not only him—not to repeat it out loud more than two times in a row, or else it could start drawing you, in its evil depths, in, and then you would fall into it headfirst and get lost, just disappear without a trace, entirely and forever.

America was ubiquitous, omnipresent. It was everywhere. There had never been a time I wouldn't have known its name, I was convinced. I must have heard it a good couple of million times already by the time I was six. Or more. But then, in truth, concerning that number, I couldn't be so sure. I only knew how to count to one hundred . . . well, maybe.

It was important to hate America and, to some extent, pity the ordinary oppressed, exploited, proletarian Americans. Every Soviet citizen was supposed to feel that way—it was one's basic patriotic duty. In the dimly lit anteroom of the collective Soviet mentality, to put it metaphorically, America loomed gigantic—a singularly hellacious place of unadorned, unadulterated evil, all bathed in toxic, deep-purple sulfuric mist, figuratively speaking. We, on the other hand—the Soviet Union, our entire nation—were the glorious society of eternal light and a radiant future, the ultimate symbol of communism-bound humankind's essential innate goodness.

In short, the infinitely wicked and historically doomed America and just as limitlessly good us—we were the world's, maybe even the universe's, greatest antipodes . . . (Antipodes? Really? . . . Okay: opposites, rivals.) When boys my age and older played war in the inner courtyard below (and sometimes, and often, Lyuba would let me watch but almost never participate in their rowdy games), it was always the youngest and weakest and stupidest and least adroit in the group who were chosen to represent America. The indomitable Red Cavalry, led by the legendary marshals Budyonny and Voroshilov (such beautiful, evocative names!), totally and with final decisiveness dispersed and destroyed America in no time flat! America had no chance against us! And yes, it was historically doomed.

(And yet . . . Oddly enough, there would always be found among that war game's prospective participants two or three weird, abnormal boys, who, notwithstanding the fact of their faces being red with shame, would actually volunteer—yes, imagine!—to be, to represent America, knowingly, braving their normal, patriotically minded peers' contemptuous looks, hissed curses, and loud shouts of derision. Clearly, much to their own mortified confusion, America held some kind of powerful, mysterious sway over them, both repulsing and irresistibly fascinating them at once, beckoning to them. . . .)

I put my father's stamp albums aside on the round dinner table in the middle of the room, took a cornflower blue chemical pencil from his desk, and, on an empty sheet of paper also lifted from his desk, wrote (I could write . . . a little!), in angular block letters, "AMERIKA."

I contemplated that word for a few moments, my head tilted to one shoulder, wondering and not quite knowing what to do with it. Such a short, simple combination of letters! And yet, just as my father's albums held within them a veritable infinity of worlds past and present, so, too, was that word, *AMERIKA*, a virtual receptacle of everything dark, dangerous, and evil on Earth, but also a lot of something dangerously and ineffably magnetic: a pole of seductive wickedness, a boundless wall of absolute darkness. And we, the Soviet Union, of course, were the wall of endless blinding light. In a nutshell.

For a while then, not quite knowing what else to do with myself, I thought of all the perfectly ordinary and warmly familiar Russian words and names probably—undoubtedly—hidden inside, as though imprisoned within that bottomless word, *AMERIKA*, as if swallowed by it: Marik (my favorite cousin's father, a well-known nuclear physicist who lived in Moscow), Arik (husband of one of my mother's oldest friends), Mirra (my mother's oldest friend, wife of Arik), Mark (one of my father's friends and colleagues at that secret research institute; he was a lot of fun and I loved him), Kira (Mark's wife and another one of my mother's friends), *mera* (measure), Karim (the kindly, always smiling Tartar *pirozhki* vendor just outside our apartment building, at the corner of Egorova and Sixth Red Cavalry streets), Aram (Aram Khachaturyan, the great Soviet composer, author of the world-famous composition "Sabre Dance"), Rim (Rome, the capital of Italy, site of the great Soviet weight lifter Yuri Vlasov's Olympic triumph), *mir* (both peace and world), *reka* (river), *ikra* (caviar), *mrak* (darkness), *kamera* (photo camera or else prison cell), *rak* (crawfish; cancer), *arka* (archway), *rama* (large frame—a window frame, for instance), *ramka* (small frame, such as one for photographs), *marka* (postal stamp), Irak (former Mesopotamia), *mak* (poppy), *kara* (severe punishment, usually by death, meted out for some ultimately unforgivable crime, such as becoming a traitor to the motherland, an American spy), and so on—an infinity of words!

I put the pencil down and gazed ahead of me at nothing in particular. Lyuba was still in the kitchen.

Old Faina was shuffling back and forth, back and forth out in the communal corridor, all along its dark, meandering length. She was always out there, shuffling back and forth, back and forth in her oversize old Skorokhod boots with no shoelaces. Back and forth, back and forth.

The long and winding, eternally dark corridor that lay outside our room and led from the communal apartment's front door to the communal kitchen, past the communal bathroom and toilet (early in the morning and before bedtime in the evening, there would be lines of apartment tenants formed, waiting for their turn to use the facilities), always presented itself in my mind as some scary, dark, bone-dry, smelly dead river with no water in it. It was static, stagnant, dead, frozen in time and space, of course—yet it still flowed, in a certain conjectured sense, through the gloomy, narrow canyon of multitiered Soviet history, so to speak, being that the slightly concave, tall walls on its both sides, all along its crooked length, were papered with layers of newsprint (*Pravda, Izvestiya, Leningradskaya Pravda*, etc.) dating all the way back to the 1920s, and up to a year or two after my coming into the world. The consecutive layers of Soviet history, superimposed upon one another, revealed their composite nature in many places in the corridor, via the visible sediment of headlines and photographs I was at the time much too little to comprehend. Yet I knew that was history incarnate. (I recognized Khrushchev and Lenin, of course, and maybe Stalin also, but not, say, Molotov or Kirov, or Chamberlain and Ribbentrop.) I had a feeling one could spend one's entire life studying those corridor walls, if so inclined—navigating that dark, dry, dead, terrible, murderous river.

Back and forth, back and forth. Old Faina, for one, most certainly was not interested in the layers of history covering the corridor walls as she paced, shuffling back and forth, out there for hours on end in those scuffed boots with time-worn soles, the ubiquitous *papirosa* sticking from the corner of her craggy mouth. She had lived through that history, after all—had flown down that river of death. Everyone called her "Old Faina."

Old Faina was viciously angry and perennially embittered, nasty even, mean to everyone. She had lived in the apartment forever—at least since the end of the Civil War between the Reds and the Whites. That much I knew, and that was all I knew about her. She would corner my mother, when my mother was pregnant with me (of course, at six, I had no idea that was how I'd come to exist), somewhere

in the corridor's fetid darkness and, blowing harshly acrid
papirosa smoke in my mother's face, would whisper to her,
"It won't be a human, mark my words. You'll give birth
to a mouse, I promise." She would, as a matter of habit,
slip slivers of tar soap in other tenants' pots of soup boiling on the communal gas stove in the kitchen, when she
found herself to be alone there. There was no specific reason. Several nights a week, she would set on the floor all
along the corridor's winding length, in a variety of random
patterns, pans and buckets filled with tap water—so that
those tenants of the male sex who tended to return to the
apartment after hours (that is, after the Kremlin Courants
on never-dormant Spasskaya Tower had chimed midnight
on the kitchen radio, followed by the fartlike opening
chords of the national anthem) and, needless to say, in a
drunken state (most of the men in the communal apartment were lifelong drunks, although my father hardly ever
touched liquor, and there also lived in the apartment with
his wife and daughter a renowned, apparently, professor of
music at the Leningrad Conservatory, who a decade and
a half or so later would emigrate to Israel and, in the end,
as a result of a characteristically circuitous set of existen-
tial circumstances, end up teaching Russian language and
choral singing at one moderately selective private liberal
arts college in the American Midwest)—well, long sentence short, all those severely inebriated men, returning to
the apartment late at night, inevitably would stumble on
and trip all over those water-filled vessels on the corridor

floor in the dark, at some early point during their wobbly progress toward their respective rooms, and would come tumbling down, fall, and spill all over themselves, and would hit the floor with a deafening thud, disgorging a furious volley of obscene words and idiomatic expressions.

That was just something that brought Old Faina joy. Shuffling back and forth, back and forth, out in the communal corridor. Pausing momentarily just outside our door. Smoking incessantly, mumbling something barely audible under her breath.

"The Bearded Men's March" was playing faintly on the radio in the kitchen. I listened to it to the end, sitting still. Then an exalted, disembodied male voice, almost howling with excitement, commenced to recite Maxim Gorky's "Song of the Stormy Petrel"—and I listened to that also, although I had no idea what it was.

Then a public announcement came on. A woman, making it—whatever information she was imparting—sound both solemn and extremely, supernaturally happy. I couldn't make out what she was saying.

"Oh my God! That is so . . . so unbelievable! Are you going to go, Faina?" I heard Lyuba say in a thrilled voice, already from out in the corridor and not very far from our door. Of all the people in the apartment, Lyuba alone was not intimidated by Old Faina—and the latter, in turn, oddly enough, didn't seem to resent Lyuba nearly as much as she loathed everyone else, with the possible exception of me. (She saved my life once, when I'd almost fallen, floated out of the open kitchen window one fragrant, velvet-soft evening. But that's a different story. Some other time.)

"Too old for that kind of stuff," Old Faina replied in her screechy voice. "All those stairs, all those damn people. No. Still, I'm going to outlive them yet, you know, mark my words! So you know. Even that young and beautiful one." She cackled at her own words, which I didn't understand and Lyuba didn't respond to, and then she launched into a prolonged coughing fit.

Lyuba walked into the room beaming, as radiant as I had hardly ever seen her before, and told me we needed to get ready for a walk straightaway. "Let's get you dressed, quickly, my love. Something very important is going to happen around here very shortly today."

"What is it, Lyuba?" I asked, also beginning to tremble inside.

"Oh, I wanted it be a surprise for you, but—fine, I'm going to tell you. We have to be in front of the Frunzensky Department Store by ten past noon, sharp, and maybe even earlier than that, because there was an announcement on the radio just now that . . . But no, I still want it to be a surprise for you. Everyone will be there, I'll bet, this whole neighborhood, so we'd better make you look real good real fast." And she quickly and deftly got me all decked out in my picture-taking best—the ludicrously childish-looking red velour short pants, pitiful wafer-thin brown flannel stockings, silly little blue corduroy jacket, and shiny black patent-leather sandals. I hated the way I looked when I was supposed to look good. But ultimately, I didn't care.

"Beautiful, my love!" she said, looking me over critically.

Lyuba and I, hand in hand, walked out of the apartment, went down the six tall flights of sticky, time-worn, fake-marble stairs, and, once out in the sunny open air, crossed the strangely deserted inner courtyard (where were all the raucous boys and rope-jumping girls and drunk dominoes players with their throaty yelps and barbaric yawps?), passed under the functionally useless brick archway connecting the inner courtyard with the outer world (the archway's inner walls were covered densely with crude chalk drawings of sundry genitalia and obscene words I wasn't supposed to know how to read), and a few seconds later were standing on Egorova Street's broad flagstone sidewalk, momentarily stunned by the scene unfolding before us. Just as our inner courtyard had been strangely desolate only several moments ago, so was our modest little street—one of the quietest in the immediately surrounding area, the only world I knew—almost impossibly thronged with people, bursting to overflow! Fellow Leningraders, denizens of the most beautiful and terrible city on Earth (one of my parents' guests in our room had said it once, and I remembered), were streaming past us in numbers infinitely exceeding my ability to comprehend, much less visualize, infinity! A river, nay, a sea of people! Some of them looked happy and excited, but most did not, it seemed. But then, it normally was only the drunks prone to smiling at no one in particular out in the street. Many had in their hands tiny miniature Soviet flags, while some had the ones with a lovely white star and deep-purple triangle, and others the ones with blue and white stripes on them.

Most of those people must be dead by now, by the way. Virtually all of them, most likely.

Yes, Egorova Street looked entirely, and therefore dangerously and ominously, unfamiliar to me that eerily distant afternoon. Everything and everyone looked entirely unrecognizable. Hard as I tried, squinting my eyes and shielding them against the pale midafternoon sun glare, I was unable even to descry, in the hazy Moskovsky Prospect–bound perspective, the ever-present, familiar, angular, ungainly silhouette of the amiable vendor Karim, who sold hot *pirozhki*, *belyashi*, from his voluminous off-white cart, spoke Russian in a funny way, and always greeted me by name with much exuberance whenever Lyuba and I went out for our daily morning walk, and, energetically gesticulating, always called out for me to come over, so that he could present me with a piping-hot *belyash*, an open-faced meat *pirozhok*—which Lyuba, smiling and rolling her eyes, would immediately take away from me, wrap in her crumpled red handkerchief, and hide in her red imitation-leather bag of sorts, telling me and Karim that she would give it to me once we were back home (as I knew she would, every time).

Indeed, Karim, with his *pirozhki* cart, was nowhere to be seen now, as if swept away, along with everyone and everything else I could identify, by that unstoppable, menacing flow of humanity. Suddenly gripped by an unaccountably strong premonition of something terribly, irremediably life-changing taking place around me, I shuddered and whimpered, clinging to Lyuba's leg.

"Are you ready?" she half-asked, her voice rich and tremulous with excitement, and squeezed my sweaty little palm lightly in her large calloused hand. I nodded, not knowing what else to do. Tears blurred my vision.

"Well, then . . . One . . . two . . . three! Let's go! Hold on to me tight!" she commanded. I closed my eyes, held my breath, nodded again—and we stepped off the sidewalk and right into that churning, silently grumbling, murmuring, low-humming, resonant river of faceless people.

It was powerful, that river! Unstoppable!

But also, mercifully, it was short—short-lived. It had a lot of tributaries, too. Soon enough, growing in size, expanding with each street block or blind alley it flowed past, it came to a halt at the corner of Moskovsky Prospect (one of the city's longest and busiest mercantile thoroughfares) and the Obvodny Canal embankment. This, apparently, was our final destination, where the river of us broadened into a veritable heaving sea of people!

Big, burly, bearlike, extremely serious-looking men with inscrutable meaty faces, clad in black slickers, too warm for the lovely and clement sunny day, were overseeing and directing, with succinct body language, the distribution of that immense mass of people over the objectively rather limited space between the oddly deserted Moskovsky and the nearest wide footbridge across the Obvodny. We were all bunched up there as densely and tightly as was humanely possible. I felt the great and still growing fear of being squeezed to near death (thus testing the limits of my inherent immortality) by two or more of those massive grown-up bodies surrounding me on all sides, although I kept reminding myself of my abiding, unquestioning faith in Lyuba's ever-ready ability to protect me from everything and everyone. Far above my head, I could see lots of handwritten or printed placards, some of which, with an effort, I actually could read: DOWN WITH AMERICA! PEACE TO THE WORLD! YANKEE GO HOME! HANDS OFF THE ISLAND OF HOPE! WE LOVE YOU, THE ISLAND OF CRIMSON DAWN! All around me, far and wide, people were shouting, laughing, hugging, slapping one another's backs, pushing and shoving one another, jostling, kicking and screaming, fighting, cussing one another out viciously. The air was full of furious sound and positively crackling with live electricity. Everyone was there, I knew somehow—our entire nation!

My head was spinning and my heart was bursting with love mixed with terror. "Lyuba! Lyuba! Let's go home! I'm afraid!" I cried, yanking at her hand with all my might. Much too excited to notice, she was also shouting something into the air, joyous, paying me no attention.

I was tiny, small, smaller than any living human creature there, the smallest little being—and I was surrounded
on all sides by a dense forest of swaying and moving in
place, menacing tree-tall bodies. Indeed, it no longer
was a river or a sea—it was an impenetrably dense forest! Throwing my head far back, I could only see a slice
of the shimmering pale blue sky of northern Russia's early
autumn—*babye leto*—womenfolk's summer, Indian summer. Autumn. The sky was beautiful, but it was empty and
there was nothing worth watching going on up there.

"Here, my love. Let me help you!" Lyuba said very
loudly, leaning down to me, finally remembering about
me. She took me in her arms, swung me up and down in
the air, kissed me playfully on top of my head, patted my
behind, and, in one last upswing, propped me up on her
shoulders.

Instantly pacified, comforted, and consoled, I smiled
happily. All was well with the world again.

Now I was soaring high above that human forest like
a . . . oh, I don't know, like some soaring-prone bird or
something; I was just soaring up there. I saw hundreds,
thousands, maybe billions, the untold multitudes of people
all around me. It didn't matter how many of them were
there. Very many, that's how many. And they all looked
the same to me. I'd only seen so many people all at once on
the small, matchbox-size, convex screen of the KVN TV
set in our room in our communal apartment when they

were showing the swelling happy crowds in Red Square on the First of May and the Seventh of November.

It was both exhilarating and, yes, terrifying to see so many of us, Leningraders, the Soviet people, in one place at the same time. And we all were waiting for something. "Amerika, Amerika," I said loudly, sitting on top of Lyuba's shoulders, just maybe so as to hear the sound of my own voice and make sure I still existed in the same way I'd always been. My heart was hammering away in my chest and in my ears. No one had heard me, and no one was paying me any mind.

Then, all of a sudden, far off on the periphery of my indistinct, blurred field of vision, I caught sight of the pale, small, almost unnoticeable, sun-dappled faces of two people I did actually know—and indeed, I knew them very well. One was my mother's old and close friend Mirra, whom I called "Aunt Mirra." (I knew that her first husband had been a brilliant young mathematician and one of the Soviet Union's most talented and accomplished mountain climbers—and, apparently, something very bad had happened to him in that latter capacity of his, as a result of which he . . . died. Ceased to exist. Because, in part, unfortunately for him, he hadn't belonged to the extremely tight circle of people covered and protected by the umbrella-like force field of my innate personal immortality. Decades later, when I would be older than my parents were when I was six, my mother, all of a sudden and for no explicable reason, would reveal to me that in reality, Aunt Mirra's first husband had committed suicide by hanging himself in the bathroom of their communal apartment.)

Of course it was her, Aunt Mirra, immediately recognizable, with her shining helmet of thick black hair. She always looked a little forlorn.

"Aunt Mirra!" I hollered in her direction, waving my hand, the one now free from holding on to the top of Lyuba's head. "It's me! Me! Over here!" I had a very loud, high-pitched, and, false modesty aside, beautiful voice; our communal apartment neighbors called me their "little Robertino Loretti," the Italian singing wonder child, loved by everyone in the Soviet Union. Nevertheless, she could not hear me, lost to the world as she appeared to be, and just continued to gaze vacantly straight ahead of her.

What was she doing there, in that spot, standing idly in the middle of a workday? But then, by the same token, what were Lyuba and I doing there, on that bridge across the awful-smelling Obvodny Canal?

Many people in the crowd did, however, hear me, and some turned to glance at me, with a nonplussed expression on their faces. One of those big, burly, and pointedly faceless men in shiny black slickers who appeared to be and undoubtedly were in charge of containing and regulating within its rigid proscribed bounds that immense human mass of which we were but a minuscule part, the one positioned the closest to us, also pivoted at the sound of my voice and gave me a cold, appraising, registering, quizzically indifferent stare—neither an overtly angry nor, most certainly, a friendly one. A mineral-hard memorizing gaze it was. Chills ran down my spine. I bit my tongue, trembling inwardly. "Shut up, love. What's wrong with you?" Lyuba hissed from underneath me, slapping me lightly on my leg and then giving my ankle a painful squeeze. I began to cry, quietly, silently . . . but then, in an instant, I cheered up some, because next to Aunt Mirra stood Mark—or Uncle Mark, to me. Fairly frail of frame, prominent of nose, quick with a smile, he, of course, was not my uncle, just as Aunt Mirra was not my aunt or Uncle Nikita Khrushchev most assuredly was not my uncle—he was just one of my father's best friends, his colleague from work at that well-known secret research institute of theirs, and also (just like my father, only probably less so) a promising young Soviet scientist. It was a little surprising to see them together, and that Uncle Mark had his arm around Aunt Mirra's shoulders. I'd had no idea they were such close friends. It was almost as if she were his wife, although both of them were married to other people. I knew Mark's wife, for instance—her name was Kira. Aunt Kira . . .

I liked Mark a lot, I loved him, and so when I saw him again, through the rainbow veil of tears, I stopped crying and, unable to contain myself, yelled again, even more piercingly than before: "Uncle Mark! I'm here! Over here! It's me! Look how high I am!"

And what do you know? Unlike Aunt Mirra, he did hear me! But of course! Immediately, with a start, he homed in on the veritable siren of my voice, like enemy radar (for that, as I would learn much later, was the area of his and my father's secret research) on the electromagnetic signal emitted by one of our heroic but outmoded Soviet submarines in the imperialist coastal waters. Our eyes met, and his handsome face expressed momentary surprise. I thought he would wave back at me with his characteristic infectious broad smile, because he loved me, as did everyone else in my world—and I thought he would right away start trying to make his way toward us through the rumbling multitudes, with sad Aunt Mirra in tow. But instead, very oddly and extremely strangely, he averted his eyes, pulled his head in between his shoulders, like a human turtle, and quickly turned away, ducking back into the darkness of the forest of people behind him. What in the world was wrong with him? . . .

In the meantime, yet again, only more sinisterly this time, the same severe faceless man in black guarding and directing our part of the entire giant crowd gave me the same steady, spine-chilling, appraising, memorizing gaze—and wilting again at once, I drew back into myself and closed my eyes in order to disappear, become invisible, cease to exist.

But then, but then . . . all of a sudden, like the loudest thunderclap ever heard, straight from the cloudless pale blue Leningrad sky of a fine September day, they, whoever they might be, were upon us! First a compact school of speedy and ferocious, shining foreign-made motorcycles roared by, all blurry white glare and black radiance, followed immediately by the terribly silent bevy of fearsome-looking, awesome, barracudalike Chaikas and ZiLs (I'd seen both on television before) with luminous black windows . . . and finally, amid a mad swarm of more motorcycles and smaller cars, far and away the greatest, grandest, longest automobile one could ever possibly imagine, the regular dinosaur (and yes, I've seen those in my *Children's Encyclopedia*) of the road, rolled into view, swiftly and yet also as if in slow motion, majestically, magisterially. It had no roof over it. Two men stood in it—one young, tall, and beautiful, beaming, radiant, magnetic, dark-haired, with a short charcoal black beard and clad in spanking-new military fatigues; the other a cue ball–bald, fatty one in a crumpled beige suit. I didn't recognize either of them at first, so smitten and overpowered I was by the otherworldly sight of the splendid cavalcade, and so totally preposterous and ludicrous was the very thought that those two men could possibly exist in reality, right in front of us, in flesh and blood, in my tiny little world, right here, amid the rotten dead smell of the Obvodny Canal and all the drunken people doubtless ambling around farther away, in the vicinity of the Varshavsky and Baltiisky train stations and . . . Oh, that was just unthinkable!

Smiling broadly, their mouths full of white teeth in one case and ugly little yellow stumps in the other, they—those two probably most famous and consequential individuals on the planet—were waving at us, all of us, the perfectly ordinary and insignificant Soviet people, the mere mortals, all of us, except me and Lyuba and my mother and my father and my grandparents and . . . and whoever else upon whom I might decide additionally to confer my unique gift of deathlessness!

Everyone went berserk. The screaming, the roaring, the sheer ecstasy, the blissful rapture, the ethereal exultation, whose extent could not normally be tolerated by a quotidian human soul without being ruptured to pieces! Brandishing minutely, as though those were aspen leaves in windy weather, the little Soviet and Cuban (yes, now I recognized those latter, too!) flags in their fisted hands and thrusting eagerly into the sky's blueness those placards of theirs, tossing the disheveled bouquets of real and paper flowers under that automotive dinosaur's enormous wheels, our entire nation emitted a joint keening howl: "Aaah! Ooooh! Ohhhh! Gloooory! Glorrrrry! Frrrriends! Forrevvvver! Deeeeath to Amerrrrrrikkkaa!"

Lyuba was screaming, too, on a single high-pitched hysterical note! "It's him!! Him!!! It's them!!!! Can you see?" she shouted up to me, raising her red, sweaty, puffed-up, wet, tear-streaked, wholly unrecognizable face skyward. "Wave, love!! Wave!! You're going to remember this moment forever! Show them how much you love them!"

"Don't leave!" I hollered back to her at the top of my lungs, pummeling the top of her head with my fist. "Stay, don't marry him, or I'll tell everybody you . . . you . . . you believe in God!"

As I already mentioned a couple of times, I had a

very strong, extremely loud voice indeed—in addition to its being almost too beautiful for its own good—like that of the fictional Italian boy named Gelsomino, the protagonist of the famous Communist children's writer Gianni Rodari's tale *Gelsomino in the Land of Liars*. Yes, I think that would be a more apt comparison than the preceding ones. Our entire nation knew and loved the hell out of Gianni Rodari! Gelsomino's voice was capable of shattering windowpane glass. Mine, just then, fueled by the energy of sheer desperation, cut right through the deafening cacophony produced by the deliriously ecstatic Soviet multitudes. Everyone, everyone heard me at that moment, within the hollow of a lull created by the pure, blunt, thrusting force of my voice! A momentary pause ensued, filled with a rippling murmur spreading through the crowd: "What? Who? God? Who said God! That child! Over there!"

"Shut up! What are you . . . doing!" Lyuba exclaimed in a crying, horrified, hissing voice, frantically pulling down on my leg, hitting me with her open palm, trying to unsaddle me from her shoulders. "God, you son of a bitch, you stupid little kike, what are you saying? Why are you doing this to me? Are you crazy? I'll kill you!"

"Stay! Stay!" I kept shouting in an overflow of fear and sadness, not knowing how to undo the damage I'd clearly just done and to make her love me again.

Now not just one but several of those severe men in black slickers were staring at me hard from different directions. A moment later, I saw them starting to push and shove their way through toward us. Uncle Nikita, standing awkwardly, like a lump on two feet, inside that beautiful giant automobile with no roof, furrowed the dull expanse of his brow, curled the corners of his fat-lipped mouth, turned to his side, and said something to someone I could not see clearly in back of him. Comrade Fidel, on the other hand, fixed me with a radiant, joyous gaze of his beautiful, luminous, bottomless eyes. "Down with America!" he roared like a lion, in Russian. I . . .

No, wait. In Russian? For real? I didn't know he could speak Russian—and of course, he could not. But no matter.

Yes, he was looking straight at me now. At me—and through me. He winked, raised his oversize hand level with his face, cocked his head to one shoulder, squinted mischievously, and, pointing a long, tapered finger at me, made as if to fire a shot: click-click. Then he threw his leonine head back and laughed happily, like a child.

I swooned. Never before had I loved anyone as much as I loved him at that moment. Not even Lyuba. If his hand had been a real gun, he would have shot me straight through my poor bleeding heart.

Flying Cranes

ON MY FIRST MORNING in our new apartment, my pet turtle, my mother's present on my eighth birthday, had managed to escape from its shoe box in the radiator corner of the living room; and since, walking out onto the balcony, I forgot to close the door behind me, before I knew it . . .

And there was a mound of hardened cement five floors below.

A Russian saying flashed through my mind: "A misfortune never comes alone."

I rushed down the stairs. The turtle was still alive. I picked it up.

A red crack ran across its shell. Feeling nauseated and heartbroken, I tossed it into a tin garbage bin.

I had no idea why I'd done this.

"Who is this?" someone said grumpily behind my back. "Is he the one whose parents work at the slaughterhouse?"

"No. That one has yellow hair. This is the one whose parents got the district prosecutor's apartment after he kicked the bucket!" replied another voice.

I turned around with a start. Two old women, their

features stern, cold, hands buried in fur mufflers, sat on an unpainted wooden bench, squinting at me.

"What is your name? And who are you? You look like a Jew. Are you one?" one of them asked.

I just gazed at her uncomprehendingly. She frowned, and I shook my head.

"The bane of humankind, that's who they are. Human locusts!" she said bitterly off into space. "They are everywhere, like rabbits! Like locusts! Their men ought to be neutered!"

That last word was unfamiliar to me.

"Hitler would make them dig their own graves!" the other old woman chimed in. "Stalin would have them hanging from every aspen!"

That was wishful thinking on her part, even though I only knew that Hitler was an extremely bad man, of course, but not—who was he?—Stalin. Not yet. I had not stood on the balcony of our new apartment in vain, regarding the dolorous otherworldly landscape of our new surroundings. Neither Hitler nor anyone else would have much luck trying to do away with me as an essential part of this new world of mine. The clay topsoil of the frozen ancient marshes, upon which Peter the Great had erected his dream city, seemed impervious even to the sharpest of vaunted German shovels; and there were no aspens, nor any other trees, in this remote suburban neighborhood on Leningrad's southwestern edge—all tectonic craters filled with dirt, and a scattering of inordinately tall construction cranes, leaning forward like the famous tower of Pisa in my *Children's Encyclopedia*.

"Just look at the arrogant grin on his little Jew face!" the first woman said venomously.

The second woman spat pointedly in my direction. I drew back, sensing danger.

Fortunately, at that moment, a gaggle of disheveled boys my age ran past, chasing two cats through the mud—one big-bellied, the other with a rat hanging from its mouth. The big-bellied cat was also being pursued by a black dog my height, whose fangs were dripping yellow saliva and snapping in the air like garden scissors.

He sank them into the cat's throat. This was all taking place as though in slow motion.

As one of the boys, scowling, swung his arm and hurled a raw-edged slab of concrete at the dog, hitting him squarely between his ears, and the rest of the boys, having overtaken the other cat, proceeded to kick it with their army boots, tossing it around like some dead thing, the two women, their bosoms shuddering with suppressed merriment, forgot all about me, as if I'd never existed.

Before I knew it, the dog and two cats lay still. The boys proceeded to run, bouncing down the narrow path in front of us, which led, meandering, to an oval-shaped mini-lake of murky water, whose serene surface gave off blinding glints of golden radiance. A half minute later, I could no longer see them behind the lopsided pyramid of scrap metal rising to the sky to the left of me. I knew I wanted to climb it. It took me a while to scale those rusty metal pipes with their slippery curves.

I paused, contemplating the bird's-eye view of the desolate terrain ahead.

"Hello, dear female citizens! How's your day going? Have you by any chance seen a bunch of no-good young derelicts running around here, chasing cats and dogs?" came a deep, husky voice from down below. I straightened up on my precarious perch on two intersecting pipes. "I am their physical-education teacher, *fizruk*, and they've just rushed out of the gym like evil spirits; something mad came over them."

Derelicts? An odd word! There still were so many words I didn't know!

A Russian saying flashed through my mind: "Do not dig a hole for someone else."

I caught my breath and glanced down. A sturdy, unshaven old man in a too-tight jacket, with both his legs cut off at the hips, perched on a dirty makeshift plywood platform on four small rusty iron wheels, which sagged in the middle under his bulk. The platform jerked forward as he jabbed his bulging gloved fists into the ground. His moist lips, which he kept licking with his tongue, were covered with bits of tobacco.

He saluted smartly at the two old women on the bench as he looked at them with a toothless smile.

He wasn't aware I was watching him.

The boys pulled away from the silty shore on two rafts.

"Boys will be boys!" said the woman who had spat in my direction. "Let them be boys, I say! We saw nobody."

I could not understand why she was lying to him. The other woman nodded in agreement.

The boys were in the middle of the mini-lake now, holding long wooden planks with three-pronged forks attached to their ends.

Those, I knew, were called "gigs."

One of the boys, the one with the yellow hair, who had killed the dog, suddenly froze, tightened his grip on his gig, arched his back, and stabbed the water with great speed—and then another boy did the same; and each, unbending simultaneously, let out a muffled triumphant cry.

"Nope. Nobody," the other woman confirmed. "Just that little Jew up there."

A black snakelike fish, an eel, or perhaps a garter snake, was thrashing wildly on one fork as it reemerged into the air and my field of vision—an otter perhaps on the other.

An *otter*? I was a city kid! What did I know from otters?

"Hey, you!" The legless man was looking up at me now, no longer smiling. "How about you? Have you seen them?" He was frowning at me.

They were sort of dancing now on their makeshift rafts, those boys. Wiggling their butts and all that. Waving their arms above their heads. Celebrating their catch.

Who built those rafts? Their fathers or older brothers maybe? I most certainly wouldn't have known how to go about it myself—and neither, probably, would my father have.

How different these wild, cruel, brutal boys—one of whom, on top of everything else, seemed to have a cigarette in his mouth at this point—were from my former first-grade classmates, children of the city intelligentsia, the neatly combed boys in mousy-gray flannel uniforms and polite, demure girls in linen dresses and lacy aprons, the ultimate little Soviet Goody Two-shoes! . . . The ear-piercing second-recess bell had just rung in the solemn, echoing halls of a stout four-storied redbrick building, my former elementary school, its tall bay windows facing the odoriferous Obvodny Canal, the city's main sewage artery. The boys and the girls of my recent past were filing out of the classrooms, where the whitewashed walls, at which I had stared endlessly for my whole first-grade year, were plastered with grainy black-and-white photographs of Vladimir Ilyich Lenin—the most perfect human being ever to walk the Earth—as well as with those of the Young Pioneer heroes, killed either by the evil White Guards with their *kulaki* accomplices or, later on, by the German invaders and occupants: Pavlik Morozov, Volodya Dubinin, Ulyana Gromova, Sergei Tyulenin, Oleg Koshevoi, and many others.

A smiling Lenin in his signature rumpled *kepka;* an animatedly gesticulating Lenin in front of the reverent, rapt crowd of factory workers; an angry, contemptuously fearless Lenin in his thirties, being arrested by the Tsar's gendarmes; an indomitable teenaged Lenin, hugging his weeping mother upon learning the news of his older brother's having been executed for his participation in the assassination attempt on the Tsar's life; and a baby Lenin, a curly-haired little angel, whose visage was embossed in gold on my red enameled Octoberist's star, a badge of honor I was obligated to wear on my school-uniform lapel forever, or until I had reached the age of ten and become a Young Pioneer, at which point I would be given the honor of wearing a Young Pioneer's bloodred neckerchief. . . .

Intelligentsia? I was only eight years old!

I pointed vaguely toward the mini-lake. The man, nodded, and then, with surprising agility, wheeled himself over to the bend in the dirt path.

"Ah! Sons of bitches!" he yelled. "There they are!"

Those poor creatures, writhing on the boys' forks in final agony! For some reason, I thought just then of the rebellious *streltsy*, soldiers in the early seventeenth-century Russian army, being beheaded and impaled on the stake by Peter the Great's guards in the great Soviet writer Alexei (not Leo) Tolstoy's novel about that time, the least cruel parts of which my former nanny, Lyuba, who had married a firefighter one year earlier, had read to me in secret, on the sly. She was not a fast or expert reader. She read slowly, haltingly, with effort. And I also recalled a TV documentary in which a mustachioed Georgian shepherd plunged a knife into a bleating lamb's body, cut its belly open in one swift motion, yanked out its throbbing heart, tossed it to his giant furry dog, skinned the carcass, chopped the meat off its leg into accurate small cubes, fixed these up expertly on a metal skewer . . .

"You're a squealy little rat, aren't you?" the man said to me, his bulky jaw set, and rammed his fists into the clay with such force that instead of lunging forward and gaining a headlong momentum of just outrage, his upper body, his entire torso, levitated for an instant above that plywood platform of his, revealing two plain clothespins sticking out of his stumps, which were like tree stumps, and fastened to the folded-up empty legs of his soiled, begrimed serge pants. "If I were you, I wouldn't be surprised if other, normal, good Russian boys decided to lay a good honest beating on me! In fact, I would fully anticipate them to do just that, and be thankful to them for not straight up killing me!"

The wheels rattled down the dirt path, and the boys, upon espying him, darted to and fro on their unwieldy little rafts in dismay!

One of them noticed me from a distance and shook his fist at me.

I climbed down slowly and went back into my entryway, my knees wobbly, my burning face averted from the two women on the bench in front of the entryway, those two old gargoyles, so—again, I couldn't help thinking—unlike two old women approximately their indeterminately ancient age from the communal apartment where I'd lived until the day before, Old Faina and Old Seraphima, if only in that the former . . .

A nice person the impossibly rude and perennially bitter Old Faina certainly was not. But at least she had enough sense to hate Hitler. One of her sons had been killed by the Germans.

As for the harmlessly insane Old Seraphima, she never said anything to me, not a word, good or bad, and practically never left her room, the second on the right from the apartment's front door, where the slightly concave walls had been hung with dark-hued religious paintings, called icons, and where no one would laugh at or rightfully berate her for her preposterous and generally anti-Soviet belief in God, unshaken within her antiquated being even by Yuri Gagarin's definitively God-defying orbital space flight. She had nightly visions of the all-seeing and gloriously bewinged archangel Gabriel, who allegedly had predicted at one point many decades ago the day when she was going to die, among other things he'd told her, ostensibly. Accordingly, every spring, in April, on the day oddly equidistant between the date of Gagarin's first-ever space flight and Lenin's birthday, she would pack all her belongings in her massive, century-old heirloom chest of drawers with its decorative cast-iron staves and ornate bronze latches, which loomed large in the sepia dusk of the endless communal corridor's perspective, close by the front door. With the familiar, comfortingly stomach-churning bittersweet smell of *combi-fat* wafting up to the unseen ceiling in pale spirals of acrid smoke, she would lie down on it in her best off-white, yellowish with time, lacy dress of a Tsarist-era Smolny Institute for Noble Maidens alumna, her arms folded on her chest, a lit candle, dripping sad wax tears, protruding from her transparent clenched fist, her eyes screwed tight to shut out the meager smoky yellow light seeping in from the kitchen and also to spare her the unlovely and totally and wholly ungodly sight of all the other eighteen or so apartment tenants lining up in the corridor to the communal toilet in their unsightly undergarments, shifting from foot to foot, scratching themselves, farting, joking, smirking, laughing at her. . . .

Rushing downstairs in the wake of the turtle's fall, I'd left the door of our apartment unlocked, like a fool— and now standing in front of it, I could hear voices behind it, too!

Old Seraphima was dead now, but the archangel Gabriel had ultimately misled her as to the presumed time frame and general circumstances of her departure from this world. Tolyan and Yulka, two other kids from our communal apartment, slightly older than I was, and I, dressed up as ghosts, or as three mini-angels of death, my mother's purloined starched white bedsheets thrown over our heads, with holes for the eyes poked in said sheets with scissors, had burst into her room, in order to make her see for herself the sheer stupidity of her religious superstitions, one April morning, some five days before Lenin's birthday.

Almost a year later, the following March, after I'd already been sent away to Moose Island, a small, quiet town on the outskirts of Moscow, to stay with my grandparents, because of the overcrowding in our room and the problem I'd been having with my teeth, I was told, by my mother, that Old Seraphima had fallen asleep forever unexpectedly in her room—a nice way of putting it, ha—and that there was no need for me to feel bad in that regard.

I was just a child. It was no more in my power to end anyone's life than to start it.

In other words, she died in March, and not in April. And that was that.

Perhaps Tolyan—a walking time bomb, an accident looking for a place to happen, in the words of some grown-ups in our communal apartment, and an overflowing receptacle of his alcoholic parents' mutual hatred, as my mother put it—should not have pushed her in the back quite so energetically that ill-conceived morning, in an attempt to convince her to kneel down and start praying to Lenin instead of God; and perhaps Yulka and I, in turn, had been overly optimistic in our assessment of the degree of her attachment to her religious paintings, or icons, as we were yanking those down from the walls gleefully. But then, she still had lived for a while after that; her death had been the result of her advanced senility, in Old Faina's words later on in the communal kitchen. It had not, therefore, been facilitated or cata . . . well, accelerated or hastened or, yes, *catalyzed* by our silly . . . prank, yes, that's all it was, of which no one but a handful of people in our apartment had ever gotten wind anyway.

It was just that her time had come. She was still around one day, and then . . .

Fear gripped my heart. There were people, strange people, dangerous people, since all people were dangerous, in our supposedly empty apartment—maybe even the infamous serial killer himself, nicknamed "the Dove" for the rumored inexpressible tenderness of his demeanor, against whom my mother and my former first-grade teacher and everyone else had warned me and all of us kids. He was young, blond, of slim build, and supernaturally charismatic; children could not resist the impulse to follow him immediately and anywhere at all when he approached them on the street or in a playground with an offer to buy them candy. Thirty-seven mutilated children's bodies had already been discovered by the militia in the secluded corners of a number of forsaken cemeteries in various parts of Leningrad.

I waited, with bated breath, as though expecting the temporary silence inside to convince me that the voices I definitely had heard in there had been but a figment of my fevered imagination. But they were not—they were repeated, this time as muted, wordless sounds.

I pushed the door ajar and peeked into the narrow, cramped hall. A naked woman was leaning back against the newly papered wall there, her eyes closed, her mouth agape, legs spread apart and bent at the knees, arms wrapped around the swollen purple neck of a fat and also naked man in the high-peaked cap of a German invader and occupier, who was thrusting his pelvis, well, his butt area, into her.

"How do you like it? Like this? Like that?" he was mumbling through clenched teeth, even though his motions seemed exactly the same to me.

"Yes, yes! A little faster!" the woman replied.

Their clothes were scattered on the floor.

The front door squeaked under my hand. . . .

"So much work still to be done in this apartment!" my father had said the night before, standing in the hall. "The bathtub is leaky; the windows in the living room are drafty as hell! The toilet constantly clogs up!"

All the elevators in our building were always out of order.

There were no elevators in our building.

Before I had time to jump back in horror, ready to bolt, both of them turned toward me, their faces still residually distorted into grimaces of what seemed like pain, bodies glistening with sweat; and the man said, breathing heavily, "Do you live here? The door was open. No big deal. No need to tell your grown-ups. Do you even know what we were doing? Well, let me explain to you, in a nutshell, the most important facts of life. As a forward-looking Soviet Octoberist, it's time for you to know where children really do come from. Including you. Your parents did the same in order to have you. It's like this, very simply: I put—"

162 Love Like Water, Love Like Fire

And the woman said calmly, interrupting him, "Shut your mouth; let's get dressed. Why do you need to dirty up this cute child's mind with all that ugliness? He is much too young to know. Someone else, some schoolyard know-it-all, will enlighten him in a couple of years. And his life will never be the same after that. But for now, he won't remember anything of what you've just said to him."

"Scram!" the man suddenly roared terribly, bulging out his bloodshot eyes at me. "Beat it, little punk!"

I flew up two flights of stairs, my heart galloping in my chest.

"Poor boy! Don't be afraid! It was all just a dream!" The woman laughed from down below.

And when I found myself on the landing of the last floor, the seventh, the pale yellow April sun touched my upturned face with its happy warmth.

A soft tentacle of an extended beam of pale northern sun, reaching down through a gaping hole in the roof-top—a reminder of the local architect's unrealized dream of an elevator shaft . . .

And for a moment, bathed in the warmth of the sky's blue altitude, where a speedy supersonic MiG fighter plane was describing one advanced geometric figure after another, the white scar of its being there gradually becoming diffuse, I felt happy, picturing myself soaring forever in that eternal sky. But when I clambered up onto the slippery aluminium banisters leading up to the rooftop, placing the flats of my palms squarely against the sooty ceiling on both sides of that hole, like a mini-replica of the human caryatid supporting the weight of the entire globe on top of one of the stately buildings in my old neighborhood, and stuck my head out, looking around and squinting against the brightness, the happy feeling was not there anymore. No longer was I soaring in the sky, which was greatly diminished by the existence of the earth below. I was gazing, through a petrified forest of chaotically slanted television antennas, at four broad-shouldered men in mud-splattered overalls, who were sitting up on the rooftop with their legs tucked under them, like those tall tales–telling hunters in the famous nineteenth-century Russian artist Perov's masterpiece *Hunters at Rest,* around a bonfire of rags and newsprint, drinking wine from green one-liter bottles, each almost empty already, and sucking into their glistening mouths slices of white meat, dripping fat, off the shining blades of the makeshift knives in their grimy hands.

One of them, probably a carpenter, judging by an ax with a cast-iron head placed across his lap, had a blackened iron rod, a monstrous toothpick of sorts, protruding from his breast pocket.

Well-cleaned chicken bones, ruby red marrow squeezed out of their flattened ends like toothpaste from a zinc tube, jutted out from the cracks between the sloping shingles of the roof around them, at the distance of a nonchalant toss over one's shoulder, forming their leisurely morning repast's uneven second circle. Gray pigeons traipsed fearlessly around its circumference on their dainty feet.

The men were talking among themselves, unaware of my eavesdropping.

"I can't believe that frigging asshole Nikita doesn't know any better than to keep frigging pushing that frigging American corn down our throats, as if nobody could frigging tell him it wouldn't grow in our frigging climate," the first man said, pulling a lumpy piece of white bread out of his pants pocket.

"And what about that frigging cane sugar?" said the second man, presumably a painter, and kicked with his gaping boot a dented bucket of drywall primer set lopsidedly by his side. "Is it a joke, or what? It isn't even sweet in my tea! And to think we're frigging sending that freeloading bearded Cuban joker our Russian bread in return!"

Blood froze momentarily in my veins. I realized that they were referring to Uncle Nikita and Comrade Fidel! How dared they! Were they mad?

The first man let the hard lump of bread fall from his hand and brought the heel of his boot down on it, hard. An audacious pigeon, its neck craned as though in an effort to accommodate the entire foursome in the crimson circle of its eye, waddled over to the mound of crumbs and began to peck at it.

"Nikita's frigging face is like his damn ass. That frigging Kennedy guy, on the other hand, looks like a movie actor," opined the third man, a plumber, twirling a socket wrench in his sausagelike fingers absentmindedly. "Pass me that bottle, will you? As frigging Churchill used to say, we get the rulers we deserve, because we—and I don't mean them frigging Englishmen—are a nation of frigging morons. . . . Hey, by the way, how's poor frigging Smertyukov doing? What's the doctors' verdict?"

Of course, they were not actually saying the word *frigging*. But I've heard so many cusswords in my life—millions and maybe billions of them—and I have used them so liberally myself, that in my mind, they have long since been transformed into some sort of placeholders of a verbal pause, placebos of quasi-meaning, if you will—the quick intakes of breath, a verbal tic, commas in a stream of unbroken speech.

"Still alive, but they say he won't last more than a couple of weeks," said the fourth man, microscopic shards of glass sparkling in his reddish hair like fake diamonds, the fine sand of the glass dust covering his hirsute hands, his butt propped uncomfortably on a deflated rubber soccer ball. He emptied out his bottle of noxious ersatz wine, his Adam's apple bobbing up and down, head tilted far back, like that of a life-size plaster of Paris Young Pioneer Bugler in front of my former elementary school building.

"Frankly, I'm surprised that frigging crane didn't finish him right off right then and there, like a frigging ant," he continued, hiccupping. "One hundred and fifty tons of frigging metal slamming down on you: That's nothing to sneeze at!"

"Nothing to sneeze at, but some people are just frigging born lucky," the second man said, wiping his mouth with his dirty sleeve. "My cousin, a firefighter, was once bumped into by a streetcar, when he was hammered out of his mind, and he walked away without even a frigging scratch. These things happen."

The first man, all of a sudden, swooped down on the recklessly audacious pigeon like a human bird of prey, pinned it down flat against the rooftop's tar-smudged concrete surface, wrung its neck, expertly chopped its head off with his ax, plucked it clean, gutted it with his knife, then skewered it with the thin iron rod in his breast pocket, held what used to be a live pigeon over the open fire . . .

"What do you mean, lucky? Wouldn't you rather be dead than frigging have to suffer?" the third man said to the second, ignoring the first one's Stone Age activities. "Let me tell you: If I already had the frigging misfortune of being born in this frigging city, floating on top of a frigging swamp, where the frigging soil can't even sustain the weight of a simple construction crane sometimes, and in this frigging country, too, where nobody could care less if you were frigging dead or alive, I'd rather be frigging dead right now!"

With that, he took a long pull from his bottle.

"You do smell like you were frigging dead!" the second man said, guffawing. "You frigging smell like all those clogged frigging toilets in this frigging building!"

"Hey, we've run out of frigging wine!" the fourth man said, sounding disconsolate and on the verge of tears.

"There, there!" the third man said to him. "Here, have some of mine! Appreciate my unheard-of generosity!"

"I've lucked upon two flagons of eau de cologne Red Moscow by going through my mother-in-law's stash," the first man interjected, slowly rotating the skewered pigeon over the smoky, sooty, terrible-smelling fire. "If push comes to shove . . ."

"Thank you, friend!" the fourth man said to the third with a feeling. "You are a real friend, real comrade!"

"Have some pigeon here!" the first man said to the other three. "It's just about done!"

A Russian saying flashed through my mind: "A titmouse in the hand is better than a crane in the sky."

Well, okay. Fine. That's silly, but fine.

I looked at the shriveled, dripping corpse of the skewered bird, which was a far cry from being done, and, unable to swallow down a lukewarm lump of nausea, I gagged, retching loudly, my chest heaving, stomach aching sharply.

"Hey, you, little frigging creep over there!" the third man yelled, finally noticing me from a distance, as a result of my having revealed my presence to them in an audial way. "What the frig you doing there—snooping on us? We sure don't like it! You'd better frigging go and bring us some more wine, if you know what's good for you! Else I'm frigging going to come to your apartment and kill your mom! I know where you live!"

The other three men burst out laughing uproariously, slapping their knees. . . .

When my first-grade teacher at my old school, my first one, teed off by my sudden and inexplicable yawning in the middle of her impromptu speech about how unimaginably lucky we all were to have been born in the Soviet Union, summoned me to the blackboard and ordered me to explain to her and to my peers why, exactly, I seemed to find the subject of our shared boundless Soviet happiness uninteresting to the point of boredom, I was so frightened and unnerved, the steely hostility of her tone was so incomprehensible to me, that my bladder gave out on me, betrayed me without a warning—and when all thirty-six of my classmates saw the awful telltale dark spot of wetness rapidly expanding down the front of my mousy-gray uniform flannel pants, they burst out laughing uproariously, ear-piercingly, sliding off the edges of their desk benches, slapping their knees and probably peeing themselves with extreme merriment. . . .

I tumbled down to the seventh-floor landing, tore down the stairs, panting and telling myself to calm down, come down, trying to think of whether my parents might have some wine in our new apartment and immediately realizing this was a preposterous notion: of course not!

Occasionally, when one or more of my father's colleagues from his secret research institute, also presumably the promising young scientists, would come over for a game of chess in our room in our communal apartment, they would bring a bottle of wine or maybe even fancy Armenian cognac, and I would be told to go to the kitchen, where all the burners on the only gas stove would be lit, glowing in the velveteen dark, and where Old Faina and perhaps two or three women from the adjacent communal apartment, which was larger than ours, would be gossiping in hushed hissing voices. . . .

"Oh for God's sake! Look at you! Pathetic! Go to the toilet and wash up! Wash yourself . . . down there! And don't come back until recess!" the teacher said in a disgusted voice, looking repulsed.

"God? Did she say God?" A whispering rippled through the classroom.

"Shush, everybody!" the teacher ordered, her face turning red.

I stood in indecision before a lopsided pyramid of cardboard boxes piled on top of one another in the middle of our new living room. The radio—a flat black dish on the wall—was playing solemn and inspiring classical music: the *Appassionata* sonata, by Ludwig van Beethoven, Lenin's favorite musical composition. "I know the *Appassionata* inside out and yet I am willing to listen to it every day," Lenin once said, according to the great proletarian writer Maxim Gorky. "It is wonderful, ethereal music. On hearing it, I proudly, maybe somewhat naïvely, think, See! People are able to produce such marvels!" He then winked, laughed, and added sadly, "I'm often unable to listen to music; it gets on my nerves. I would like to stroke my fellow beings and whisper sweet nothings in their ears for being able to produce such beautiful things in spite of the abominable hell they are living in. However, today one shouldn't caress anybody—for people will only bite off your hand; strike, without pity, although theoretically we are against any kind of violence. Umph, it is, in fact, an infernally difficult task!"

Lenin. Good God. An infinitely evil man.

Most everything of what we owned was still in those boxes, from my brother's stockings to my mother's favorite perfume, Red Moscow.

Only our black-and-white KVN TV set had already been unpacked, in addition to a bunch of my father's technical and scientific books, and plugged into the wall. I had no idea which one of those boxes contained the glass jars with grandmother's homemade preserves and pickled mushrooms, but this was the one I had to find, because I knew that, of course, breakable objects belonged together.

I pulled up a chair, climbed onto it, and reached up for the box on the very top of the pyramid, the smallest of all, which was not sealed up with isolation tape like the rest of them.

Homemade preserves. Pickled mushrooms. Sunflower oil. Vials of perfume and nail polish. A jar of mayonnaise. Stain remover.

Vinegar . . .

Vinegar! It was drinkable, was it not? It was wine, of sorts, wasn't it?

"What the frig is this?" the first man said, chewing, too drunk to be genuinely surprised, when a full, sealed bottle of vinegar rolled slowly down to his feet. "Where in frigging hell did this come from?"

A dizzying smell of eau de cologne was in the air.

"That stupid frigging little Jew head over there, sticking out of that frigging elevator shaft over there like a frigging head of lettuce," the second man said slowly, with an effort, his words slurred and his own head drooping and dropping to this chest. "That . . . that frigging head . . . did it."

And the fourth man was already dead asleep, snoring deafeningly, like Old Faina in our old communal apartment.

My father never told my little brother to close his mouth and breathe through his nose, like all normal people. . . .

"Vin . . . vinegar? What the . . . You . . . damn kikey moron! Is he, what, making frigging fun of us?" the third man, who for some reason seemed to be wide awake, bellowed, making as though to rise on his haunches. "You just wait; I'm frigging going to get you, you little vermin! You and all the rest of you! I . . . I know where to find you!" He almost managed to scramble up to his feet, but at the last moment lost his balance. . . . I flew down the stairs.

And it was already afternoon. The sun stood high in low-slung northern sky.

There was nothing for me to do in our apartment other than to turn on our tiny KVN TV in the empty living room and, sitting on the newly varnished floor, start watching, for the tenth time maybe, a rerun of the last decade's most famous movie, starring the Hero of Socialist Labor Pavel Kadochnikov—the most attractive man in the entire Soviet Union, by nationwide consensus.

How come I was not feeling hungry?

I went to the kitchen and had a piece of boiled cow's tongue and a glass of cranberry *kissel* from an otherwise empty refrigerator.

Kadochnikov played a Soviet secret agent among the top echelons of enemy leadership, liquidating dozens of ludicrously stupid and inept German invaders and occupiers, who spoke Russian with a heavy and extremely unpleasant foreign accent Their truncated bodies, riddled with righteous bullets, careened awkwardly through the air, their distorted mouths emitting ear-piercing screams of final agony.

Rivulets of black blood trickled down the tiny TV screen. I felt good.

And it still was the same endless afternoon, dragging on.

I went to my room. I had a room of my own now! I shared it with my little brother. There, I clambered on top of our bunk bed and lay down.

And as always in my dreams, I kept hoping, while still inside the dream, that I could still remember the dream I was dreaming when I woke up. But it never worked that way. I could only remember my dream while I was dreaming it, it seemed.

And then, when I opened my eyes, I could tell it was already evening.

Could I even tell the time, incidentally, at eight years of age? Had anyone bothered to explain to me how to translate the unstoppable monotonous swinging of my parents' heirloom grandfather clock's bronze pendulum in our room in our old communal apartment into hours? Had my father ever mentioned to me the possibility of buying me a wristwatch—of course not; where did that even come from?—when I became a red-neckerchiefed Young Pioneer? . . . That grand old grandfather clock, my Old Bolshevik grandfather's wedding present to my parents, was now temporarily stilled, silent, muted, constrained within one of those boxes in the living room.

Time, time . . . What was it? . . . Yeah, well, you know. . . . That's deep.

In wintertime, it was dark outside for most of the day, and come summer, it was never dark. That was all one needed to know, really, timewise.

A Russian saying flashed through my mind . . .

No Russian saying flashed through my mind just then.

And when my parents came home . . .

And then my parents came home with my little brother, who had spent the second half of the day at my mother's work; and it was therefore already seven o'clock.

My mother walked to my bed and leaned over me, taking off her overcoat.

"Sleeping," she said quietly. "He's taking this whole new thing hard. I worry about him."

"He'll get over it. It's only natural. . . . Are we going to eat?" my father said.

"Let's finish unpacking the box with the utensils first," she said.

"I wouldn't mind eating with my hands," he said, chuckling. "And I wish we had a bottle of wine, too."

"What about me?" my little brother asked.

"You are going to bed," my mother said. "Those women back at work gave you more than enough food—cookies and other such stuff."

"No fair! Too early!" he protested.

"Look at your brother," she said. "He's already turned in for the night, it seems like. Of course, we'll still have to wake him up in a couple of hours, I'm afraid, to make him brush his teeth and change into his pajamas. Adherence to routine is important, especially in a new place. It's comforting."

But my toothbrush was still in one of the boxes sitting on the floor in the living room, and my green Chinese pajamas with red dragons disgorging balls of fire from their open maws in another.

And the evening just went on, slowly.

My parents were in the living room, in the yellow light of an unshaded bulb beneath the low-slung ceiling. The radio on the wall was playing Civil War songs, my brother was snoring happily in his lower bunk bed, and as I tiptoed out into the hall, with it squeaking linoleum floor, I saw my parents embracing in the living room, swaying slightly, as though listening to some pleasant, lovely music, rather than the sounds pouring from the radio. My mother's chin was resting on my father's shoulder, her eyes were closed, and the expression on her face was the happiest I had ever seen.

I pressed my lips into the crook of my elbow and, unaccountably even to myself, expelled air from my lungs forcefully, producing an obnoxious farting sound.

They recoiled from each other, startled.

"What in the world are you doing standing there?" my father said, smiling. "Instead of sleeping? Are you spying on us or something?"

"We almost forgot about him!" my mother said in a sad voice.

"Who did? I didn't. But are we supposed to think about him twenty-four hours a day? He's a big boy," my father said, winking at me. "Well, of course we are. But still . . . I wish he wouldn't be creeping up on us like this."

"What time is it anyway?" my mother said. "Is there some movie maybe on television? How are we going to celebrate—any thoughts? I wish we had some Crimean champagne."

"Four," my father said absently, looking at his wristwatch. "No, wait a minute, that couldn't be right! My watch must be broken! Rats!"

"Would you like to go out for a movie?" my mother asked hopefully. "There's this great one playing in a local theater somewhere around here, with Alexei Batalov and Tatyana Samoylova. You've seen it. Let's go see it again."

"No, not really, I'm sorry," my father said. "Tired, frankly, and don't feel like spending a good hour or however long wandering around this wilderness looking for a movie theater."

With that, he headed for the kitchen.

"Well then, I think I'm going anyway," my mother said stubbornly. "Alone."

"No, please don't," he replied. "Please reconsider. Let's do it another night." Then he opened the refrigerator, looked inside, and said, "Who, I wonder, ate all the cow's tongue?"

She looked sad, dejected.

I ran up to her, threw my arms around her waist, wedged my face in between her legs.

"What is it, silly?" she said. "Are you trying to say you want to go to the movies with me? No, I don't think so. Go back to bed!"

And she pushed me away gently.

I hugged her again, clinging to her ever stronger.

"Oh, what am I going to do with you?" she said, laughing. "Fine, let's go. At least *someone* wants to go out with me. Put on your warm clothes. It's chilly outside— and what if your dad is right and we don't find the movie theater right away?"

But we did find it, of course—and very quickly, too. It was just a short walk away, even though there was hardly anything else in that dark wilderness of what I, growing up in old, large, densely populated midtown Leningrad, was accustomed to seeing all around me on my walks with my nanny, Lyuba, or my grandmother: no metro station, no train station, no public bathhouse, no laundry place, no bus stop, no streetcars or trolleys, no crowds of people everywhere, no District Party Committee office, no *pirozhki* kiosk, no beer stand, no *kvas* vendor's cistern, no *kolkhoz* market, no Lenin statue, no military commandant's headquarters, no shooting gallery, no old buildings with lots of inner courtyards, and no . . . anything else, really. Only a two-story meat and dairy store with boarded-up windows squatted darkly and ominously next to an incomprehensibly defunct and altogether incongruous parachute tower and the rusty tip of an endlessly long felled construction crane at the edge of the boundless wastelands spreading out to the invisible horizon of no-man's-land, where the muffled outbursts of shrill cries for help could be heard.

"It's nice, isn't it?" my mother said with forced cheeriness as we approached a very large cube of blue ice made of glass and steel, illuminated by an otherworldly glow from within, on top of which the flickering neon letters, each taller than I was and some of them dark, missing, read s ace f ight f lm t eater. "Enough of those gloomy, cold old stone buildings! This is what I call modern architecture! We could live and have a good life here, don't you think?"

"Yes," I said, although I didn't really understand what she was saying.

But when I saw a fake marble sculpture of a mortally wounded Soviet soldier, with a cussword already stenciled in fat black ink across his bare chest, standing guard in the doors, I did actually begin to feel better inside; it occurred to me at that moment that yes, maybe I could get used to living here, amid all this strangeness, after all.

We went inside, and my mother bought two tickets.

How much did the tickets cost? Fifteen kopecks each, I believe. But I wouldn't bet on it. Just the year before, Uncle Nikita's monetary reform, otherwise known as the "highway robbery of the decade," had gone into effect, wiping away most people's meager lifelong savings.

And then we hung around the foyer, amid potted rubber trees, studying the autographed photographs of the famous movie stars of the world: Nikolai Kryuchkov, Boris Babochkin, Pyotr Aleinikov, Lyubov Orlova, Inno-kenty Smoktunovsky, Mark Bernes, Nonna Mordyukova, Gina Lollobrigida, Gérard Philipe, and many others. And then the bell rang, twice. The film was about to begin. . . .

That night, which was no different from any other night in Leningrad, of all the four-plus million people populating it, we were among only a few other movie-goers in that movie theater in the middle of nowhere on Leningrad's southwestern outskirts: a young man in mud-spattered coveralls, with greasy long hair, slouched in his chair in the middle of the front row and emitting the complex odor of ersatz wine, vomit, and eau de cologne; a young woman with a baby seated directly behind us; two old women in the middle, their eyes narrowed and sheer pewter, mouths full of sunflower seeds; and a few boys my age, jostling and giggling and whispering and cursing and cussing, catcalling all the way in the back. I kept gazing around nervously while the opening credits were still rolling down the screen, because . . . Because.

The young woman unbuttoned her blouse and held her gurgling baby to her chest. The baby was a he. It was hot in the darkness of the theater, and when she unwrapped its oilcloth swaddling bands, I saw that his thing . . .

Give me a break.

The man in front of us was a menace, and so were the women and the boys. Because they were strangers. I didn't know them, and I had no idea what was in their heads. They were not the same as we were.

A Russian saying flashed through my mind: "Two deaths you cannot have, and one you cannot avoid."

But then, I was just eight years old. Death? Seriously? No.

But then I realized that if I started fearing all the people with whom I might cross paths with over the years, my life would become frigging unbearable—which, I suspected, it would anyway.

I suspected no such thing.

But then I noticed that my mother was sniffling, as if this were a wedding or a funeral. . . . At that time, I had not yet been to a single wedding or a funeral.

And I tapped her on the elbow to remind her that this was only a movie. She was dabbing at the corners of her eyes with an unadorned handkerchief. And I had to admit it: The main hero experienced an exceptionally beautiful death! All those spinning and whirling birch trees and flying cranes! All that space, all that sky, into which he fell . . . all that love!

And his heartbroken fiancée would always, always remember him!

I leaned in to my mother's ear and whispered, "I would like to die like that!"

And she squeezed my hand in the dark and said, in a quiet voice full of love, "I know."

April 1st, Sunset Hour

WE WERE WALKING along the canal, my hand in hers. In the darkening golden sky, bled of all its afternoon paleness, blackbirds dived and fluttered, fretful and slow, like so many soot flakes above the silent tongues of flame. It was, in all, a lovely tableau.

I thought, in passing, of the fearsome square gaping mouth of the floor-to-ceiling ceramic wood-burning stove with the pipe-smoking Peter the Great in full stride depicted on each one of its uncountable glazed cornflower blue tiles back in our family's single room, small and kidney bean–shaped, in the ever-rancorous communal apartment on the third floor of the tall, off-red, century-old building, owned apparently at some point in the unimaginable past by the second husband of one of the last Tsar's favorite female friends, three brief street corners away on the other side of the humpbacked little bridge across the dead canal with which the two of us had just drawn level, in that strange, oddly eternal, liquid and molten, crimson-golden, blood-disquieting light falling slantwise from the low-slung Leningrad sky.

Directly in back of us, two ordinarily drunken men were cursing good-naturedly at Eisenhower and Adenauer, using a variety of bad words. That light, both ominous and too beautiful for words, was making me feel like crying and laughing at the same time. I had no idea what was happening to me. I was very little.

Everywhere I looked, casting my eyes low, as befitting my utmost smallness, giant oblique shadows moved silently on the tired gray asphalt: a veritable forest of shadows, through which we walked, she and I. We had no clear, set destination in mind, it would seem to me, nor were we in any great hurry to get anywhere. An evening, though heavy with suppressed foreboding, was just an evening. My life, however plenty long already, had not even properly begun yet, at least in comparison to the malevolent ancient woman from our communal apartment, Old Faina, who had lived there forever, since shortly after the Great October Socialist Revolution, and who had told me recently, in a hissing whisper, for no identifiable reason, cornering me in one of the communal corridor's manifold recesses, just that: I hadn't even begun to exist yet.

In three months, I knew, I was going to be five years old. Would it be fair to say that sometimes I had a feeling, even at that negligible age, as if I had existed forever? Yes.

I shook my head now and then, as we progressed, to empty out its contents. In the shallow niche in the stone wall close by one of the two adjacent train stations jointly forming the angry, roiling heart of the Obvodny Canal neighborhood of my early childhood, in the very heart of what the unaccountably happy people on the radio sometimes referred to, cryptically, as "Dostoyevsky's Petersburg," a bronze Lenin stood, life-size, squinting knowingly at the ceaseless flow of faceless passersby, my fellow citizens of the great and terrible city built by the mad and abnormally tall Tsar Peter yet named after that little bronze statue, Lenin, smiling imperceptibly with the corners of his harsh bronze mouth, as though he had all of us, the living, figured out, once and for all, unto eternity, and in the most minute and exhaustive of details, too, which undoubtedly he had, obviously, if only for the simple reason of his being the most perfect and immortal genius in mankind's history, the most unimaginably and wonderfully indescribable and perfect and immortal human child ever to be brought into existence by the stork cranes of human history. Everyone—and this went without saying yet still needed to be kept in mind—was duty-bound to love and adore him more than one loved and valued one's own life itself. Every time I walked past him standing there, in that shadowy shallow niche in the train station's wall, I saluted him smartly, yet also quite subtly, a bit surreptitiously, for fear of drawing the rays of random strangers' unwarranted attention to what, I felt, perhaps a little smugly and unbelievably, was an intensely private gesture.

Walking without purpose seemed to be the purpose of our walk that evening. It was all I could do to keep pace with her, half-running in mincing steps in my tiny galoshes-shod *valenki,* amid the merry, high-pitched, fork-on-pewter-plate screeching of unseen streetcars a couple of small bridges away, across the Obvodny, in back of us—in the near vicinity of the city's, and maybe even the whole Soviet country's, second-largest department store, with its truly wondrous selection of wooden rifles and stick horses.

She kept progressing forth, my hand in hers, in determined, regal, Peter the Great–like strides—for she did not know, in point of fact, how to move in a more leisurely or languid manner—with her majestic head held high, gazing straight ahead of her, guarded yet confident of disposition, and only half-pausing briskly now and then to exchange a few brusque words of socially relevant greetings with someone she knew from the neighborhood, or in her capacity as one of the local Party committee's active lay members.

Did I find it puzzling when, virtually after every single one of her visits with our family, the women in our communal kitchen voiced surprise at the fact that, considering how undeniably beautiful she still was, especially for her age, she apparently never had a man in her life, since forever and eternity, and did not seem to be interested in the least in finding one, either? Yes. Did my little heart fairly swell with wholly unmerited pride every time the two of us walked together? Yes. My father never knew his father, which, it appeared, somehow, was the reason for my not having a second grandfather. It was too early for me to understand, much less come to grips with, such things.

On we went. That's what I remember, if anything.

One tongue-tied stranger, owner of a lopsided, puzzled-looking, and visibly inebriated shadow, likely making his laborious way home from one of the immediate train station area's basement vodka-shot shops, complimented her, in a terribly convoluted, diffuse language, addressing her repeatedly as "dear comrade beautiful woman" and jabbing the swollen shadow of his gnarled finger at my shrinking shadow, additionally commenting on how well behaved and clean-looking her little son was, in his nice oversize flap-eared, high-peaked Red Cavalry *budyonnovka* felt helmet hat with our bright Kremlin star in its dead center: one true-blue future motherland's defender, no question about it! He hiccupped delicately.

In response, she issued a peal of lilting laughter, tossing back her full, glimmering head of unruly raven wing's–black hair, and squeezing my sweaty palm reassuringly, told him to go on and stop pulling her leg with his silly flattery, blabbering like that perhaps in baseless hopes of her giving him a ruble to buy more vodka, because she was fully aware what day it was today, even if he didn't happen himself to remember: the first of April, April Fool's Day, when no one in her right mind would believe anything said by anyone one didn't already trust! Go on, comrade! Be on your merry way!

Do I actually remember her saying that? Yes and no.

The drunk's shadow shoved off then, deflated, mumbling unintelligibly under its grotesque nose, and I pulled

down on grandmother's hand impatiently, jumping
up and down in excitement, and opened my mouth to
ask her what exactly the April Fool's Day of her reference was. . . . But just then, as the two of us, my grandmother and I, stood there, immobile in the amber of that
pointlessly memorable moment, next to one of the narrow humpbacked bridges across the dreadful Obvodny
Canal, Leningrad's main open-air sewage artery, awash
in that strange shimmering golden northern light of the
presunset hour of April's first day, the first of April, a
distant rumbling spread across the sky and, materializing seemingly out of nowhere, like a coagulation of that
thick, heavy sky radiance, and falling with the speed of
a thrown stone, a wayward dove dived in low over the
bridge, and its sudden shadow smashed into mine and
shattered both to smithereens, causing me to recoil in
wide-eyed horror with the thin shriek of a stuck streetcar, and I commenced to trip over myself, mortified, panicked, careening backward inexorably, at which point my
grandmother stepped in with ready agility and gathered
me up into her arms and, by turns laughing and cooing,
proceeded to remove my *budyonnovka* and stroke my hair
soothingly, there, there, telling me that everything was
all right, she was with me, I was safe, everything was
fine with the world, it was, it was, except for that strange,
ominous, dangerous-looking, heartbreaking light, which
must have gotten the best of me, yes, evidently, so now,
before we headed back home, I needed to close my eyes

for a spell, just screw them tight and keep them closed for a while, to make the world disappear, to give it a little time to rest and set itself straight again during my non-presence in it.

Which, in the end, was exactly what she herself did, nearly blind and beset by constant pain, some four-plus decades later, on the other end of the world, in the beautiful and remote city of San Francisco, one of inclement summers and snowless winters and ludicrously steep hills, where people spoke a language she didn't know and the fog rolled in from the ocean like a hushed army of the merciful angels of death, and where her only son—in whose life alone she ever had found the true justification for her own existence—had been buried seven years earlier. Getting up with difficulty from her La-Z-Boy recliner in the living room, in front of the TV permanently set to a Russian-language channel, she went into her room, lay prone on her bed, facing the shadowy ceiling, breathed out deeply, closed her eyes, and willed the world and herself along with it to disappear for good.

First Death

THE NUMBER OF STEPS from our house to the nearest bus stop on the Moskovsky Prospect was eleven times fifty and twenty-three.

It was late April, and the streets were all covered with deep, oddly shaped brown puddles and lopsided mounds of dirt.

If my mother had been walking alone, without me by her side and holding her hand, the number of her steps between any two points along our journey that day would have been considerably smaller.

The bus came in fifty times eight plus twelve. It was empty, due to this being a workday morning. I knew it was morning still because the noon cannon, heard distinctly, if distantly, in our part of the city also, hadn't gone off yet over at the Peter and Paul Fortress, where I'd never been.

The bus was a bus was a bus. I'd ridden buses before, at least four times since I'd started having memories. My mother, sniffling her nose and sighing heavily, and even seeming to fight back tears, gave two large dull coins to the severe ticket woman in a square-shouldered man's jacket at the front of the bus, and we went to sit all the way in the back. In the back of my mind, I wondered what was wrong with my mother, why she was so strangely sad, and why she was not at work on a workday to begin with, in her capacity as a junior engineer in the Children's Gym Shoes department at the world-famous Red Triangle rubber-goods factory, over on the dead-watered Obvodny Canal embankment, a mere four street corners and one small humpbacked bridge away from our apartment building.

It was a short bus ride: fifty times eight and twenty-eight.

"Two Balls" was the name of the world's best high-top imitation Keds sneakers, made in China. One of the older boys in our building's inner courtyard was rumored to own a pair of those.

I loved the lush illustrations in the thick, heavy book of Chinese folktales our live-in nanny, Lyuba, frequently read to me from.

The number of steps from the bus stop of our disembarking to the entry of the Institute of Technology metro station was fifty and fourteen.

I'd ridden the metro three times previously. Make it four. Everything about it was just enormous. I knew that its escalators were the longest in the world, leading halfway to the center of the Earth, because of their pulling also the double duty of being the world's most indestructible atomic bomb shelters, for the obvious reason that the pernicious American Imperialism was constantly on the lookout for an opportunity to kill us all. I found it amusing that the Leningrad metro and I were the exact same age. It was so much bigger than I was!

We reached the bottom of the station in fifty times four and fourteen. Fifty plus twelve after that, the train arrived, full of roaring and pushing ahead of itself an invisible tight wave of hot air.

"We all think we're going to live forever, but guess what," my mother said suddenly to no one as we stepped inside the near-empty train amid the sliding doors' snake-like hissing all along the train's great length. "Life passes very quickly. One day, it feels like it still is too early to tell your loved ones you love them, and then, before you know it, it already is too late."

"Don't be unhappy," I told her.

We took our seats in the middle of the car.

Momentarily overcome with sadness, I felt like telling my mother not to worry, that she was never going to die, and neither were any other members of our extended family, or any of our close friends, protected as we all were by the invulnerable and invisible shield of my personal immortality: the wondrously unique gift I alone possessed of all the people in the world. But then I decided to say nothing.

You can't do two things at once inside your head.

In fifty times six and thirty-five, we arrived at the Insurrection Square metro station. In fifty times four and forty-four, we got off the upward-bound escalator there.

Fifty and sixteen later, we already stood at a bus stop outside the station, amid the incessant flow of a veritable river of faceless people, our fellow Leningraders. The bus my mother said we needed had rolled up to the stop in fifty times three and forty-eight. In fifty times seven and eleven, we already had been riding it, toward wherever it was we were going, for quite a few stops, when, just beyond yet another tight street corner, I saw something so beautiful, I felt as though an unseen iron fist or small horse's hoof had punched me smack in the solar plexus. "Below the little spoon," as everyone in Russia calls that vulnerable spot on the human body.

"Mommy, what is it? Over there?" I cried, jumping up and down and sliding off my seat, and then climbing back onto it, and pointing eagerly with my hand.

She pulled me back down. "Be quiet," she said. "We're not alone in here. That statue is called the *Bronze Horseman*. That man on the horse is Peter the Great. He was a very powerful and cruel ruler, in addition to being an extremely tall man. He was the founder of our city. Lots of people perished, having been sucked in by the swamp we're floating on top of, during the laying of this city's foundation. There really shouldn't have been any city built up here. I'm sure you've heard already about Peter the Great, and more than once, too. That horse is just his horse. Its name is unknown, at least to me. It may never have actually existed. Peter the Great was not a good horseman. He was freakishly tall and not well coordinated. *The Bronze Horseman* is the name of Pushkin's famous long poem. Pushkin, right? We've read you many of his poems and fairy tales. Of course you know him. *The Bronze Horseman* poem is about the terrible flood on the Neva that took place in 1824. Lots of people perished in it. This city was ready-made for such natural disasters. *The Bronze Horseman*'s main hero, a young man named Yevgeny, loses his mind and goes mad with grief after his fiancée drowns in that terrible flood. Her name was Parasha. It is a very old-fashioned name, the diminutive of Praskoviya. The only living person I know by that name is that repugnant woman in . . . Never mind. He—Yevgeny—starts shouting and screaming and stomping his feet and brandishing his impotent little fist at the bronze Tsar over there, cursing and berating and blaming him personally for the unspeakable tragedy befalling his ill-starred dream city. He carries on in that vein for a while—until finally, and completely unexpectedly, Peter the Great gets tired of all that verbal abuse being hurled at him, and he and his horse get off that slab of rock they're perched on and start chasing poor mad Yevgeny through the empty, devastated, perfectly straight, and soulless streets of Leningrad, or Saint Petersburg, and then . . . Oh well. But—listen to me babble on. Sorry, baby." She cut herself off with an apologetic smile, and put her cool hand on top of my head.

"Life can be a pretty tragic affair indeed," she said abstractly.

"No kidding," I murmured absently.

I was staring avidly out the greasy bus window. Beyond it, the most beautiful city in the world was unfolding majestically, unfurling like a dream within a dream made of water and stone. A flock of curly little white clouds moved across the low-slung pale gray sky with considerable speed. My heart contracted painfully. This, I knew, was my city, Leningrad, the city of my life— only it wasn't the Leningrad I'd ever experienced before, because for all the five years of what felt already like a plenty long life, I'd inhabited a different, much angrier and edgier and more crowded, and more decrepit, too, part of Leningrad's midtown core: the city's very roiling, Dostoyevskian (that was an incomprehensible word one of the tenants in our communal apartment, a professor of music, liked to pepper his speech with) heart, or perhaps its liver or solar plexus, where the streets were strewn carelessly with all manner of dirt or buried under the great mounds of snow and offered a passing stranger no half-gorgeous vistas, and were lined haphazardly with the buildings run down in an unabashedly nonpretty way, presenting to the world their scuffed countenance with natural barefaced candor.

Overflowing with ardor, with a dire surfeit of instant happiness, my little heart was galloping away in my chest. Tears welled in my eyes. Perfect and absolute was the eternal beauty I was beholding.

It occurred to me just then—and the thought startled

me at once with its pure streamlined simplicity, as well as with the very fact of its having visited my head—that it would be impossible, or nearly impossible, for someone growing up amid these staggering spaces, with this immutable view reflected by his retinas at all times, to end up becoming a bad, dishonest, dis-har-mo-ni-ous person, let alone a criminally inclined one; that the number of good, decent, noble, and spiritually uplifted people, therefore, had to be higher in Leningrad, or at least in this particular area of Leningrad, than anywhere else in the Soviet Union, let alone the rest of the world. The rest of the world, my foot! The rest of the world, stuck forever as it was on the planet's dark side, could just go to hell, for all I cared. . . .

I was breathing fast, my nose pressed to the bus window.

Oh, how lucky indeed I was to have been brought into existence in the Soviet Union, by a Soviet crane, and subsequently to have been found in a cabbage patch by a Leningrad rabbit! Not only was I living in the most wonderful country in the world, hands down, but I also happened to reside in that wondrously wonderful country's best and most beautiful city—the most beautiful city in the whole world! It was simply unbelievable!

Someday, I told myself fervently, someday, when I was a grown-up, I would be coming here, to this very spot, every single night, in order to keep becoming progressively a more infinitely good person, amid this eth— ethereal symphony of water and stone!

That meaningless phrase—"symphony of water and stone"—having popped into my brain out of nowhere, kept bouncing off the inner walls of my head, ever so annoyingly. I knew it was too advanced for a child my age. I shook my head energetically, like a wet dog, to purge it from my mind.

"Oh!" I cried out, unable to contain myself any further. All this was just too much for me. Happiness was engulfing my whole little being with its relentless bonfire.

"Our stop," my mother said, looking at me sternly. She took my hand, and we got up and headed for the bus doors.

Twenty-three. Thirty-two.

At that instant, the air all around us was torn to shreds by the roaring of the noon cannon over at the Peter and Paul Fortress just across the wide, wide river from us! I covered my ears with my hands and hunkered down on my haunches, but my eyes remained open. I'd been seeing photographs of that most trenchant of the symbols of Leningrad ever since I'd started having memories—and now, what do you know, there it was, right there, towering majestically in plain view just across the river from me!

The river was called Neva. It was the most beautiful river in the world. I had never seen it before with my own eyes, either.

I couldn't bear to look directly at that shining gold spire across the water—it was just too blindingly magnificent.

Twenty-seven. Forty-nine. Fifty and six.

Wide was the embankment, tall the granite parapet bordering it, sharp the cries of large white birds overhead, wet the wind, silvery and everlasting the river.

So much stone. So much river. So, so . . . much of everything.

My mother was scrutinizing her face in the small round mirror in her palm. The number of those little white clouds moving speedily across that pale gray sky above us was twelve . . . twenty-three . . . fifty and nine . . .

Done looking at her own reflection, my mother pointed at the imposing granite building facing us directly on the other side of the empty embankment.

Tiny was the number of Leningrad's private car owners back then.

Fifty and nine was the number of steps it took us to get across the embankment and inside the granite building of our destination—where, in contrast with the faded grandeur and noble proportions of the building's facade, the air was musty and damp and smelled like the toilet in our communal apartment did, and was filled with large whirling particles of black dust, the black moths otherwise known as soot. The number of the time-worn, tired, thinned-out, dirty pale marble steps of the steep staircase leading all the way up to the landing of the last, the sixth, floor in there was fifty times two plus eight.

We stood before a massive cotton-padded, grimy black door all the way up there, on the sixth floor. It didn't look all that different from the front door of our own communal apartment. The door was a door was a door. My mother, her hands shaking slightly, once again gazed intently at her face in that small round mirror in her palm, stretching her lips into a frighteningly unnatural smile and touching the corners of her eyes with her pinkie, first one and then the other. Finally she exhaled and pressed the lower of the two little metallic buttons sticking out of the unruly cotton padding at the door's edge. A distant, muted ringing deep inside the space behind the door reached our ears. Twenty-nine, thirty-five. There came the slow, deliberate shuffling of heavy, unwieldy feet. It grew louder, drew nearer.

An old, kind-featured, rotund woman with pale eyes and a worried look on her pancake-flat face, having unlocked and unlatched the door from within, materialized in front of us.

"Come in, come in," she said hastily, crying a little and moving aside to let us in.

"How is she, Praskoviya Petrovna?" my mother asked in a perfunctory manner, looking past the woman. It was clear she was not expecting any substantive response from the latter. The two of us stepped inside the cluttered hall permeated by the blended smell of sweet dried flowers, chlorine, various medical substances, tobacco, mothballs, metal rust, unwashed human flesh, mice droppings, and something else—something . . . something truly dreadful I couldn't quite put my finger on.

"Still the same, only worse yet," the woman replied plaintively. "We're losing her, we're losing her, our dear sweet angel Roza Aronovna! O, woe is me! How am I going to live without her?" She began to weep openly, crossing herself and rapidly bowing her head, the way the backward old women in babushkas in our apartment building's inner courtyard were wont to do on occasion, when they thought no one was watching.

We went into the room situated on the right of the hall. Inside, there were my grandmother—my mother's mother, who lived in Moscow but had come to Leningrad two nights earlier and had been staying with us, although I barely had seen her since her arrival—and, prone on her back on the bed, her sister, my great-aunt Roza, or Auntie Roza, whom sometimes, infrequently, I called Grandma Roza. She was my real grandmother's older sister, but while her patronymic was Aronovna, that of my real grandmother was Alexandrovna. I wondered how that might be possible. Had they been raised by two different fathers? I realized, at that moment, that I hadn't seen Auntie Roza in a really long while—a week maybe, or maybe a month, or even three months. Forever, in a word. Her eyes were closed, the lids papery, her cheeks sunken, the skin on her face and on her hands sallow and yellow and crinkly. She looked altogether frightening. Through her cavernous gaping mouth the air went in and out, in and out, with a hollow whistling sound. My grandmother was sitting close by the edge of the bed, slouched in an old armchair with a tall carved back.

The small, cramped room was chock-full of ancient-looking books, sundry knickknacks, and dried flowers in cracked ceramic vases. The walls, papered rather sloppily in blue-gray, were hung with very old photographs. Auntie Roza lived alone. Her two sons, I knew, had been killed during the war. I didn't know if she'd ever had a husband. I wasn't supposed to know such things, either. I was only five years old, after all. I had no idea, for instance, where babies came from. I'd never been in this room before. Auntie Roza was almost unrecognizable to me now. This was not the Auntie Roza I'd known and loved all my life, ever since I'd started having memories: the ever-authoritative, self-assured doctor Roza, assistant director of a local polyclinic, who always walked fast and had a husky voice and spoke in short, assertive sentences.

My mother went over to the bed, too, pulling me in close behind her. "Say something," she whispered to me urgently.

I cleared my throat. "Auntie Roza! It's me!" I said feebly.

"Roza, Roza!" my mother said. "Look who's here! Take a guess! It's someone you really wanted to see. You wanted to see him, remember? Well, he's here now."

"She probably can't hear you," my grandmother said in a bleak, exhausted voice. "The nurse from the polyclinic came an hour ago, and gave her a large dose."

Twenty-seven. Thirty-two. Forty-five. Fifty and three.

But apparently, although that did seem unlikely, Roza still could hear and understand.

"Come here, my love. My dear boy! Tell him to come to me," she said with a slow effort, in a rustling, barely audible, entirely strange voice. Her eyes continued to be closed. It occurred to me, completely out of the blue and much to my inner shuddering, that she never was going to open them again.

But no, that couldn't be.

Twenty-two. Forty.

After a brief hesitation, my mother gave me a light nudge in the back, causing me to take two further small, mincing steps toward Roza's bed. Now I was standing next to her.

"Roza, he's standing right next to you," my mother said.

"Dodik, my love, is that you?" Roza asked in the same spooky, rustling voice. Her emaciated hand had lifted off the bed's flat plane and was groping weakly in the air.

Dodik? Who was Dodik? I was no Dodik! What kind of name was that—Dodik? For a moment, I panicked.

"Say nothing; just keep quiet!" my mother whispered in my ear. "Don't be afraid. It will be over in a moment."

She took the bird's foot of Roza's hand and placed it on top of my head. Eight, nine, twelve. Roza's hand, though seemingly weightless, was, in point of fact, as heavy as if it were made of cast-iron or plaster of Paris. It felt hot on my head.

"Your hair is curlier than it used to be," Roza said distantly, dreamily. "What happened? Have you been walking in the rain?"

Twenty-three, thirty-two. I just stood there, with her hand on top of my head. It was all I could do not to burst into tears.

My mother, sensing perhaps the state I was in, pulled me out gently from under the weight of that terrible spectral hand, and it fell heavily, lifeless, back down on the bed by Roza's side.

"Go wait for me out in the hall," my mother told me quietly. "I'll be right with you."

Never before in my life had I been quite as glad to leave a room.

Eight, seventeen, twenty-five.

"Soon, soon it will be over," said the fat old woman with the kindly face who had opened the door for us, stepping now out of the condensed shadows of some strange pieces of furniture and piles of clothing items in the hall. Only now her face was not kindly, but, rather, dark and joyously angry. "Soon, soon, thank God!" She was wiping her wet hands on the dirty-white kitchen apron tied around the middle of her shapeless body; a bunch of ugly, carnivorous-looking red cockerels was printed on the apron's rough fabric. "And your dear mother and your high-cultured grandma from Moscow, they better not even think of laying their grubby Jew hands on her room," she continued in a deepening tone. "It is mine. Mine. By all rights, before God and the city municipality. I've earned it, through the very fact of living for twenty-five years in here, alone in the same small apartment, with a damned Jew, right next door to her, cooking my food in the same kitchen with her, going to the same toilet, washing myself in the same bathtub. That must count for a lot of suffering, let me tell you, in Jesus' eyes. And now that she's dead—"

"She's not dead," I said, interrupting her and taking a quick step back from her, just in case. I didn't know what the word *Jew* meant, nor what she was talking about on the whole, but I didn't like her wheedling, gloating voice or the triumphant fury animating her unremarkable features. Nor did I like it, either, that she was talking as though to herself, as though I weren't even there, standing right next to her in the hall. "She's not dead," I repeated stubbornly, in a quavering voice. "And she's not ever going to die, either. I can tell you that right now. So, you're wrong."

Emerging from her apparent reverie, she shook her head and gave me a curious look—one of pitying condescension and ironic contempt. "She's not, huh?" she said, chuckling. "Is that what you think, my cute little Jesus killer? Well, if you say so, it must be so! That changes everything! ... My, but aren't you just adorable! ..." Then she, too, as if on cue, put her hand, which smelled of fried fish and was rough and damp, on top of my head. What was wrong with everybody today? I squirmed out from under that revolting paw of hers.

My mother, her eyes rimmed red, came out of Auntie Roza's room. Without saying a word, she took me by the hand, and we started on our way back home.

Fifty times fifty and five.

The Beginning of a Long Road

ARLIER TODAY, in a conversation with a friend, I recalled the preposterous little novel I wrote at the age of thirteen: my very first literary work of any sizable scope. The year was 1968; the month was August; the location, Roshchino, a middle-scale lakeside resort community some forty-five minutes away from Leningrad by suburban train.

Titled *The Beginning of a Long Road* (*Nachalo Bol'shogo Puti*), the narrative followed doggedly, over the full ninety-six handwritten pages of a standard-issue school notebook with a cornflower blue oilcloth cover, the peregrinations all across the United States, on foot, in a fruitless job search, of three typical unemployed representatives of the American working class: Jim, John, and Jack. Jim was a metalworker; John, a baker; and Jack, a carpenter.

The whole faux–*Grapes of Wrath* premise—and to be sure, at the time, my awareness of Steinbeck's existence was no greater than his of mine—served as but a pretext for me to utilize and show off (if only for my own benefit) my newfangled knowledge of U.S. geography and its regional economies, gleaned solely from the 1953 *Abridged Soviet Encyclopedia*—a hefty set of massive, thousand-page-long tomes (each weighing at least five kilos and, if hurled with sufficient force from a close distance, capable of serving as a potent lethal weapon against an oncoming enemy), filled to trembling overflow with Stalinist propaganda, and one of my primary sources, back then, of all the factual information about the world at large.

All across America, from state to state, the hapless, destitute trio hoofed it, for days and months on end, looking for some kind of gainful employment—and not finding any. America—the dying, historically doomed citadel of the pernicious International Imperialism—was mired in a perennial economic depression of cataclysmic proportions. There were no new jobs to be had. None, zero. It was an altogether desperate, extremely hopeless situation.

What did they eat along the way? Scraps of rotting food found in garbage dumps—and also whatever paltry morsels of barely edible crap they were tossed, now and then, by the contemptuously wealthy people residing in the stately mansions and sprawling cattle ranches the three men happened to pass by periodically, in exchange for performing some minor, psychologically degrading menial chores, such as trimming the hedges on the property, clearing the brush, mowing the lawn, shoveling the snow, brushing the dog, petting the cat, raising a barn. . . . Where did they sleep? Oh, wherever the nightfall would find them: along the roadsides, in abandoned factories and unguarded apartment-building entrances, in snowbanks, in rat-infested, dank alleyways, in the leafy shadow of young girls in flower . . . well, no, actually—not in any immediate, potentially explosive vicinity of the female sex. Jim, John, and Jack, three typical American proletarians, were too impoverished, too chronically underfed and penniless, and too brimful of indignation, so to speak, over the rotten state of affairs in America and the dying capitalist world on the whole to be interested in girls. Girls sucked, you know, to put it bluntly; they were nothing but a massive distraction from the truly important issues pertinent to the awakening of one's class consciousness. . . . At thirteen, I kind of agreed with them on that latter point.

On a whim, in a clever (I thought, proudly) flight of novelistic fancy, I made Jim, John, and Jack walk all across America, from state to state, in alphabetical order: from Alabama to Alaska, then straight on to Arizona, then directly to Arkansas, etc. In that sense, *The Beginning of a Long Road* was an Oulipian text, if you will—although, needless to say, entirely unbeknownst to me.

The three friends constantly felt puzzled themselves by the fanciful pattern of their wanderings.

"Why in the world are we moving around like this?" Jim would wonder cantankerously. "Instead, you know, of the natural, continuous fashion? That's totally crazy, goddammit! What's wrong with us?"

"Yes, I know!" John seconded. "Why, goddammit, can't we make it so much easier on ourselves by taking the time to look for jobs in two adjacent states in a row, then two other ones, and so on? Why must we just keep marching repeatedly through a

whole bunch of states, clear across the goddamn country, in order to start looking for jobs in earnest? Frankly, I'm exhausted, as I know the two of you are also! My feet are hurting something awful! My shoes are falling apart! My vital inner organs are all out of alignment! Why, goddammit, must we dash around like those old chickens with their heads cut off? . . . Ah, chickens! Speaking of which. When was the last time I've seen one on my plate? Or out in the open, for that matter? What, goddammit, wouldn't I give right about now for a juicy drumstick or a healthy spoonful of hot chicken soup!"

"Friends, I have a strange feeling, or premonition, that this is something we're not meant to understand," Jack interjected after a pause, creasing his narrow brow. "There's some greater force at play here, I sense, governing our circumstances: some omnipotent alien intelligence, armed perhaps with the all-powerful Marxist theory. If you know what I mean. Or maybe it's some other, equally potent theory. I'm not sure. The whole thing just gives me the creeps. Better not think about such spooky, unknowable matters. . . ."

From Alabama to Alaska, then straight on to Arizona, then Arkansas, then . . .

Ah, but no! Not so fast! Not in that exact order! Therein, you see, lay the additional rub, with regards to the narrative's geography: Idaho, and not Alabama, was where their journey had originated—and from Idaho (Moscow, Idaho—well, naturally) they headed straight for Iowa (that's right), and only then went to Alabama, then Alaska, then Arizona, then Arkansas, and then

Wyoming (yes, Wyoming, goddammit!), then Washington, then Vermont, then Virginia, then Wisconsin, then Hawaii (oh, sure, absolutely; they managed to stow away in the bowels of a Honolulu-bound tourist ship, you see, and then repeated the maneuver to get back to the mainland—after the manner of Tom Sawyer and Huckleberry Finn's trip down the Mississippi), then Delaware, then Georgia—well, you may be getting the idea already—in full compliance, in other words, with the order of letters in the Cyrillic alphabet (rather than the Latin one) and the way the U.S. states are spelled commonly in Russian.

Utah, thus, turned out to be the final point of their monthslong ordeal: the frenetic, schizophrenic journey of supposed self-discovery.

In the end, inevitably enough, Jim, John, and Jack come to realize the urgent imperative of joining the U.S. Communist Party, led by the faithful friend of the Soviet Union, Comrade Gus Hall. For a short while, they also entertain the idea of up and emigrating outright to the Soviet Union—the workers' paradise, the glorious land of their dreams, and all the rest of it—but then, ultimately, they decide against it. First off, Russian must be an extremely difficult language to learn, and, frankly, they're no great linguists; and second, and most important, it is revealed to them, in a fateful dream shared mysteriously by all three of them at once somewhere in the howling steppes of East Texas, that, even despite the accidental misfortune of not having been born in the Soviet Union, a self-respecting American proletarian must not be a lame-ass quitter and shirk, for whatever ostensibly noble reason, his moral responsibility before the future generations of Soviet Americans to wage the unrelenting class struggle against, ugh, those hateful top-hatted fat cats from the oak-paneled backrooms of the Pentagon's Wall Street right here, at home, in America, thereby helping to hasten, however perhaps minutely, the ignominious final demise of the pernicious International Imperialism.

The novel's ending, if memory serves me, went, roughly, as follows:

"We must stay right here and fight!" Jim stated emphatically, hammering his fist against his concave chest and breathing a bit laboriously from the considerable exertion of climbing one of the lovely little hillocks and mountains surrounding the economically depressed and culturally and spiritually dead-as-a-doornail city of the Salt Lake.

"Yes, we must, comrades!" John echoed, coming up from behind with a conspicuous limp and putting his calloused hand with six fingers [I forgot to mention: He was, in a bid to be more interesting to the hypothetical reader, somewhat of a minor freak of nature] *on Jim's frail shoulder. "We will destroy this ugly capitalist realm of exploitation and injustice, and on its ruins we'll build the new, the beautiful world of . . . well, you know, harmony and equality and all that! Comrades, I'm so damn excited! I just can't hide it! Well, now what? I mean, what's the next step? I suppose we start by locating the office of the Utah state branch of the Communist Party, right?"*

"Right," confirmed Jack, also emerging on the mountain-top—despite his high fever and the hacking cough fairly ravaging his emaciated body—and, in his turn, placing the brittle bird's paw of his hand on John's shoulder. "Well, comrades! One for all, as the saying goes, and all for one! There're no obstacles we couldn't overcome together! We're yet to see—to quote the great Russian writer Anton Chekhov, whom I have no idea as to how I can possibly know, goddammit—the sky sparkling with diamonds!"

They stood up there, on the windswept mountaintop in the state of Utah, the three of them, in single file, bunched close together, barely alive with fatigue—and yet, unaccountably happy, too, and filled with extreme resolve, even though they knew full well that this was only the beginning of a long, hard, superarduous road ahead!

In short, it was a bunch of unself-consciously opportunistic nonsense.

But so what. I was just a Soviet kid. What did I know?

I remember that August of 1968 well. I went on a couple of successful mushroom hunts; swam (and, on one occasion, nearly drowned—I was a pretty bad swimmer, and still am) in the placid Roshchino lake; exchanged several progressively more soulful and maudlin pieces of correspondence with the lovely girl from my high school who I had a crush on at the time; played for hours on end with the impossibly cute, bearlike little Caucasian shepherd puppy my parents gave me as a birthday gift the month before (in fairly short order, growing in leaps and bounds, he would turn into a veritable Hound of the Baskervilles—much too large and mean a creature, in other words, for our cramped three-room apartment in a concrete-block building in one of the less picturesque Upper Kupchino "Khrushcheville" microdistricts on the outskirts of Leningrad; but that, of course, is a whole different story); raised my personal record for consecutive two-arm chin-ups to an impressive thirty-five (these days, I wouldn't be able to pull off just one, even if my life depended on it—which it occasionally does, incidentally, in one of my recurrent nightmares . . . well, not really); met one afternoon, randomly, over at the local park (where he was trying to keep an eye on his rambunctious toddler of a grandchild), and proceeded gushingly to introduce myself to, the famous Soviet children's and young-adult writer Lev Kassil, author of my favorite novels, *The Black Book and Schwambrania* and *The Great Opposition*—who subsequently, smiling wryly, presented me with an autographed bookmark bearing his sagacious Semitic likeness and imprinted at the bottom with one of his hallmark pithy sayings: "If only children thought more frequently about what they will be like when they grow up, and the grown-ups recollected more frequently with regards to what they were like as children, old age would never be in any hurry to come to people, and wisdom would never visit them too late."

As the summer of 1968 wore on and drew to a close—in a development that had little to do with my own tiny little thirteen-year-old existence—the heroic Soviet army occupied brotherly Czechoslovakia, in order to save the latter from sliding irrevocably into the nightmarish cesspool of Capitalism and International Imperialism. My Old Bolshevik grandfather rejoiced at the news, seated in an easy chair out on the porch of our rented dacha with the *Pravda* newspaper (all aglow with the black fury of its ruthless headlines) unfurled across his lap: "Well done! Way to go! We should've done this earlier!" In my book—as far as I was concerned, at the time, that is to say—he never was and never could be wrong. However, from my parents' whispered conversations behind half-closed doors, their meaningful sidelong glances and eye rolls at the *Pravda*-reading grandfather—and from the certain sotto voce exchanges between the stern-looking, poorly shaven city strangers milling around the Roshchino park in the dark—I began to gather the uneasy notion that the truth of the world as it had been known to me thus far might not, in point of fact, be such a clear-cut proposition. Something stirred inside me, darkly exciting, like a flock of blackbirds.

Also around that time, my great-uncle—my father's de facto adoptive father—died. One of the leading Soviet experts in the cellulose industry and owner of a very large library of old books in several languages, he lived in a rambling, spacious apartment in midtown Leningrad, just around the corner from the Dostoyevskian apartment building where I was born and spent the first eight years of my life. An inveterate long-distance swimmer, he nonetheless, somehow, managed to drown during a routine morning exercise, when crossing some narrow northern river, while attending a cellulose-themed symposium. A sudden muscle spasm, apparently.

Everyone in my family was crushed. . . . I loved him a lot.

Jim, John, and Jack. Three unemployed American workers. If it were up to me now, I would have those three bums up and hired by a Red Lobster somewhere in the vicinity of Coxsackie, New York, say—provided there is one up there, which there must be—and be done with them.

But for better or worse, I won't be able to do anything with them, or about them, now—not now and not ever—even if I wanted to, because back in 1993, when I was relocating to New York from Minneapolis (where I had completed my two-year stint as a visiting assistant professor), the large cardboard box containing that old standard-issue school notebook with its cornflower blue oilcloth cover (among sundry other sentimental mementos, such as scores of childhood photographs, a few slim stacks of adolescent love letters, drafts of unfinished youthful stories, that Lev Kassil–autographed bookmark, the oil painting of an oversize and idiosyncratically angled crawfish on a wet pub table next to a massive half-empty mug of Zhigulevskoe beer that my late father had bought for me on the occasion of my departure for America, et al.)—the only truly irreplaceable box out of the twenty-four comprising the sum total of my earthly possessions that I had shipped off to a friend's address in the Bronx—got lost without a trace in transit.

Sad

I N   A   C A B. Montreal. Corner of Saint-Viateur and Saint-Urbain.

CABDRIVER: Can I quickly speak with my brother on Bluetooth?

ME: I'm sorry?

CABDRIVER: With my brother. I must. Quickly, quietly. I have Bluetooth. You don't mind?

ME: Sure, go ahead. I don't care.

CABDRIVER: Do you know why I must speak with my brother?

ME: No, I don't.

CABDRIVER: Because I stopped my marriage. Today.

ME: You stopped your marriage.

CABDRIVER: Yes. Today. Marriage next week, but I stopped it.

ME: I'm sorry to hear that.

CABDRIVER: Don't be sorry.

ME: Okay, I won't be.

Cabdriver commences to speak with his brother, in a quick, urgent whisper, for a couple of minutes. Finishing the conversation, he remains silent for a few seconds.

CABDRIVER: In my heart I'm very sad.

ME: Are you okay to drive? Would you like me to get out and get another cab, so you could take a break in solitude?

CABDRIVER: No. I'm okay. Do I look okay to you, on my face?

ME: You seem to be okay, but what do I know.

CABDRIVER: I'm not okay inside. But don't worry, I'm not going to do anything bad. Do you know why I stopped my marriage?

ME: No, I don't.

CABDRIVER: Because of her friend. That woman, she never saw me or heard me, but she is saying all kinds of bad things about me. I said, I don't want that woman, your friend, at the reception. She said, Then there is no reception. I said, Then I stop the marriage. And I stopped it. I did the right thing, yes?

ME: I have no idea. It's a complicated situation. What do I know?

CABDRIVER: You lived a life.

ME: Yes, but not your life. My life.

CABDRIVER: I think I did the right thing. . . . You bought
    bagels in your packet there back on Saint-Viateur?
    Smell good.

ME: Indeed. That's where you picked me up.

CABDRIVER: I like from Fairmont better. I think I did the
    right thing. I do, but in my heart I'm sad.

Blue

AN OLD BLIND MAN in a long wintry line to the beer kiosk told me once, decades ago, in another lifetime, in a world no longer in existence, in a glorious and terrible city that has since been re-renamed, that when he was a young prisoner in an Eastern Siberian Gulag camp, he wrote poems for an imaginary fiancée at night, in pitch-darkness, on scraps of cement paper bags, with an illicit stub of lead pencil, by the light of his own eyes. I told him that was a nice metaphor, and he said in response, a little huffily, that it was pure nonmetaphoric truth. "Why do you think I've been blind for so many years now?" he added in a wistful tone, turning to me his desiccated face with empty eye sockets. "I burned them out then. Still, no regrets. Just imagine that blue light in the night!" I told him, feeling a shiver of strange unease scamper down my spine, that I sure hoped his imaginary fiancée had subsequently appreciated those, doubtless lovely, poems of his.

Almost Nine

I T WAS MORNING. A teakettle was hissing on the stove. Mother turned on the light in the kitchen. "Hurry up!" she called. Dad unplugged the razor in the bathroom. "You don't have to shout!" he said.

Mother looked at him with reproach. "Are you mad at me?" she asked. "Don't you love me anymore?"

"Of course I do!" Dad said.

Mother pressed her face to his chest. "I'm sorry about last night," she whispered. "It's just that when you come home so late, I get angry."

"Let's eat!" Dad said.

They sat at the table. Mother yawned and glanced at her wristwatch.

"The news!" she reminded him. "The weather!"

Dad nodded and reached up to the radio. It was a round felt dish on the wall. They heard the announcer's solemn voice. It delivered the Supreme Soviet's statement.

Mother shook her head and sighed deeply. The First Moscow Boys Choir began to sing. Dad pushed his plate aside and leaned back.

"Unbelievable!" he said. "That stupid ass Nikita is gone!"

"Is it good or bad?" Mother asked.

"How do I know?" Dad replied.

"Anyway, he is listening, so maybe let's not," Mother said. She shrugged and poured a glass of milk from the carton. Five drops fell and trembled on the oilcloth. In a moment, there was a small lake of milk. Mother frowned and mopped it up with a towel.

"Drink!" she ordered. "I don't have all day!"

"That's right!" Dad said. "And please quit just staring at me like some kind of creature from another planet!"

"Don't shout at him!" Mother said.

"Oh, for god's sake!" Dad slapped the tabletop. The three cups clinked and rattled on the table. "They simply kicked him out!" he said. "Well, serves him right."

The Kremlin Courants began to toll.

"Is there someone else?" Mother asked. "Can't you simply tell me the truth just this once?"

"What on earth are you talking about?" Dad said. "Don't you understand what just happened?"

Mother sighed. Dad hugged her. "Please don't cry!" he said.

Mother shook her head and sniffled. Dad stroked her hair. It was still a little wet. Dad took his hand away.

"It's still a little moist," Mother murmured. "I bought this new Czech soap the other day."

Dad smiled and whispered something. Mother's face reddened a little.

Dad's fingers slid under her robe.

"No, let go!" Mother breathed out.

"Could we go to the bedroom?" Dad said.

"My parents are there!" Mother reminded him, giggling.

"Could we, then, go to the bathroom?" Dad said.

"The little one is there!" Mother laughed.

There was a pause. They heard a tiny child's loud singing. A jet of water gushed into the tub.

"Unbelievable!" Dad said. "Six people in one crummy . . . little . . . apartment!"

Mother bit her lip, as if in pain.

She was breathing heavily, with an effort. An ugly vein throbbed on her forehead.

"Turn to the window!" Dad said. Mother sucked in air through clenched teeth.

"Stop being so apprehensive. We're not doing anything bad or unnatural!" Dad said.

His neck swelled up. He grunted like a pig.

It must have begun to rain outside. The fog of night, so dense only an hour before, had receded. Still, there was nothing to look at there but one's own indistinct reflection. It appeared to be streaked with flowing shadows. This weather couldn't be seen, only guessed at. What was that patter of so many little feet up above? It might have been the pigeons slipping off the roof in the rain. One would hope for snow, but winter was too slow to come. This was by far the mildest fall in nine years.

Or almost nine. Eight years and eight months. Eight years and eight months, and eight days.

"The thaw," said a voice on the radio, "will be over shortly." Neither Dad nor Mother seemed to be listening.

"Are you comfortable?" Dad said. "Relax!"

The ceiling was snow-white, all in swirls of stucco.

The refrigerator hummed in the corner. A scratch ran across its enameled front. Two cockroaches traversed the sticky floor.

"Twenty-eight days till our country's glorious forty-seventh anniversary!" the voice said. "How are YOU going to celebrate it?" The national anthem started to play.

Mother seemed to have difficulty talking. "Go to the corridor!" she said pleadingly. "Go to your room and get dressed!"

"He's gone!" Dad said. "Don't worry!"

The door screeched. It was still dark in the hall. One had to wait a while to start seeing things there. The sweet smell of dead flowers was strong.

"God! It's almost nine!" Mother gasped.

"We're out of mustard!" Dad said, opening the refrigerator.

The kitchen door squeaked and whined.

"We need to have those hinges oiled," Dad said.

There were shards of teacup glass on the floor. Mother's pink slippers were under the table. All the windows in the tall nine-storied building across the street were already illuminated. Gloomy silhouettes drifted, weightless, inside their suspended cubicles of bright light.

It was warm and damp in the kitchen.

The yolk of a half-eaten egg quivered on the glistening plate in the yellow glow of a shaded bulb. Dad's new white nylon shirt was unbuttoned.

Mother stood at the stove with a hairbrush in her hand. A scattering of crumbs on the table had formed a small mountain ridge. Everyone was awake now. Mother's parents shuffled in.

Dad was eating bread with bologna. "Bastards!" he mumbled. "Liars! He is a fool, of course, but . . ."

"Maybe he was, in fact, ill," Mother said. "Why couldn't that be true?"

Dad winced and turned off the radio. "Let's hope it'll be all right," he said from the corridor. "If I were you, I'd take a very hot bath. Just a suggestion. Don't take it the wrong way. Just to be on the safe side."

His steps echoed down the stairs outside. Mother took a knife and made a ham sandwich.

"Here's your lunch," she said. "Hurry! I know you start late this morning, but still."

It was time to go to school.

Life: How Was It?

SOMEONE I HADN'T SEEN in forty years recognized me the other afternoon at the Strand Bookstore. In middle and high school back in Leningrad, he had been one of my closest friends. He was buying a coffee-table album of New York pictures (something along the lines of *To See New York and Die*; for his mother-in-law, he told me, winking), and I'd stopped by on my way to a friend's house in the neighborhood.

A burly, broad-shouldered, handsome man of vaguely Levantine aspect—a cross, of sorts, between Hitchcock and . . . oh well, those crosses and parallels tend to make nothing more vivid; a cross between Alfred Hitchcock and Angelina Jolie: How's that?—he hailed me good-naturedly in Russian as I was passing by the cash register: "M! M! Is that you? . . . Is Mishka already up north?"

That was an old running high school joke between us. Mishka Up North had been one of the most popular brands of chocolate bar in the Soviet Union. Its wrapper pictured a dignified-looking polar bear strolling along a massive floe of Arctic ice. Mishka is the common loving diminutive for any kind of bear in Russian—be it black or polar. Mishka, of course, is also the diminutive, highly irreverent, and childlike form of Misha, which itself is the diminutive of Mikhail, which is my name. For someone to be "up north," in the general Soviet parlance, meant his having been arrested and sent off to one of the Gulag destinations for his political activities—or, more likely and pertinently, the looseness of his lips, the pointless frivolity of his speeches.

"D.D.!" I exclaimed (not his real initials, but close enough), already quite certain it was indeed him, recognizing him even despite my general propensity for recognizing those from my distant past whom I'd never met before. "Is that you? What a strange meeting! But how did you know it was me? I cannot believe . . . Don't tell me I haven't changed beyond any, you know, possibility of recognition since high school!"

"Oh, you most definitely have," he assured me with a smile. "It's just that I saw a picture of you in a newspaper back home, maybe five or six years ago. Plus, I'm on Facebook, technically speaking, although I hardly ever am there. . . . It's true, though: There's very little in the face you have today from the one you used to have back then. Sorry if that sounds upsetting to you, maybe. . . ."

"Oh no," I said, waving my hand. "That's how I tend to think of myself, in any event, at present—being on my second, wholly separate life. You know, it's like that old joke about the historical museum in Genoa's having on exhibit two skulls that used to belong to Christopher Columbus: one as a child, the other as a grown man. In every joke . . . there's a kernel of joke, as the saying has it."

He paid for the book for his mother-in-law, and we moved away from the cash register and started talking animatedly, though he only had a few minutes (he was running back to his hotel to collect his wife and elder daughter to head to the airport and home).

He told me the abbreviated story of his life. After twenty years of being a merchant marine and having circumnavigated the world many times over, he was now living in Yekaterinburg. "It's a long story," he said in response to the puzzled look I gave him. "My wife's from there, her father—a mini-oligarch of sorts, locally, and he offered to invest in the tour agency I was starting then, fifteen years ago, if I relocated there, and so on. So I thought, Why not? Saint Petersburg, of course, is great, but Yekaterinburg has its certain advantages. It's a nice-enough city. Just very far away from everything, to be sure. But—them's the breaks. You can't always want what you get, you know."

We reminisced. Some of the key episodes from our shared childhood and adolescence neither of us could recall, as though they'd never happened—or rather, as though we'd never lived through those moments of our own lives. Memory either confirms or refutes the very fact of our own existence.

He couldn't recall, for instance, that I once hurled an ethnic slur at him—his family has North Caucasus origins—during one of the heated moments in an intramural soccer game, after he'd mowed me down brutally from behind. (Both of us were the stars of our school soccer team, which, admittedly, is not saying much.) This was one of the most shameful episodes of my youth, and I had been rehashing it in my mind for a long time. But he didn't seem to remember it—and not the vehemence, either, with which he'd rushed at me with a piece of stone in his hand, blind rage distorting his genial features. He seemed to have blocked it out.

I, in turn, could not remember having on another occasion burned my lips almost clear off my face after biting off a chunk of small red pepper lying around the kitchen in his apartment, despite his jocose earlier warning not to touch it—that their native cuisine was way too hot for the uninitiated. Subsequently, I'd spent, according to him, a good half hour in a delirious state, with my face stuck under a stream of cold water in his kitchen sink, and my lips were swollen something awful, to the point of my not being able to say a single word for hours afterward.

Well, but some things we did remember jointly, of course. The girls we had crushes on, the soccer games of special import, the pranks we pulled on the teachers . . .

We looked at each other with a mix of tenderness and befuddlement, moist-eyed. It was clear to both of us, after the five or ten minutes of our hasty conversation, that this chance meeting was the last time we ever were going to see each other. I would never find myself in Yekaterinburg, and he wouldn't be returning to New York or going to Montreal. We wouldn't have seen each other, either, had he not recognized me a few minutes ago in this unlikely locale, in the middle of a bustling New York bookstore.

But that was okay. Knowing we would never see each other again—it was okay. When you're young, you think there'll be plenty of time for everything in your life: counting all the grains of sand in the Sahara Desert, seeing all the people in the world, becoming greater than Jesus and Lenin and Lomonosov and Pushkin and Einstein all rolled into one, reuniting at some point with everyone you've met once in your life, befriending every man, falling in love with every woman. . . . Life is a process of gradually coming to terms with the meaning and the very concept of neverness. Never—well, so be it. Quoth the raven: Oh well, them's the breaks. Get used to it. Get over it. Life is a perishable proposition of rapidly diminishing returns. You could've become this or that; you could've been here and there and everywhere; but that didn't happen—and well, so be it. There won't be, in the end of your life, a joyous, transcendentally meaningful regathering of everyone you've ever met on your path, with stories shared and wine flowing and laughter lilting and happiness abounding and life never-ending—well, so be it.

"Well, so—how was it, in all?" I asked him just as we were about to part ways and give each other an awkward farewell hug.

He understood me. "Life, you mean?"

"Yeah, you know . . . life," I said, with an embarrassed chuckle. "What did you think of it?"

"It was okay. Good. Better than one might have

expected," he said pensively. "I can't complain. How was it for you?"

"Interesting," I said. "Yeah, definitely. Pretty interesting. I wouldn't know what else to say about it. I, too, can't complain—and it would be pointless to complain, too, because . . . well, whom or what would one complain to? It was interesting."

Love Like Water, Love Like Fire

There is love like fire, and there is love like water.
—The Chassidic Masters

1

IN THIS FADED, BLURRY PHOTOGRAPH taken, according to the slanted, barely legible purple ink note in my mother's hand on its reverse side, in August of 1939, near Gomel, Byelorussian Soviet Socialist Republic, one can see my forebears. Grandfather is the only male in the picture, and Grandmother, half-smiling and looking sideways, is third from the left. Their nine-year-old daughter (my future mother) is fourth from the left, gazing directly into the camera with grown-up seriousness, her right elbow resting easily on Grandmother's knee. Grandmother's younger sister is the last one on the right, with her toddler of a daughter in her lap, while her ten-year-old, wide-eyed and beribboned, doe-like and quietly joyous in her summery white dress, is on my grandmother's left. Grandmother's nameless niece is towering on her knees in the back with an expression of uncertain merriment on her face. And finally, with a hint of a smile or frown in the corners of her pursed lips (especially terse-looking on account of being unaccustomed to posing for photographs, one would imagine), is Grandmother's mother—my great-grandmother, who died before I was born.

When, exactly, did my maternal great-grandmother die? I don't know, and it is somewhat puzzling to me now why it never occurred to me to ask that question back when everyone who could have answered it was still alive or capable of answering questions. I don't think she was killed during the Holocaust, because I probably would've known about that—at least *that*—although maybe not, much to my shame, considering that the Holocaust was a taboo subject in the Soviet Union, a nonexistent word denoting nothing, and ours was not exactly a taboo-breaking family; we were just the ordinary big-city Soviet

Jews—which is to say, hardly Jewish at all, considering our near-total unawareness of all things "Jewish," including our own familial roots. One might say we were Jews in official Soviet designation only.

It occurs to me now that the only piece of information about Grandmother's childhood ever made known to me was the family legend, according to which, one uncommonly rainy morning back in 1908, at the peak of Russian Jews' migration to America, when she was five years old, Grandmother's family was set to follow so many others' suit, having sold their cramped wooden house and nearly everything they owned in order to purchase nonrefundable tickets for steamboat passage from Odessa to New York, but the horse cart carrying all of them and all of their scant remaining possessions got stuck in the impassable mud of an otherwise rather short and easy road between their Byelorussian shtetl and the train station at Gomel (or Homl, in Yiddish; the site of the infamous Jewish pogroms of 1903), and as a result, when they finally arrived in the faraway port city of Odessa, it turned out that their boat had already departed, taking with it their one and only chance of leaving behind forever the misery of life in the Pale. They'd missed it by about half an hour.

As a teen, I often marveled about those thirty-odd minutes, each time feeling awestruck by life's sheer dark randomness. Indeed, unless that admittedly contrived-sounding story had been but an innocent flight of my grandmother's fancy, a figment of her childish imagination

transmogrified and hardened into unmitigated truth with
the passage of decades, the entire difference between my
existence and nonexistence, being and nonbeing, had been
determined by that infinitesimally small drop in the ocean
of time: a mere half hour's worth of horse cart–ride delay
caused by a wholly unforeseen, unusually heavy rainfall in
the vicinity of Gomel, Byelorussia, one unverifiable morning in 1908. It was, to the adolescent me, a fascinating
notion—that from that one accidental distant downpour
several of my short lifetimes earlier, everything that would
result in the auxiliary outcome of my insignificant persona's emergence in the world flowed and followed with
the inevitability of a wholly predictable movie plot that
would unfold thusly: Dead broke and brokenhearted, my
future great-grandparents would have no other recourse
but to return to the old shtetl in order to try to restart
their old life from scratch there; some sixteen years later,
in the bitter winter of Lenin's death, one of their daugh-
ters would leave the dullness of the Byelorussian provinces
and come to the newly renamed, coldly majestic Leningrad, the beating heart of the imminent worldwide proletarian revolution, to study health science and human
biology at the venerable University of Physical Education
there; a few months after that, during the great Leningrad
flood of 1924, while helping to organize the boat rescue
of old people in the city center, she would meet a soft-
spoken yet passionately eloquent, curly-haired, and soft-
eyed young Party and Komsomol activist, also originally

from a Byelorussian shtetl, one outside Bobruisk, and the two would proceed to fall in love, get married, and have my mother; and then, finally, my mother, in due course of her blooming youth, would meet my father, who lived just around the corner, in the very same Leningrad neighborhood, and who went to a boys high school one block away from her high school for girls. . . .

Just one measly half hour! My head was swimming pleasantly at the incomprehensible thought of how unimaginably close to eternal nonexistence, in the form of never being born, I had come some six decades earlier and many hundreds of kilometers from Leningrad. I looked around me, just to make sure my world was real. It was. My small room, which I shared with my younger brother, was perfectly, if dismally, real. Outside, beyond the window of our three-room *cooperative* apartment in a standard-issue five-story cinder-block building on Cosmonauts Avenue, in one of the dozens of identical and rapidly multiplying *Khrushchevian microdistricts*, the dolorous flatness of Leningrad's southwestern outskirts stretched out in all directions. It certainly was no America, this unlikely locale—but it was my world, the only one I knew and rightfully belonged to.

But I digress.

The year is 1939. Stalin's Great Terror, barely past its apogee, still rages on in the land. All across the vast country's eleven time zones, and especially in its two largest cities, countless people of all walks of life are being *disappeared* on a nightly basis. In Leningrad, my future grandmother lives in a constant state of gnawing fear. She knows—or at least suspects strongly, with the dreadful intensity of near certainty—that at any moment, the same fate could befall her husband, especially considering his highly visible status as an up-and-coming young Party activist and citywide Komsomol leader—that is, someone already, by default, existing permanently in the ominous zone of the *organs*' unremitting attention. Just in the last nine months, three of her husband's former close friends of long standing, his fellow young Party leaders and Komsomol activists, also born and raised in the Pale, have been *unmasked* and *disappeared* as foreign spies and enemies of the people, vanishing without a trace in the night, with their wives following them into the same darkness a few nights later in each case, *disappeared* presumably as their husbands' accomplices and enemies of the people in their own right. Two of those families lived in the same apartment building with her and her husband and their daughter—an old massive structure with six stairways. Due to its semiexclusive designation—it is partially reserved for the young Party and Komsomol *nomenklatura*—there is just one single, sparsely populated communal apartment per floor landing. The young woman who would be my grandmother witnessed all four of those *disappearings* in their initial and final stages down in the inner courtyard, watching surreptitiously, breathlessly, frozen, petrified, from behind the window curtain. Everything unfolded silently and almost routinely, matter-of-factly, inescapably, but also slowly, too, as if taking place underwater or in accordance with the awful logic of a lucid self-aware nightmare one knows better than to even attempt awakening from, or else. Every time, come morning, she would open her eyes with a fleeting hope she'd dreamed it all up. But no.

Every time, come morning, she would say nothing to her husband about what she'd seen in the night—not a word—knowing that she, his rock of kindness and stability, would be the last person he'd expect to be the bearer of the heartbreaking and infuriating news of yet another one of his friends and Party comrades having turned out to be a despicable traitor, counterrevolutionary snake, wretched foreign spy, contemptible lackey of International Imperialism, sheep in wolf's clothing, Trotskyite-rabid-dog enemy of the people. Learning this from her would probably devastate him, despite his being a man supposedly made of ferocious proletarian steel, steeped to the eyebrows in the ruthlessly ironclad Marxist-Leninist theory, the Party's tireless foot soldier, the Komsomol's passionate trailblazer and path beater. It would break his heart if she were to become an agent of utmost pain in his life, for she is the only person in the world with whom he can allow himself to be fully and defenselessly human: weak, confused, and prone to helpless tears of sorrow. And he has a congenitally weak heart, too—a minor defect from birth, nothing imminently lethal, but still . . .

She knows him so well—much better than he knows himself. He is so altogether predictable in his one-dimensional mental rigidity coupled with childishly naïve optimism! He has no fear of being *disappeared*. She wishes she could be like him: someone shielded safely against life's harsh reality by boundless faith in the Party's eternal wisdom, the *organs'* absolute fundamental infallibility and, more obviously than words could ever express, the Great Leader's transcendental supernatural genius for being the greatest and wisest genius ever to walk the Earth and the true immortal heir to Lenin's deathless greatness. She wishes she, too, could live without fear, cocooned securely in the unquestioning belief that for as long as one knows with utmost certainty that he himself is *not* an enemy of the people, there cannot possibly exist, not even in some abstract theory, any conceivable chance of his being *disappeared* by the *organs*. But unfortunately, she cannot be like that—she's not him. She is incapable of possessing his halcyon serenity of spirit, his sacred trust in the Party, the *organs*, and, most especially, the Great Leader. Secretly, she trusts no one, not even—much to her own anguished dismay—the Great Leader himself. She suspects she may be sick in her head—but if so, so be it. There is nothing she can do about it.

Hence, this blurry old photograph. Grandfather's presence in it almost certainly has been her sole doing, the result of her sustained effort to talk him into asking his Party and Komsomol superiors for some time off from his tireless ideological pursuits, so that—a white lie, yet still a lie—he could join his wife and daughter at a long-planned family reunion in her birth town of Gomel. That certainly could not have been an easy request for him to make, and he must have felt keenly embarrassed doing so, because true Bolsheviks and Komsomol activists, the tireless stormy petrels of the imminent world-wide proletarian revolution, do not take vacations. After all, as everyone knows, the Great Leader himself never sleeps a wink.

Here they are, then—in soporific, provincial Gomel, where the obligatory *purges* and *disappearings,* while still being carried out with proscribed regularity, in keeping with the quotas determined by the Byelorussian NKVD in Minsk, proceed nevertheless at a markedly slower and more relaxed pace—and where hardly anyone in the local *organs* structure would pay much heed to some young Leningrad Party and Komsomol hotshot's private visit to their neck of the woods.

Here, in this photograph, she looks relaxed, at peace with her life, as she and others in the clearing wait for her younger sister's husband—and Grandfather's good friend, an ebullient, burly, bald Jew, also a Party member, of course, and someone rather important at the Ministry of Construction of Heavy Industry in Moscow—to line up the shot, laughing in his booming voice. (And incidentally, for some reason, I remember him more clearly than some of the much more central characters of my childhood, even though he lived in Moscow, hardly ever coming up to Leningrad, and died when I was still little.)

Before long, however, the three of them—my future grandparents and the girl who would become my mother—will be returning to Leningrad.

2

IT IS PAST MIDNIGHT in midtown Leningrad. The year is 1939, the month January. A young woman, already on the verge of drifting off to sleep in her family's square single room in a scarcely populated, spacious communal apartment on the fourth floor of a tall, massive, one-hundred-year-old building, hears the muffled rumbling of an automobile outside as it swerves off the empty street and pulls in under the low-slung archway leading into the interior courtyard. Instantly, she is wide awake. An automobile. Not a truck. Automobiles still are few and far between in the city, especially at night, and they almost never appear in the courtyard, because why would they? That hardly ever happens.

Hardly ever. But not never.

The young woman knows right away what this means. She just does. She can't believe this is happening again, here. That would be grossly unfair on life's part. Lightning shouldn't strike the same apartment building twice, let alone five times, even given this particular apartment building's somewhat special status. Enough is enough . . . no?

But then, she tells herself, on the other hand, maybe this time it's nothing. Despite all her certainty to the contrary. Nothing to worry about. Maybe it's just her overactive, excessively pessimistic imagination. No reason to panic just yet.

Her heart thumping dully in her chest, she slips out of bed, ghostlike in her long white linen nightgown in pitch-darkness, and tiptoes over to the room's only window, careful not to awaken her husband, who is snoring peacefully and almost melodiously in the dark, or their nine-year-old daughter, sound asleep under the fluffy goose-down comforter in her own smaller bed in the ten-square-meter room's warmer corner, the one closest to the ceramic woodstove opposite the window and farthest from the door—the latter, incidentally and apropos of nothing, has been painted red, for some reason, by one of the room's previous occupants. No panicking, she admonishes herself. There's no cause for panic yet, at this point. There are six separate stairways in the building leading to six separate landings—dozens of communal apartments. Why jump immediately to the worst of conclusions? Why be so pessimistic? Why must it necessarily be this particular apartment's turn tonight—or that of any one in the building? She is so self-centered, she tells herself. That's an unpleasant, backward, bourgeois character trait. And even assuming for a moment, just for abstract supposition's sake, that this indeed is what she is almost certain it is—and if, furthermore, it does turn out to be their stairway and their apartment whose turn it's going to be tonight—still, there are other people living in the apartment, too, so there does actually exist a larger-than-zero possibility that it could be one of them . . . right?

Unfortunately, no. Sadly, no way. There are only five other tenants in this large, rambling apartment with a long and narrow corridor: two perfectly harmless and altogether inconspicuous working-class retiree couples and the perennially downcast, yet equally unobtrusive, hard-drinking grave digger over at the Smolenskoye cemetery. She must be brave enough to face the truth of the situation: If anyone, it's got to be him—her husband. Who else? His being a prominent up-and-coming young member of the city's Party and Komsomol *nomenklatura* is, of course, the reason they have so few neighbors in such a spacious apartment in the first place—an enviable living arrangement, to be sure; tonight, however, it only could work to his, and hers and their daughter's, extreme disadvantage.

Bating her breath, clutching her nightgown at her throat, the young woman stands beside the window in the dark, her back pressed against the wall—and then cautiously, fearfully, ever so slightly, she lifts aside the corner of the cheap chintz window curtain. Craning her neck, she peers outside, into the acutely narrow triangle of night's darkness. There is fresh snow on the ground. A long, humpbacked black automobile, a *black raven,* its lights turned off, completely lightless within and casting no shadow on the snow, is pulling into their courtyard. It angles slightly toward their stairway and then grumbles to a halt, still shuddering minutely for several more seconds. Then it gets quiet.

The night has its stillness back.

The automobile's single door opens slowly, as though reluctantly, with an effort, and two soldiers in winter overcoats and peaked caps climb out, their pawlike hands bright red, followed by a short man in a long black leather overcoat, wide-brimmed black hat, and round steel-rimmed spectacles. His hands, unlike the soldiers', are gloved, and his small round face with a studiously cold expression bears no distinct, notable features. (This, it occurs to the young woman as she looks at him, with horror and revulsion, may be the main reason behind having a face like that, too: forgettable to the point of being almost memorable. She is certain she's never seen him before. Those black-clad others, who looked just like him, climbing out of the *black ravens* down there in previous instances, were different individuals, at least nominally so.) The short man in black glances around him briskly, then proceeds to rock back and forth on the balls of his feet, gazing upward: straight, it seems—but no, that couldn't be!—at her, the young woman by the window. In the night's moonless monochrome, his steel-rimmed specs give off a sharp, cruel refractive sparkle—a blinding diamond white razor of light.

Instantly, involuntarily, she recoils from the window, her heart fairly leaping up into her throat; but then, almost immediately, she realizes the foolishness of her reaction, because there simply is no way he could see her up here, peeking out from behind the curtain in the room's total darkness. She needs to stop losing her mind for no reason. That's not going to help or solve anything. Besides, she reminds herself again, more sternly this time, nothing has even started happening yet—and until it does, *if* it does, it is nothing and has nothing at all to do with her or her family. Get a hold of yourself, she tells herself. Don't be a frightened, foolish little girl. No panicking just yet.

Without turning his head, the short man in black says something curt through barely parted lips, pointing upward with his stubby index finger at some indefinite spot simultaneously above and below her window—and the soldiers follow his hand dutifully with their empty eyes, then give an indifferent nod, and one of them yawns. The man in black says something else, this time gazing directly at the soldiers with a lopsided grin, and the soldiers half-smile and nod again in response; and then all three start walking toward the apartment's stairway, silently crunching fresh-fallen snow. In no time—but then, what is time, anyway, when sometimes a minute lasts a lifetime?—they disappear from the young woman's narrow conical field of vision. A few moments later, she can hear their confident, hefty footsteps all the way downstairs, in the lobby. They start ascending the stairs.

It actually *is* happening. It is.

The young woman, her back pressed against the wall, eyes shut tight, hands clasped together in front of her, starts praying, silently, fervently. She is not fully aware of what she is doing, and no coherent, distinct words one might credibly associate with an actual prayer of any kind pass through her mind—yet still, her lips are moving silently. She does not know any prayers, needless to say, and has forgotten, once and for all, the ones she was taught as a child in the shtetl—and she certainly would've been offended and downright outraged by anyone's ridiculously outlandish suggestion to the contrary. She is, after all, a proudly ordinary Soviet citizen, a highly educated, future-bound young Soviet woman, a member of OSOA-VIAKhIM (that, as every Soviet child knows, stands for Society for Aid to Defense and to Aviation and Chemical Industries), a high school teacher of human biology, wife of a prominent young Party activist and Komsomol activist, someone steeped fervently to the eyebrows in the unyielding, beautifully blood-soaked Communist dogma; she also, one should know, is a sophisticated and acculturated Leningrader, long since liberated forever by the Great Revolution from the misery of her Pale of Settlement origins and never considering herself anymore (nor being considered by anyone else, either) as merely a Jew, some hapless Sholem Aleichem–like type of caricature, a perennially downtrodden yet stubbornly optimistic shtetl character (the sort her poor parents used to be, and still are, through no real choice or fault of their own). She is neither a Jew nor a non-Jew anymore, but only and exclusively a non-ethnospecific member of the glorious and entirely unique breed of human beings—the Soviet people!

So, in a word, no: She most certainly is *not* praying. Her lips are moving of their own accord. She is not responsible for her lip muscles, given the pressure of the moment. Besides, she thinks, whom would she be praying to anyway, even if she knew or still remembered any prayers, Jewish or any other ones? Only the coldly indifferent, impenetrably dark, sinister wintry Leningrad sky would listen to her now.

Her parents. They know all the prayers. She wishes she could be a little girl again right now. Her parents, they know all the prayers.

Those steps, heavy and ponderous, deliberately slow. How loud they are already, down there, even while still only on the first flight of stairs. The staircase flights in this building are long and steep. At this rate, it would take those three a good three minutes to reach their landing.

Even though this actually is happening—her worst nightmare apparently being realized—there still may not be enough of a cause for full-fledged panic, she tells herself. Stay calm. It still might not be the end of the world—not for the three of them in this room at least. Still no need to panic. Not just yet. No need. There are other people living in apartments below theirs—admittedly, none more prominent than her husband, in terms of their *nomenklatura* status, but still: Some are semiprominent enough. And who, after all, said one's *nomenklatura* status was everything in such matters? This still could be nothing, although . . . it clearly is *something*. Regardless, she mustn't go crazy with panic now. That wouldn't help anything. She could, in point of fact, be fast asleep and having an exceptionally vivid and realistic nightmare right now, for all she knows!

Those steps down there. She's not listening to them. She's ignoring them. Nothing there to hear, or fear. That loud footfall up the staircase has nothing to do with her.

Oh God. She is so lost. She doesn't know what to do. She doesn't know anything about anything anymore. Maybe it would actually have been better if her parents . . . But no, she is *not* going there in her mind, in that dangerous direction; not allowing herself to seek solace in insanity. She can't believe she has almost allowed that treasonous, poisonous thought to enter her mind. A severe mental crime! . . . Oh, but what can she do, what must she be thinking at this moment, what imaginary straws to be grasping at for a second's worth of relief from panic, what with those merciless, echoing footsteps down there, climbing up the staircase? Yes, she thinks, in spite of everything, maybe it *would* actually have been better, for her and for everyone else, if her parents and she and her siblings, back when she was a little girl, had in fact made it to Odessa in time to get on that boat to New York! There! The unthinkable thought has been had! Damn those thirty minutes of being stuck in the clayey mud on the road to the Gomel train station! Damn that crazy biblical rain over Belarus that goddamn morning thirty-one damned years ago! At least then, had they made it to the boat on time, she wouldn't have been in this impossible situation right now—frozen with horror, wild with panic in the night! She would've been someone else entirely in America, and completely unreachable to the *organs*!

Of course, then, in that unimaginably far-fetched scenario, she would never have met her husband—this naïve, childlike man snoring in the dark here—and the two of them would never have had a child together, their daughter; it would've been some other girl or boy she would, or would not, have given birth to there, in America, obviously, and that, of course, would be totally inconceivable. . . . And yes, she would've been someone else there, too—in that hellacious, historically doomed America! She—or rather, that strange woman representing her American self—might not even have been able to survive there, in America, for very long, either, given that millions of ordinary Americans, apparently, keep dying routinely of starvation or crushing hopelessness every year, right in the middle of American cities, like stray dogs—the ordinary innocent people whose only crime was to have been born in America. . . .

She is staring off into darkness with unseeing eyes. Her heart is beating rapidly in her chest. Thinking about being an American, no matter the context, is a mental crime—she knows that. Maybe she *does* deserve to be *disappeared*.

Those footsteps out on the staircase. Those footsteps.

She doesn't know anything about anything right now. Nor does she know anything about the brief moment in time in which she and her husband and their daughter and everyone else in the vast Soviet land are trapped like millions of hapless antediluvian insects in one giant pool of the cooling-off resin of history.

Still, she does know something, and that's plenty for her.

She knows that in the last few months, three of her husband's former close friends of long standing and his fellow up-and-coming young Party and Komsomol activists, also born and raised in the Byelorussian part of the Pale—two of whom used to live in this very apartment building with their families—have been *unmasked* and *disappeared*, vanishing without a trace and soon followed into the same void of nonexistence by their wives. That's how she—a very light sleeper, especially of late—has come to know the ominous meaning and sinister purpose of those humpbacked automobiles, *black ravens,* one of which is biding its time down in the courtyard right now, with its lights off, darker within than it could've been had one been looking at it with one's eyes closed. She'd watched from behind the window curtain as all this unfolded, repeatedly. Each time, everything happened quickly, but also slowly, somehow, and with the soul-crushing sense of terrible, inescapable matter-of-factness, as if in one of those monstrously realistic nightmares one knows better than even to attempt to awaken from, lest one find out immediately that there are much worse things than death in life. She didn't want to watch any of those *disappearings,* but she just couldn't help herself, and she couldn't stop watching. It was mesmerizing. She saw her husband's friends being led out of their respective stairways into the courtyard by two soldiers, with a man in a black hat and long black leather overcoat, his steel-rimmed specs glinting merrily, stepping casually in the back, bringing up the rear; and she saw them, those two already former, *unmasked* friends of her husband's being shoved unceremoniously inside the *black raven*'s belly. She heard the *black raven* immediately starting to purr and growl, temporarily sated, taking off into the night. She also saw, several nights later in each case, the wives of those two—the friendly and cheerful young women—also being taken out into the courtyard, rather in the same fashion, except that the soldiers held the women's arms on both sides less tightly and the short man in black, walking leisurely in the back, seemed to have a lopsided smirk on his forgettable face. She saw all that: all four of them, her husband's former friends and their wives, being *disappeared* into darkness. And the night swallowed them all.

Then, as now, her husband was peacefully asleep in their bed, snoring gently, almost melodiously, while she stood by the window, frozen, petrified. Each time, come morning, she would just keep silent, letting him have a few more peaceful hours of merciful not-knowing, some small measure of relative calm before facing the inevitable storm of the day. She would leave it to the *organs* to inform him and his Party and Komsomol colleagues about the previous night's developments, with a brief and terse phone call to their respective district Party and Komsomol headquarters. Then and there, he would not be able to show any personal weakness, which would be totally unbecoming someone in his position—a man of Marxist-Leninist steel, the Party's faithful foot soldier. He would have to swallow the pain and despair and get to work immediately, for it would be his and his comrades' task to set in motion the daily surge of anti-imperialist, anti-enemy-of-the-people hatred, preemptively stirring up the masses, Leningrad's working class and its proletarian *intelligentsia,* by way of providing the vital informational assistance to scores of local Party and Komsomol representatives directly responsible for organizing the impromptu rallies of fury at factories and academic institutions all across the city, in the course of which it would be announced, in a limited variety of booming iterations, that owing to the heroic *organs'* ceaseless eagle-eyed vigilance, in the past several days, including as recently as the night before, another vicious pack of rabid Trotskyite dogs of counterrevolution, contemptible yellow earthworms, flunkies of International Imperialism, deplorable traitorous foreign spies and enemies of the people, evil saboteurs and harm-doers, who for years had been able cynically to conceal their repugnant subhuman true inner selves under the guise of Party and

Komsomol activists, had finally been *unmasked* and *disappeared*, and were now going to face their deservedly severe punishment at the hands of the infinitely righteous and ruthlessly merciful proletarian justice.

A roar would spread across the roiling sea of humanity. "Traitors! Loathsome yellow earthworms! Rabid Trotskyite dogs! Deplorable enemies of the people! Contemptible lackeys of International Imperialism! Sheep in wolf's clothing! Exterminate those dirty vermin! Stamp 'em out! Death to them! Death!"

"Unimaginable!" her husband would exclaim, raising his desperate, helplessly angry red-rimmed eyes at her. Every time after one of his former friends' *unmasking*, he— granted, not the shrewdest man in the world perhaps (but so what, if he loves her, which he certainly does, and she loves him, too!)—would return home in the evening utterly crestfallen, crushed, ashen-faced, causing her to briefly worry about his congenital heart defect. "Unbelievable!" he would repeat in a quavering voice. "He was my friend! My Party comrade! We just about grew up together! I thought I knew him almost as well as I know myself! How did this happen? When? How in the world has he been able to pull the wool over my stupid myopic eyes so thoroughly for all these years? It's . . . it's just incomprehensible! Oh, the snake! The disgusting vermin! Sheep in wolf's clothing! . . . Oh, my love, my dear," he would continue after a dejected pause, "how endlessly wise, as ever, the Great Leader is when he tells us, if not in those very same words, that no one can be fully trusted these days, not even the people you think you know inside out and trust completely by implication! Not even your comrades, your Party peers, not even them, at least not always—even if, admittedly, by default, most of the time you simply have no choice but to rely on their judgment while working alongside them for the greater glory of the revolution. . . . Yet still, not even while trusting them implicitly on a day-to-day basis can you trust them completely! Not even we ourselves can always be fully trusted by ourselves! Only the Great Leader can always be trusted—and in my case, you. You! The Great Leader—and you! Him—and you! Just the two of you! And no one else! I am so unjustifiably fortunate to have you! You are so wise, my love—so tell me, explain to me: How did this happen? How on earth could I have been so unforgivably blind, not recognizing much earlier, years ago, that traitor's true nature, his poisoned enemy heart? . . . I've let the Party down, once again! I deserve to be punished!" His voice would trail off, and a quick tear would roll down his cheek. Never once, not for a second would it ever cross his mind that the man who only the day before was still his old friend and fellow Party and Komsomol activist, an equally ardent believer in the imminence of the beautifully blood-soaked worldwide Communist revolution—and now, all of a sudden, the newly *unmasked* and *disappeared* enemy of the people and imperialist spy— might perhaps, even if only in remote theory, through some unfortunate fluke of cosmic disturbances, be, well, innocent of all the terrible charges leveled against him: no, never! Not one time! Never a moment of doubt! The *organs* had *disappeared* his lifelong friend, as a foreign spy and enemy of the people—and therefore, ipso facto, he was guilty and no longer her husband's friend. The *organs* were infallible by default. They only *unmasked* and *disappeared* the rotten apples in the society, the counterrevolutionary element, the traitors, the enemies of the people. Every Soviet child knew as much. "Traitors! Snakes!" her husband would exclaim quietly, shaking his head and sobbing a little. "How could they?"

And she would just lower her eyes, bite the inside of her cheek, nod demurely with a sigh, pull him in closer, cradle his bent curly-haired head in her arms, and say nothing. What else was there for her to do?

It would never become known, either to him or to her, in the years and decades to follow, what, exactly, happened in the end to those three former friends of his and their wives. Not one of them ever reemerged on the surface of life after Stalin's death and Khrushchev's subsequent mass amnesty of the victims of the Stalinist *repressions*. The three men, as everyone would have to assume, must have been shot dead, because of the unforgivably grave nature of their crimes in the eyes of proletarian justice, while the women most likely had been sent off to one of the Gulag camps up north or in Eastern Siberia and, at one point or another, died there quietly, in complete oblivion. That would come to be the belief on the grandparents' part.

Those steps on the staircase. Heavy and ineluctable, unforgiving. Stone on stone. They're up on the second-floor landing now, she can tell.

Right now, dead still in pitch-darkness, petrified, her heart pounding in her ears, her back against the wall, praying without praying while listening without listening to those ponderous, measured steps on the staircase—they grow louder, get nearer!—the young woman doesn't know, nor would she want to know or even imagine, what, exactly, will happen to her husband or to her if they—he tonight, and she a few nights later, inevitably—are to be *disappeared.* Her mind goes blank beyond the point of their being shoved inside their separate *black ravens.* Then—nothing. No empirical knowledge. All she knows is that if this were indeed to come to pass, she would never see either her husband or her daughter again. And that would be the end of it all for her. The end of her life, if not her physical existence. That's all she knows, and that's more than enough for her to know.

There is only so much horror the human heart and mind can take, and sometimes just one extra drop of it could kill one on the spot. In the past, she did wonder briefly a few times as to what, exactly, in terms of the bare sequence of infernal, spectral events, happened to those three former friends of her husband's and their wives after they'd been swallowed by the night. Right now, however, that would be the last thing she'd wonder about. And rightly so.

It would serve no good purpose for her to know any of those gloomy details: that from the very first moment each one of those three men arrived at the NKVD prison, all three were beaten relentlessly, fairly pummeled to a bloody pulp for days on end, without reprieve, both during the grotesque pseudointerrogations and afterward, in their overcrowded cells, by the easily bored and just as easily entertained criminal element in there, with much sadistic relish, just for the fun of it and also because thieves and murderers, despite their antisocial behavior and criminal proclivities, still considered themselves to be the patriotic Soviet people, and as such they hated and despised the wretched enemies of the people and foreign spies. That's the way it was then. It would do the young woman in the night no good to learn, further, that initially, in the first few days or maybe even the entire first week of their being there, in that netherworld of slanted shadows, each one of those three men, just like countless others before and after them, would stubbornly, and pointlessly and counterproductively, refuse to admit his guilt and confess to being a despicable traitor, enemy of the people, and foreign spy, but eventually would come to his senses, realize the sheer futility of his mulish obstinacy, and would sign, meekly and even gladly (because after that, at least those endless beating sessions under the guise of interrogations would cease), everything put before him: every single page of rough gray paper filled densely with the near-blind typed text of his thoroughly detailed and, needless to say, completely and totally voluntary "confession." Only once, while in the process of signing those pages without actually reading them, dully and automatically, with hollow bovine submissiveness, would each one of those three men flinch momentarily, pause and recoil within himself in a spasm of infinite despair, when coming upon the list of names of his supposed accomplices and coconspirators—many among those his friends and good acquaintances, his fellow young Party and Komsomol activists—with his own wife's name fairly leaping out at him from the top of the page. At that instant, each one of them, those three men, would wish ardently, the way he'd never wished for anything before in his life, that he could just have a lethal heart attack, right then and there, or knew of some feasible way of killing himself instantaneously. He would sign that page with his wife's name at the top of it, to be sure, one interminable second later, even knowing that by doing so, he was effectively sealing her already preordained fate as his coconspirator and enemy of the people in her own right. He did sign it. Human flesh is weak and prone to admitting defeat even while the spirit still wants to fight on. He just couldn't stand the thought of continuing to be beaten and tortured by his interrogators. Everyone, or the great majority of people, confessed to everything and signed everything in those circumstances. That's just the way it was then. Those steps on the stairs. Those heavy footsteps. She doesn't want to listen to them. It certainly would've caused the young woman in the night nothing but acute heartbreak and severe mental anguish to find out in similarly concrete and graphic detail how those three men, her husband's former close friends and fellow Party and Komsomol activists, spent the final span of their nominal, post-*disappearance* existence: how each one of them, having become numb to any human feelings after signing the above-mentioned "confession" of his, completely broken down, nearly deaf and blind and with half of his teeth missing from the still-ongoing interminable beatings in his cell, barely human anymore, his hair turned ghastly gray, was, at some indeterminate point in time, several days or weeks later, dragged out of his cell, taken to another location within the same NKVD facility, and made to stand in front of the so-called revolutionary troika, three make-believe NKVD judges, who would proceed seemingly to ignore the condemned man's ghostly presence in the room, pretending to be conferring among themselves in lowered voices for a couple of minutes, casting from time to time angrily bored glances at the gray cardboard tie-up folder containing the rough gray pages of that "confession" of his, before clearing their throats and announcing, quickly and mundanely, in a dull monotone, that for his unpardonable counterrevolutionary activities aimed at causing grave and irreparable harm to the Soviet state and conducted in the capacity of an imperialist spy, the sworn enemy of the Soviet people, citizen such and such was being sentenced to death by shooting. And that was all. That was that. That's just the way it was then. The young woman in the night, luckily for her, would never know how then, afterward, a few more senseless, insensate days or weeks later, every one of them, those three men, each in his own turn, again was taken out of his cell, hauled out into the prison yard, shoved into a covered truck with the warm word BREAD stencilled on its side, along with dozens of other convicted enemies of the people, and then driven to the city's remote outskirts, a dolorous postapocalyptic wasteland, where everyone inside the truck was ordered to disembark and line up along the jagged edge of a clayey ravine, with his or her back to the detachment of the *organs'* dispassionate, perennially overworked executioners, and was thereupon shot dead, promptly and quickly, efficiently, mundanely, and prosaically, without much ado and with much practiced dispatch, and finally ceased to exist forever, even as a spectral shadow of his former self, as did all the others standing naked meekly on both sides of him, disappearing once more, permanently and literally this time, one after another and all at once, their bodies falling into that shallow clayey ravine on their own, under the inescapable pull of Earth's gravity: layer upon layer of emaciated corpses, to be covered subsequently with shovelfuls of limestone, out of the basic sanitary considerations, prior to the arrival of the next batch of the condemned ones in a covered truck with the word BREAD on its side.

The young woman in the night, her back against the wall, frozen with horror and trying not to listen to the heavy, resonant steps of three pairs of feet of stone on the staircase, her hands clasped in front of her, lips moving silently, doesn't know any of the above, but she senses she should be grateful to the darkness she's in for not knowing any more than she already does. And that certainly is true. For one thing, had she been made aware, at this or any earlier time, of the existence of those long confessional lists of supposed accomplices and coconspirators and enemies of the people that the three former friends of her husband's had been forced to sign, she would've been going out of her mind with worry now, wondering endlessly, with dreadful foreboding, whether or not (and if not, then—and it is, admittedly, a horrible, unthinkable thought with truly terrible implications—why not?) her husband's name might have already been placed by the *organs* on one or more of those deadly lists or might yet appear on one or more of those, perhaps even the very following day, for someone to be *disappeared* tonight or tomorrow night to sign. That's what would've been on her mind right now, most certainly, had she known more than she already does. She would've gone mad with mental torment. She would've been torturing herself, too, ceaselessly, with the unbearable vision of her husband, broken down, gray, toothless, beaten to a bloody pulp, lost to the world, insensate, signing meekly, with a shaking hand, in pale purple ink, his own such list, with her name at the top of it. Unbearable. Unendurable.

She knows all about the inner workings of the human body, about the unstoppable circulation of dark blood in one's veins, but she has no distinct notion as to what having been *disappeared* and swallowed by the night does to one's human spirit. She knows we don't know ourselves, but she doesn't know the extent of that not-knowing. She does sense viscerally, however, that blessed not-knowing is her sole shield against insanity.

Those steps. She's not listening to them. They are getting nearer, louder. She's not listening to them.

And those men's wives? Again, it would serve absolutely no good purpose for her to learn that the wives of those three former friends of her husband's—the cheerful, easygoing, happy-go-lucky young women she used to like and laugh with, who were *disappeared*, each in her own turn, a few nights after their husbands, as the knowing aiders and abetters of foreign spies and enemies of the people in their own right—were plunged into a hell of their own: that each one of them, upon having been deposited at the women's section of the NKVD prison, was raped by a waiting pack of the criminal element, the subhuman gaggle of thieves and murderers gathered at the prison entrance area on their *organs* supervisor's orders in anticipation of yet another female enemy of the people's arrival, especially for that purpose, with an official dispensation to have their way with her, in order to break her will right away, from the very first moment of her entrance into the netherworld; and that each one of them, those three women, also was beaten continually after that, day in and day out, with merciless mundaneness and routine rage, by her nominal interrogator (additionally peeved, in the case of a young female in his charge, by the fact that he was free to beat and torture her to his heart's content, but, unlike that criminal slime, was not allowed to have his way with her, in his official capacity of a Soviet officer, under the portraits of Comrades Dzerzhinsky, Ezhov, and Beria), as well as by her hardened female cellmates; and that each one of those three women also, in a matter of fairly short time, signed everything she was told to sign, fully and unequivocally admitting her unpardonable guilt and confessing to her treasonous counterrevolutionary activities, also validating formally with her weak, wavering signature her own page-long list of her own supposed accomplices, fellow counterrevolutionary saboteurs, foreign spies, and other such enemies of the people, with her husband's name at the top of the page. She would, by then, already have been shown her husband's signature at the bottom of the analogous page from his own confession—the one, accordingly, with her name at the top. She would catch with the edge of her blurry gaze a small, smudged pale blot of dried blood in the rough gray page's bottom corner. She would wonder for an instant why people cannot just will themselves to die when death is all one wants from life anymore. She would sign the page.

That's the way it was then. One doesn't choose the time and place of one's birth—or one's death, for that matter. My grandparents would be correct in their later assumption that the three women's lives indeed were spared, unlike those of their husbands, but that all three of them did, at different times during the war years, die in their respective Gulag camps: one of pneumonia, the second of extreme exhaustion and complete loss of the will to live, and the third from being beaten to death one evening, just for the fun of it, by her bored criminal-element barrack mates. That was just the way it was then.

As for those three *disappeared* couples' children—and the young woman in the night did from time to time, with a sudden pang of sadness, wonder what might have happened to those two young girls and three little boys— they were transferred to special *organs*-supervised orphanages for children of the enemies of the people, where in a matter of weeks they learned to be intensely ashamed of their treasonous parents, to despise and hate those contemptible earthworms and rabid Trotskyite dogs of International Imperialism with every fiber of their little beings; and where they also had their last names officially changed to some other, blandly commonplace and overtly *Russianized* ones, in order to have their pure, innocent souls cleansed, once and for all, of the ugly stain of having once been the offspring of the despicable, subhuman, anti-Soviet enemies of the people.

That's the way it was then.

The young woman in the night does not know or care about any of this at the moment. She is not thinking about anyone or anything but herself, her husband, their daughter, and the three men out on the staircase. She is wondering why this is happening to her right now—to the three of them in the room. She cannot understand why life—her life, her husband's life, their daughter's young life—must be like this, all of a sudden: just so absolutely terrible. What has happened? Who is punishing them, and what for? Why must this night be like this? Her life—what is it? What has she done to deserve this night? Is she her own self right now? She feels as if she might be someone else. Who *is* she anyway? What makes her, her: someone other people think of as her? Where, if anywhere, deep inside her is the presumable unbreakable center, the indelible core of her being—the *real* her? Does it even exist? Does she exist? What is she doing here—in this night, this room, this city, this country? It is, she knows, a strange and dangerous line of rumination, the perniciously individualistic thought of an enemy of the people, and she'd better not allow it to enter her mind any further than she already has, if she knows what's good for her, which she doesn't think she does right now. Still, though—why? Why is she, why are the three of them right here, in this room, right now? What is going to happen to them tonight? Are they going to survive it? Is she? She certainly is never going to forget it—that's for sure, not for as long as she lives. And even if she's allowed to survive it—an enormously big *if*—is she going to remain the same person afterward, or be transformed by this night irrevocably into someone else entirely—an inwardly broken ageless woman crippled permanently by the unremitting fear ceaselessly burrowing into her bone marrow like so many shining black worms or small snakes, and causing her to be listening constantly, involuntarily, for the sound of an automobile engine down in the court-yard past midnight, for the echoing heavy footsteps on the staircase? Is she still going to be able to laugh or to make love to her husband? How do other people manage to keep themselves alive, having survived a night like this?

Stop it, she tells herself. Just stop it. Cut it out. Enough with this decadent, defeatist, self-pitying, individualistic, thoroughly bourgeois inner whining. Is she not an optimistic, future-bound Soviet woman? One must always keep one's dignity intact.

Those footsteps. They are getting closer and closer, louder and louder still. They are downright deafening now. For an instant, an entirely insane thought darts through her mind: If they ring the doorbell now, those three, in a few seconds, in a minute or so, then maybe she could just be done with it all quickly, once and for all, just get it all over with, immediately, instantaneously, just disappear for good on her own terms, cease being here or anywhere at all, escape through this window, just fling the damn thing open in one brutal, ferocious motion, even in spite of its frame's having been "winterized" to the point of near-total impenetrability, impervious to any application of effort to open it, with multiple layers of starch and glue and thick yellow tufts of hardened cotton—but so what, people can be unnaturally strong in desperate circumstances; she's read about this and is feeling it to be true in her own case right now—and then leap up onto the windowsill and, yes, just throw herself out into the night, and out of this terrible moment, and out of life, forever . . . no? Right? Why not? . . . Oh. The things they're making her think. *They*! Damn *them*! No, but really: The apartment is on the fourth floor, and these are tall floors up long flights of stairs, so she would pretty much be guaranteed mercifully instant death upon hitting the snow-powdered ground, or maybe even (and wouldn't *that* be a perfect ironic manifestation of some ultimate cosmic justice!) landing on top of that lightless hump-backed black automobile, the *black raven* down below, crushing to death the driver in there, completely invisible right now amid the absolute blackness inside and only guessed at by the red dot of the *papirosa* cherry floating slowly, appearing and disappearing, just beyond the automobile's windshield. Wouldn't that be a beautiful thing?

Such terrible, shameful things they're making her think! *Them*! Sure, what a wonderful idea: for her to escape into the safety of death all by herself, like a damn coward— and to abandon her husband and their daughter, leaving it to the two of them to suffer through a lifetime of nonexistence, either virtual or real! What in the world is wrong with her? Such disgusting selfishness! She truly is a horrible human being. She may well *deserve* to be *disappeared*.

She can't take this any longer. She feels like running out into the corridor and flinging open the front door herself, right now, for those three to walk in already and for her and her husband and their daughter to start being done with it all. It's taking all the inner force she can muster not to let out a low howl of sheer primeval despair. But what good would that do? What would it help to resolve? Nothing. Besides, she tells herself again, as insistently as she knows how, besides, still, maybe, just maybe, even if those three do ring the doorbell now, it still wouldn't absolutely necessarily mean they have come for her husband. Still. It wouldn't. It still wouldn't have to be the end. They still could've come for one of the neighbors. The pensioners. The grave digger. Still. Against all odds. Just maybe. The probability of that . . . that alternative scenario—it still would be larger than zero. Mathematically speaking. Far-fetched? Yes. Admittedly so. But impossible? No. Nonsense? Yes, probably. But total nonsense? Well, yes and no, and maybe not. Not in abstract theory at least. Miracles do happen, don't they?

No, they don't.

The heavy, resonant, booming steps outside are closing in on their floor. As everywhere else in the building, there is only one apartment on their floor. The entire staircase is shuddering and reverberating under that relentless footfall. She is astounded no one else seems to hear or be paying any attention to it—and that, most important and heartbreaking, her husband and their little daughter are still sound asleep. Granted, the nine-year-old knows nothing about any of this, and isn't supposed to know anything, except that enemies of the people are everywhere and need to be exterminated like rabid Trotskyite dogs—she's just an ordinary, happy Soviet child—but *him*? Her husband? He is amazing to her. He really must have an entirely, totally, and completely unburdened conscience and perfectly untroubled soul. Such a wonderfully lucky man! Just snoring away in their bed in the dark, peacefully and gently, almost melodiously.

Snoring! Snoring away! Fool! Stupid fool! She must do something, *any*thing, right *now*, this very second—wake him up, tell him to run, no time to explain, no time to get dressed, just run, my love, run, run, no matter where, just somewhere, run, anywhere, or maybe just hide under the bed here, yes, what the hell, under there, sure, but no, of course not, not there, well, but somewhere inside the apartment still, where else, lock yourself up in the bathroom, but no, not there, either, oh God, I don't know, hide in the grave digger's room, he's always drunk and wouldn't hear or see anything, his door's unlocked, maybe they wouldn't look in his disgusting room, what with the putrid smell of booze and piss in there, but no, that's not it, either, oh God, I don't know, just do something, anything, my love, do something, jump out the damn window maybe, yes, and hope against hope to land safely down there, by some miracle, miracles do happen, even if they don't, they still do, and run for your life, off into the night, yes, barefoot, no matter, yes, naked, yes, just in your underpants, so what, who cares, yes, across the snow and into the night! *Stop snoring; they'll hear you!*

She needs to calm down. She must stop going

crazy. Nothing has happened yet. Calm down. Breathe. Breathe. Think of something completely different. Something. Anything. If her parents had actually been able to make it to Odessa on time that day back when she was a little girl, she wouldn't be in this predicament right now. She would be in America. Yes, that's true, but then, on the other hand, some other husband would be snoring in her bed right now, if she had a husband there, in America, in that horrible, hellacious place, lair of International Imperialism—and also, of course, some other girl or boy would be sleeping in that hypothetical American room of hers right now, instead of her daughter, if she had any child at all, which would be unthinkable. America, she thinks. Unimaginable. She's already forbidden herself to think about all that, hasn't she? Yes, but so what. Who cares, at this point. What are they going to do to her—*disappear* her? This is not about that anymore. Not about mental crimes, although it always is, of course, in one way or another. This is about the crushing strangeness of life, of how everything in life is intrinsically interconnected. Every single moment in time changes people's lives forever, or at least for generations to come. By doing or not doing something right now, we are altering the future, both our own and that of countless other people near and far. America, she thinks. Unimaginable. If only her parents had made it to Odessa in time for that boat to New York. That would be a disaster, though, too, wouldn't it? But no, this is not about America anymore. Mental crime or not, thinking about America right now is a waste of time, and she has only seconds or, at most, a couple of minutes left. Think again, she tells herself, think of something different, something completely unlike this night, this moment—something wise and beautiful and eternal. Something to sustain her and make her stronger in the darkness about to engulf the three of them in here. "Like fire or like water," as she heard the rabbi in the shtetl synagogue saying once or twice when she was a girl. Like fire, like water. That was something having to do with love, if memory serves her. Love, yes. Love. What's love got to do with any of this? Nothing. Love is not going to pull her through this darkness. It's not what she needs right now. Like fire, like water. Now those words are stuck in her head. Like fire, like water. Like water, like fire. Like the fires of hell! Yes. Mostly hell. Mostly hell. Where did that come from? Spinoza. Yes. Spinoza, the philosopher? Ridiculous. What would Spinoza do in this situation? He would've been *disappeared* and shot through the head a long time ago.

She remembers now: While studying dialectical materialism back at the university, all those years ago, just before the flood of 1924, the year of Lenin's death, at one point she was assigned to read, from a strictly critical perspective, an article by Georgi Plekhanov—former famous Marxist, or an infamous one, rather, a *menshevik*, a deeply flawed and ultimately counterrevolutionary thinker, but also young Lenin's sometime mentor. The article, to the best of her recollection now, was a disquisition on the medieval Dutch philosopher Baruch Spinoza, of all people, and that relatively short text on Spinoza's supposed determinism, the meaning of which last word she hardly could explain anymore, had somehow, fleetingly, piqued her curiosity with regard to that man himself—in part probably because he also came from a shtetl, only in his case it was called a "ghetto," back in feudal times in Holland, and partly because of his childishly funny last name, in which the corporeal, sturdy words *spine* and *nose* were hooked together strongly in a strange and somewhat beautifully discordant fashion. There were no other reasons. She was just curious about him. So she spent a few extra hours at the library, on a couple of quiet evenings, reading up on that medieval philosopher, Spinoza, with no distinct purpose in mind; and at one point she came across a random piece of manifestly superfluous information, which, again for no reason, moved her to a surprising extent—specifically, that on the front of the house in Holland where the solitary philosopher, he of the bent spine and hooked nose, lived for a couple of years in the middle of the seventeenth century, there was, etched into a limestone wall, a quote from some poet friend of his, stating, "Oh, but if all men were wise and acted accordingly! Earth would then be paradise. Now it is mostly Hell." Yes, that's what that inscription said, at least in Russian: *mostly hell. Po preimushchestvu ad.* Mostly hell. She didn't know why she felt quite so . . . stirred, uncharacteristically agitated by those strange and, frankly, frightening words, in spite of their absolute ideological preposterousness and downright counterrevolutionary perniciousness. Mostly Hell. Mostly Hell. That's what an enemy of the people would say—that life *everywhere* on the planet is mostly hell. But not so! Not here, in the USSR! Nothing could be further from the truth! Still, she couldn't help repeating those bizarre words, *mostly hell,* for days afterward in her mind. It was ridiculous, really: to feel emotionally affected by something she'd stumbled upon as a result of perusing some random and generally useless article by the ideologically wobbly and dangerously myopic Plekhanov—some totally retrograde religious absurdity etched into the wall of the ancient Jewish philosopher Spinoza's temporary quarters. Mostly hell? Hell no! That's only true if applied to the capitalist world! Although, objectively speaking, this moment she's in right now—well, it's mostly hell, for her, in all frankness. Such is the terrible truth of her current predicament. It's mental crime, obviously: for her to be having this thought about hell. But to hell with it, for now. Mostly hell. Not true. Yes, true. Mostly hell. There is only one hell in the world, and it's called America, the citadel of International Imperialism. Here, in the USSR, by contrast, the paradise of the radiant Communist future is being built right before our eyes! America and International Imperialism are historically doomed. Mostly hell. Mostly hell. Those steps! Those steps! Mental crime. Stop it!

Her husband needs to stop snoring, *now*. They'll hear him! She must wake him up!

Last month, the geography teacher in their school, a silly and very young girl, fresh from a pedagogical vocational institute, fell asleep, such a stupid little thing, during the weekly *politinformation*, delivered, this time, by a new lecturer from the district Party Committee, a younger and more alert and severe-looking one than the older and slightly deaf, orotund man normally assigned to them; and unfortunately, on top of merely dozing off (which, after all, could've been partly understandable, seeing that she was about to get married the following week and likely had stayed up until dawn the night before, making out and talking about the future with her fiancé, in some dark entryway somewhere in the neighborhood . . . silly, reckless youth!), she also started snoring a little, too, gently and softly—just a tiny bit, quietly and almost inaudibly, but still, apparently, loudly enough for the new lecturer's professionally trained ear to pick up on that near-silent sound coming from one of the middle rows of chairs in Lenin's Hall. He broke off mid-sentence (something about the pragmatic new anti-imperialist international alliance between the Soviet Union and National Socialist Germany) and, having quickly located the poor girl with his cold gray eyes, fixed her with an implacably hard, unblinking stare. Another teacher, one of chemistry, a more mature woman, sitting right next to the girl, elbowed her in the ribs sharply, causing the silly little thing to awaken with a start, her uncomprehending

wild-eyed face all blotched with sleep, flushed with fear
and confusion—but it was already too late. The *politinformation* resumed, after a momentary pause, but for her
it was all over already, and everyone could sense this to
be the case, too. Two days later, she—that young geography teacher—failed to show up at school, and then the
following day, and the one after that, too—and then, just
like that, she was never seen again by anyone. Someone
else, another teacher with basic knowledge of geography,
took over her classes. She had been *disappeared*, vanished
without a trace into the black void of oblivion, and no one
at school would ever speak about her or even mention her
name again, as if she'd never existed . . . which, in a certain
cruel, larger scheme of reality, she never had.

So terrible, the young woman in the night thinks.
So sad. It was her own fault, of course, that silly girl's,
but still: Was it, ultimately, such an altogether unforgivable crime, in the end, from the *organs'* perspective—that
unintentional light snoring of hers, even if it took place
during such an ideologically important event as a *politinformation*? Why did they have to *disappear* her for that, to
extinguish her life forever, so brutally and irrevocably—
just for that one admittedly stupid yet still accidental
and, frankly, minor transgression? It's as if people were
mere motes of dust to them. . . . *Them*? *Them*—who? *The
organs*? *Them*? Yes.

All of a sudden, the young woman in the night is filled
with pure red-hot, scorching rage. She is fairly burning

with fury inside! She is mad as hell! She can hardly contain herself! She wants to scream at the top of her voice! Bastards! Cruel monsters! She hates them, she . . . she hates and loathes them, with absolute, blistering passion! She hates their guts! She despises and detests them all! All of them! Every single one of them! She hates and detests those three out on the staircase, too! *Especially* them! She wishes them dead! She wants them to burn in hell—yes, she knows there's no heaven or hell after death, but no matter, she hopes they'll be burning in hellfire unto eternity, because that's where they belong! She hates, loathes, despises, detests, and hates that heartless, soulless lecturer, that low-life *politinformator* who destroyed the poor silly young girl's life just one week before her wedding! And for what? For nothing! Just because the poor thing fell asleep during his dull, boring talk! Murderer! She . . . She just . . . And she also hates the . . .

But even in the enraged, frenzied state she's in, something is holding her back, and she still is afraid to admit, even to herself, even in the privacy of her boiling mind, that she hates—yes, that's right, she does, and how!—the Great Leader himself, Lenin's rightful heir, the beloved father figure to all the oppressed people on the planet, the wisest and most human and humane and brilliant immortal genius ever to draw breath and walk the Earth! She hates him, but she is fearful of admitting as much even to herself, especially with those three out on the staircase, closing in on their landing.

She hates him. She hates him. There, she did it; it just happened: She just had that unspeakable, unutterable thought—and not for the first time, either!—and . . . well, she's still alive! Maybe not for long, what with those three on the staircase, but—she's still alive in the night! The Great Leader cannot read her mind, apparently, from his always-lighted office in the Spasskaya Tower in the Kremlin, or from the quiet solitary premises of his secret suburban dacha! He is not all that omnipotent, is he? Or maybe he is but just doesn't care about the infinitely insignificant thoughts of the likes of her. Or maybe, again, those three out on the staircase have actually been sent by him, the omnipotent, clairvoyant Great Leader, in advance of her having that thought, because he knew with his supernatural foreknowledge that she was about to have it? Well, perhaps, but who cares now. She's still alive, that old lightning didn't strike her, and the night didn't swallow her whole . . . yet! And yes, indeed: Now that it's all out in the open, she *has* had this monstrous, unthinkable thought before, too—twice! To be sure, on those previous occasions, there was not any kind of premeditated reflection on her part, but, rather, just something that flew in and out of her head for no apparent reason, like a big black bird, leaving her dazed and horrified in its wake, but—a mental crime is a mental crime. She's not making excuses for herself. She hates him, she hates him, she loathes and detests and hates him! There! She hates him more than anyone in the world would ever know! She hates and loathes and despises the Great Leader! She cannot help it! She . . . She is fully aware she is committing the gravest mental crime of all, but what can she do—she just cannot help it. This is stronger than she is. It isn't even she who hates the Great Leader with such relish—it is her inner enemy of the people taking over her entire being. Yes, that's right. She's not in control of herself right now. Her mind and her heart do not belong to her in such moments. They betray her, turn on and against her, having been taken over, taken hostage by that invisible enemy of the people dwelling inside her! That's the truth of it. But, again—no excuses. She is her own worst enemy. She is an enemy of the people. Yes, that's who she is. She probably should be *disappeared*. Only after that, the enemy of the people inside her is going to die, or otherwise leave her body and leave her alone. She can't bear this any longer—this terrible mental sickness of hers, this ugly rot in her heart. She almost wishes those three out on the staircase, already practically here, on their landing, were coming for her tonight, instead of her husband. That would be much fairer, too, even though she knows her turn will also come, no worries. She *deserves* to be *disappeared*. She hates the Great Leader. She does. That's a stubborn fact. She can't help it. She hates him intensely. She loathes him with a vengeance. Her hatred for him is like a wildfire, like a mighty waterfall. It's irrational. Hatred like this, so strong, is almost like love in reverse, actually. Love in reverse, that's right. Like water is fire in reverse, and vice versa. And love in reverse—well, what is it, if not just love, only the opposite kind of itself? Love by any other name is just love. Love is love. Could it be, then, that she actually *loves* the Great Leader, and madly so, while thinking she hates him? Could this be the case? Then, if so, obviously, she does *not* deserve to be *disappeared*. On the contrary. On the contrary—what? Oh, this is such nonsense, just a bunch of stupid sophistry. She hates him, and that's all there is to it. She is sick; she disgusts herself. She wishes—oh, how she wishes!—she could talk to someone, anyone about this: someone to whom she could confess this abominable sickness of hers, this inner fire eating her alive! Then maybe this awful nauseating tightness in her chest frequently bedeviling her, that python squeezing her heart with its lethal coil so hard that she can't breathe—perhaps then she would no longer be experiencing that, either. If only such a person existed somewhere within her reach—someone who would just listen to her, kindly and understandingly, nonjudgmentally! But she knows that's but wishful thinking. There is no one like that in her world—not even her younger sister in Moscow, her one true soul mate, as they used to say in old classical Russian novels, because it would be too unconscionably unfair to saddle that golden heart and innocent mind, her little sister's, with such an impossibly heavy moral burden, such an unspeakably ugly and, possibly, contagious mental crime! Her sister's whole being might then also start being taken over by her own, theretofore dormant, inner enemy of the people, and she would not be strong enough to resist that awakened monster inside her—and who would be, realistically speaking?—and she almost certainly would start losing her mental bearings; and then, in a desperate attempt to preserve her rapidly diminishing sanity and remain a good future-bound Soviet mother to her two girls and an optimistic wife to her husband, she likely would feel compelled to share her older sister's unthinkable secret with her husband, who is a Party member, obviously, and a prominent figure in the Ministry of Construction of some kind of important industry. And then what would happen to all of them? Their lives would be ruined forever, inevitably and irreversibly, that's what. Everyone would end up being *disappeared*. . . . No, confiding in her younger sister would be out of the question. And as for her own husband . . .

The idea of telling her own husband of her hatred of the Great Leader is so outlandish, grotesquely preposterous, and downright absurd on the face of it, the young woman has never even so much as entertained it seriously for one second. She may be sick in her head, but she is not insane. Never, under no circumstances, not even in the slightest of whispers or in the middle of the scariest of nightmares. Not for as long as the a priori deathless Great Leader is still alive. Impossible. It's as simple as that, and she doesn't have to rationalize or explain this to herself. If it needs to be explained, it doesn't need to be explained. . . . Well, for one thing, to start with, a revelation like that could simply kill him on the spot, and quite literally so. His congenitally weak heart, unable to cope with a shock of this magnitude, could just give out instantaneously. And second . . . Of course, the first reason alone would be quite sufficient, in and of itself, for her to keep her silence on the subject. Still, there is much more to it: Specifically, she knows—and she does know this with absolute, clear-eyed certainty, too—that no matter how much he loves and cherishes her (and in that respect, again, she can and should consider herself a truly lucky woman indeed, because he does love and adore her, absolutely and unconditionally!), he still, without a question, most assuredly, would report her to the *organs* right away. Yes, that's right. He would. Indeed. He would turn her in. Definitely. He would sacrifice her, putting this in obsolete religious terms, on the altar of his immeasurable love for the Great Leader. He would, too. Like a burnt offering or something. He would . . . Oh sure, he would be completely crushed, absolutely, totally heartbroken, brokenhearted, in the process of turning her in, and he would be crying copiously, too, yes, most certainly, but he still would go through with it, while still loving and adoring the hell out of her, totally, and assuring her, through spasmodic wet sobs, that he was doing this for her own ultimate good, in order to salvage and preserve unto eternity the unblemished innate purity of her immortal future-bound being, her quintessential sublime *Sovietness*, for the sake of her rightful belonging in posthumous Communist tomorrow, so that she could be cleansed thoroughly from within, scrubbed clean of her inner enemy of the people and thus reclaimed from the dark infernal forces of counterrevolution and International Imperialism, salvaged for future generations' metaphysical memory by the restorative, curative means of an inevitably and necessarily long and harsh but also merciful (in terms of its being preferable to a bullet to the back of the head) Gulag term, and . . . oh, and so on. What's the point in even thinking about this? He would do it, and that's all there is to it. All that matters. Her husband and her best friend, the love of her life, the father of their child—he would do it. Out of love, presumably. But not merely out of love for her alone, either. Oh no. Yes, of course: He would do it—turn her in, give her up, sacrifice her for her own transcendental good as he is capable of comprehending the latter, *precisely* because he loves her so—sure; but he also, and most crucially, would do it because his love for the Great Leader vastly and naturally, by a factor of foul infinity, surpasses his love for her or anyone's mere mortal love for another human being throughout history: The two loves are just altogether noncomparable and noncompatible; they are two entirely different kinds of love! Like fire and water, indeed! His love for the Great Leader, it . . . well, one cannot really view it as *love* per se; it is not love, strictly speaking, but, rather, an enormous, limitless, and constantly expanding, indescribably ardent and fervent devotion, utmost selfless dedication, boundless passion, something that lends the ultimate meaning to his existence, along with that of hundreds of millions, maybe even billions of other hopeful future-bound working people of the world! Without that all-encompassing, all-abiding passion for the Great Leader, in the absence of that all-devouring flame burning inside him, she knows without quite knowing how she knows it, he would be nothing and no one, lost in darkness forever, blind, empty and hollow inside, bereft of meaning, dead, either literally or metaphorically! Without the Great Leader, there is no Party, and without the Party, there is no dream and no hope and no salvation—and thus no reason to live. Without the Party, he's back in the shtetl, in the Pale—in other words, no one, someone not yet born. Without the Great Leader, he has no inner fire to burn in. And he does need a fire to burn in.

She looks at him, sound asleep in the dark, in their bed, snoring peacefully—an overgrown innocent child, really, blissfully unaware of what is about to happen to him in a matter of minutes. Her heart contracts momentarily with an almost unbearable, suffocating tenderness. He is a child, a baby. *Her* child. She is being unfair to him. He loves her. He cannot love her any more than he already does. It's not his fault that he loves the Great Leader more than her, and with a very different kind of love. It's she who is a bad, rotten person. He is good and innocent, much better than she. There is no ugliness to his soul. He would never give her up, betray her. He loves her. He would rather die than . . .

No, he wouldn't. He wouldn't rather die *than*. And in any event, that's a moot question at this point. It's too late now. Too late for everything.

And now the terrible, ponderous joint footfall out on the stairway—heavy, fateful, confident, inescapable, stone on stone, if partly drowned out by the roaring of blood in her ears—has reached their floor. This is it. She braces herself. This is the moment. They are here now, probably looking at the door of the apartment. She holds her breath. A quiet shuffling of feet outside, or maybe it's just her imagination. Doesn't matter. Then nothing. Silence. The crashing waves of blood in her ears subside. They're standing out there in silence, those three, catching their breath, biding their time. Enjoying themselves, too, relishing their unlimited power to instill mortal terror in people's hearts while doing nothing but merely standing silently on a landing. Silence. She goes dead inside. She is stone. Stone. Now, then. Now this is going to happen. The doorbell will ring, and then everything will be over for the three of them in this room. Do it already, you bastards! They will never see one another again. Her parents really should've made it in time for that boat to New York, back then, when she was a little girl. They really should have. Everything would've been different now, there, in America. And now, in a second or two, everything will become different forever here. Everything changes in the world with every instant, every breath one takes. She holds her breath. For as long as she can stay breathless, maybe the world will remain unchanged.

Arzamas, she thinks, out of nowhere. Arzamas. Arzamas . . . What's Arzamas? Strange word, popping into her head for no reason. Why not some other one? It's got something to do with Tolstoy, she vaguely recalls. Lenin's favorite giant mirror of the Russian Revolution. Something she read at the university also, or heard at a lecture on the origins of Tolstoy's worldview. The so-called Arzamas horror, that one night he spent in that town, Arzamas, while in his thirties. One interminable night of endless horror without a clear cause or reason. Not her case right now, for sure. He never was the same person afterward, apparently. Only after that interminable fateful night in Arzamas did he become the great genius known to the world as Leo Tolstoy. Well, to hell with him, she thinks. Who is he to her right now?

She is stone now. Stone. She will not let them see her humiliation.

One must always have dignity. Must one? One must. But then again—no. Who cares. To hell with that also. Who needs her dignity anymore? She must do something to come alive, to be able to move again before this all happens, to unstone herself, this very instant! To do something, anything! She has to wake them up, both of them, her husband and her daughter, right now, so at least they can say good-bye to one another just between the three of them—without those demons in the room! Before it's too late.

It already is too late now, though. Yes, maybe, but still. Even when it's too late, it still isn't too late, or at least may not be. Even when it's too late, it's not too late still. Yes. She doesn't know how she knows this. Isn't it something Tolstoy wrote about somewhere, too? Well, he was wrong about that also, that rich count. She attempts to move and fails, finds herself unable to force her body to become hers again, to stir herself into motion. She must try again, even if only to fail again. She tries and fails again. She fails once again, too. Try again. She tries again. Finally, she manages to shake herself out of her petrified, frozen state, to unpeel herself from the wall and take a small, tiny step into the room's simultaneously deepening and receding darkness, toward her husband and her daughter.

She starts moving—but then, immediately, she stops. She freezes again, because just at that very instant, simply and ordinarily, mundanely, flatly and prosaically—as if this were no big deal, but, rather, something perfectly par for the course, the presence of those three outside the door: just some armed strangers in heavy boots, two in soldier's uniforms and one in an ankle-length black leather coat, lounging out on the staircase in the middle of the night, just hanging out, whiling away the time with nothing better to do, that's it, nothing more, with a *black raven* waiting down in the courtyard, its engine silent and lights cut out—the footsteps resume, but their sound is less ominous now, somehow, as the three, apparently, start moving away across the landing and proceed to climb the last, the fifth, flight of stairs. There is, of course, one more floor above this one—how could she possibly have lost sight of that simple fact? The last, the fifth, floor—that's where they're headed! She can't believe herself, her stupidity. What a fool. She was so panicked and, as a result, so insanely and ridiculously self-centered from the very first moment of hearing the sound of the automobile, so preoccupied with her own dire premonitions and forebodings, she completely overlooked the glaring circumstance that there might actually be some other *disappearance*-worthy people in other apartments in their stairway. Truly shameful of her! Shameful is the degree of her bourgeois self-absorption! Really! Just because her husband is the only prominent young Party and Komsomol activist among the tenants in apartments below and above theirs, that doesn't necessarily and automatically mean that . . . Oh God. What *does* it mean? It means nothing. Anyone can be *disappeared* at any time, on any given night, that's the truth of it. She doesn't know what to think. Nothing here to think about. Nothing means anything right now. She's a fool, and that's all. She is pathetic. Those three from the *black raven*, they were merely taking a quick respite, a breather outside their door. The flights of stairs in this building are tall and steep. Such a damn fool she is.

And now what? Is it over, then? That, she thinks, would be unimaginable. *Is* it over, though? It depends on what *is* is. And what *it* is, too. Suddenly feeling cold and naked in nothing but her flimsy nightgown—even though she knows it's hot in the room—she slides down the wall and sits up on the floor, shivering minutely, filled with emptiness, her arms encircling her drawn-up knees. It's over, she tells herself, unable to stop shivering. It's over. Over . . .

And it is, or seems to be. Their lives have been spared, for the moment. For the time being. They've been allowed to keep on living for a while longer—the three of them in this room. Summer will come, she thinks, shivering, and they'll be strolling along the Nevsky in summery clothes, the three of them, smiling at the sky, buying ice cream from dignified street vendors in white smocks. Summer will come, as it always does. Young people in love will be kissing right on the street. Old people will be cooing over their grandbabies. Life is life, for as long as one's not dead, and it always reasserts itself in the end, no matter what. Always. No matter the *black ravens* down in court-yards. No matter the heavy footsteps past midnight on the staircase. No matter anything. Life is life. People can get used to everything.

She feels exhausted, hollowed out. Nothing is over yet, she knows. This time, death has decided to let them keep on living for the time being. It took one quick, cursory look around the room and decided to move on, for now. But there have been no promises made, no guarantees given. Death could be back at any time. Lightning is under no obligation not to strike the same tree twice—or even ten times in a row. . . . She is crouched on the floor in the dark.

So then, she thinks dispassionately, it's going to be someone else tonight—one of those up in the only apartment on the fifth floor. There are seven tenants in that apartment on the fifth floor. She knows who it's going to be tonight, too. The one about to be *disappeared*. That's no great mystery. There's only one prominent, *nomenklatura* couple of any potential interest to the *organs* up there. It's going to be the husband. She is friends—well, not really friends, but sort of friends, friends in a manner of speaking only, not really close friends or anything, not even distant ones or friends at all, strictly speaking, just acquaintances maybe, and not really very good ones at that, just in case the *organs* might want to start wondering at some point, which hopefully they won't—with the wife of that man about to be *disappeared* tonight: a reasonably nice (but then again, who can know anything for certain these days as to who is nice and who, on the contrary, is just a deceptively friendly covert enemy of the people?) woman in her early forties—head of their district children's library, which is an ideologically important position, of course, and one almost certainly necessitating a Party membership, as well, if not quite a *nomenklatura*-level one. And that woman's husband certainly is a *nomenklatura*-level person. So it's going to be him tonight. Well, so be it, then, the young woman thinks. That's life. And that's death, too. Or maybe it actually could be both of them, she thinks, the husband *and* the wife, because she, that children's librarian, could also turn out to be an enemy of the people in her own right, irrespective of her husband, who for dead certain is about to be *disappeared* tonight. Still, whatever's going to happen, right now or in a few minutes or seconds, that librarian woman is a reasonably nice person, the young woman thinks, at least on the surface of her public persona. So if it turns out she is not in fact an enemy of the people herself, that would be sad, because her life is going to be ruined irrevocably in any event—although, on the other hand, one must have faith in the *organs'* judgment. The *organs*, as everyone knows, never make any mistakes. Who knows, who can tell anything for certain these days? . . . She feels exasperated. That's not up to her to try to figure it all out—who is or isn't an enemy of the people. That's up to the *organs* to determine. If the *organs* say she is an enemy of the people, then she must be one. The fact of one's having been *disappeared* by the *organs* is all the proof of one's incontrovertible guilt any Soviet court would ever need. The *organs*, as every Soviet child knows, are infallible. . . . Oh, rubbish. Nonsense. Enough. In any event, what's it to her, the young woman in the night? She's got her own family and her own life to think about. It's not like she's some kind of bosom pals with that librarian, let alone her husband. Her husband—well, he's another one. There is nothing openly, overtly objectionable about him, nothing to put your finger on in that respect, on the face of it—he's invariably polite with everyone, though maybe a little *too* polite, and also a little too curt and impersonal in his manner, as if constantly immersed in deep thought, which probably could actually be the case, considering he, apparently, is the chief engineer at one of the city's largest paper-goods factories: obviously, a Party *nomenklatura* position, which is why it's his turn to be *disappeared* tonight. . . . His turn, yes. His turn? Yes. His. They give the impression of a perfect Soviet couple, those two: goal-oriented, future-bound, publicly responsible, socially useful and optimistic. These days, however, who can tell anything with any certainty? No one. Only the *organs* can. She is going around in circles in her mind. Enemies of the people are everywhere. They just keep multiplying. Extremely devious and resourceful they are. Snakes, rabid dogs, sheep in wolf's clothing! That's enough, she thinks. Anyway, she never felt too close to them. Not in the least, actually. As a matter of fact, if one were to ask her about them—which, hopefully, would never happen, because why would anyone do it?—she'd say she always experienced some certain distinct unease being around them, that couple, whenever she bumped into one or both of them occasionally outside the apartment building or on the staircase. She's always harbored—yes, that's the word: *harbored*—some vague suspicion as to their innermost core. Not enough of a suspicion to warrant alerting the *organs* perhaps, or even her husband, but still . . . definitely some distinct unease. She knows nothing of any substance about them. At least they don't have children, those two, she thinks, suddenly pierced by a needle of sadness. That's a bit of a silver lining.

She's listening to the steps out on the stairs. Those three have almost reached the last floor landing already. And now they have. Again, momentary silence.

It's unfortunate, an unfortunate circumstance, she thinks, an unfortunate coincidence that those two occupy the room directly above theirs. (And how does she know this? one might ask. Has she ever been inside their room? Huh? No, no. She knows this because . . . well, she just knows it, that's all. How could she not? Seriously.) Thankfully, she probably—well, certainly—will hear nothing of what's going to happen up there now, in a minute or two, because ceilings in this old and sturdy building are tall and thick and the floor in that room directly above theirs must additionally be covered with a lush Uzbek carpet (she's never been inside that room, so she doesn't really know for certain about the carpet, see?), as a result of which those two up there can, or could, literally never be heard down here—not their steps as they move, or used to move, about their room, nor the footsteps of any of their hypothetical guests, and certainly none of their conversations. No conversations of any kind! Never, absolutely not—neither their own up there nor, much less, those of their presumptive guests, so there really would be nothing for her or her husband to tell the *organs* on the subject. Much as they would've been eager to tell the *organs* everything, of course.

But they've got nothing to tell. Nothing at all, or else she and her husband would've informed the *organs* right away a long time ago. They—she and her husband—have nothing to hide. But should there still be any lingering doubts in that regard, then someone from the *organs* could come in here, into this room (although, to be frank, hopefully not), while having one of his colleagues walk around or stand still and talk loudly to himself or someone else up there, in that room directly above, already occupied by some lucky family of the *disappeared* couple's former apartment neighbors—but empty at the moment, for the sake of the experiment's purity—and then any objective person, as all the people working for the *organs* are known to be, without exception, would be able to hear, or *not* hear, rather, for himself. There is absolutely no acoustic penetration down here from up there, through the ceiling—zero, none. Nothing to report. Unfortunately.

She feels nauseated by the shameful strain of her thoughts. It's sad, she thinks. It's just sad. The way it all happens. Tonight it will be him, the polite engineer—and then, a few days later, inevitably, his wife, the librarian. It's their turn to be *disappeared* this time. There's nothing to be done about it. It's terrible, really. But then again . . . Oh, she doesn't know. She doesn't know anything. At least they don't have children.

Her breathing is shallow, spasmodic. She tells herself she needs to calm down. She must be strong now, stronger than before, especially considering her husband's congenitally weak heart, because it was a very close encounter with *disappearance* they had tonight, the three of them. She needs to be stronger than before for their daughter. Whatever that might mean. She doesn't know how, exactly, her being stronger than before could be of any help the next time the *black raven* materializes in the inner courtyard below, but she knows she needs to be strong, which means she should be prepared for anything. Because of everything.

She holds her breath, for as long as she can, while counting to ten, perhaps a little too quickly, before exhaling slowly—and to her surprise, it works. She takes three more deep breaths. There. Better now. She can breathe again. That's life, she tells herself again, although she doesn't quite know what she means by that. That's life. Life is life. It is what it is. Life is life, and life is the way it is. Things happen to people all the time in life. All kinds of things. Mainly bad ones. That's just a fact of life. Every night it has to be someone's turn, it just must be, and that's all there is to it—that's life's mandatory-participation lottery, and all lotteries are alike, in terms of the total randomness of their outcome, only this one is a bad, negative lottery, one with a minus sign drawn across its every ticket; a lottery whose winners are its losers, the accidental ill-starred recipients of the worst of luck. Tonight it's the engineer's turn, up there, in that apartment directly above, and then his wife's. They might well turn out to be real enemies of the people, too—who knows? Probably not, but—who knows? That's not the point, or not the whole point—although for them, those two, obviously, it's the end of everything. The point is . . . But she doesn't know what the point of it all is. The point is, life is life, and there are no time periods in history, and no geographic locations, free of the negative lotteries of their own. Because people keep dying constantly, for one thing—and what is death, in most instances, if not an unlucky lottery ticket? Every one hundred years, the entire population of the planet disappears forever, as if washed away by a giant tsunami wave, and is replaced by an entirely new human multitude. And so it goes. At this very moment, as she is sitting on the floor in the dark, in the impenetrable boreal night, in a square room with a red-painted door in a communal apartment in an old apartment building in the middle of one of the world's unlikeliest and most artificial and beautiful cities in the seabound northwestern part of the world's largest and strangest and cruellest and most incomprehensible and most terrible country, one or more people within the same city area have died of a heart attack or a stroke, or have finally succumbed to cancer. For them, those newly dead, it's all over now, for better or worse. Nothing more to fear, to fret about, or to aspire to. They're done with life, so they can rest now in their eternal nonexistence. Their work in this world is over. Their task—to go through life from the very beginning to the very end, from one nonexistence to the next, a more permanent one; from a newborn's cry to the silence of a chunk of dead protoplasm—is complete.

They're done here. Good for them. Lots of those still living envy them. But everyone has to wait for one's own turn. When it's time, it's time. No earlier and no later. . . . Oh, what is she thinking about in the middle of the night! So stupid. Her thoughts have a bourgeois cast to them, a touch of historical determinism, the kind Plekhanov ascribed erroneously to Spinoza—or maybe not. She has no idea about anything. At least they don't have children, those two in the room overhead. Life is life. It's more than most people can cope with. It can be a terrible thing. She needs to go back to bed.

There comes, from the floor landing above, a distant, muffled, yet still confidently insistent sound of a doorbell ringing.

She is sitting there, on the floor, in the dark, in that square room with the ceramic woodstove and red-painted door, with her eyes closed. The year is 1939.

In a few months, it will be spring, and then summertime, she thinks again. The streets will be filled with smiling people in bright clothes made of breathable fabrics. People will be buying ice cream and thick glass mugs of cold *kvas* from dignified street vendors in white smocks. Everyone will be looking happy. Life will be good to everyone. But still, every night, without fail, after the midnight hour, scores of hunchbacked black automobiles, *black ravens,* some with their lights turned off and some not, will be taking sole possession of the deserted city streets, speeding along with unyielding, ironclad purpose and suddenly and seemingly on a whim swerving now and then under some low-slung blind archway and into the silent interior courtyard of some large or small apartment building, and shuddering to a halt there, in front of this or that ill-starred stairway. A few seconds later, the heavy automobile door will be pushed open from within, slowly, as though reluctantly, and three men will emerge into uncertain visibility: two armed soldiers and a nondescript short character in a long black leather overcoat, wide-brimmed fedora, and round steel-rimmed spectacles. The night will be perfectly still. Inside the looming dark building, in one or more of its communal apartments, people will be watching, peeking out through the narrow crack between the curtain and the window's edge, mortified with dread, their hearts pounding in their chests. Everything will be the same. Nothing will be different here.

She doesn't want to think of anything anymore.

In that old 1939 photo, Grandfather gazes right at me, through the multilayered distance of sixty-nine years, but Grandmother's eyes are averted. She is half-smiling, while he is serious. She seems happy. Both of them are young and alive. Their nine-year-old daughter—my mother—is looking into the camera with grown-up solemnity. No one knows what lies ahead. That's the way it was, then.

He would die at sixty-nine, of a third consecutive heart attack—and incidentally, had he been living in our time, I've been told by people who know such things, he would've had a routine bypass surgery in the morning and been back home the same evening; but sadly, one doesn't get to choose the time and place of one's birth—and she would have her first and lethal heart attack seven years later, while standing over his grave at Leningrad's Jewish cemetery. Sounds contrived in a cloying "literary" way, I know—too "written," too overtly dramatic to seem credible—but that's exactly where and how she died. Life can take a lot more strangeness than any fiction ever could. It has no truck with verisimilitude and is under no obligation to unfold in accordance with our notions of reality, especially at the moment of its collusion with death.

The young woman gets up off the floor, tiptoes back to bed, and slides in under the blanket, next to her sleeping husband. It's over, she tells herself again, over, over—although she knows that's not true. Nothing is over. Nothing ever is.

She can hear steps above her head.

U.S. Border, Midnight

C USTOMS BORDER PATROL OFFICER—a tall, burly, somewhat goofy-looking young man—waves me over, saying something I cannot make out because of the general din in the large, echoing space.

ME (approaching, handing him my passport, taking off my hat): Hi, how are you?

CBPO: Professor?

ME: I beg your pardon?

CBPO (chuckling ironically): Are you a professor, by any chance?

ME: Yes I am, actually. How did you . . .

CBPO (grinning): Didn't you hear me just now, when I said *professor*, looking at you? I immediately thought, when I saw you, This man must be a professor; he just looks like one. That's why I said *professor*! And you're telling me now you actually *are* a professor?

ME: Yes, I actually am. Huh. This is really funny.

CBPO: You could say that again. It's kinda hilarious.

We look at each other, smiling, for a couple of seconds.

CBPO: Well, and where and what do you profess, professor, if I may be permitted to ask?

ME: At a university up in Montreal. Creative writing, literature . . . you know.

CBPO: Creative writing? You mean stories and stuff?

ME: Yes. Stories and stuff.

CBPO: I was in a writing workshop once, in high school. Wrote a story about a man who's, like, driving on a highway all through the night, and it's, like, pitch-dark outside, because it's nighttime, but then it gets to be dawn, in theory, and then morning and so on, but it's still just as dark everywhere, endless darkness, and he realizes, much to his horror, that it's going to be like this forever now, going forward—the sun's just forgotten to come up, like, for the first time in a billion years, so he'll always be doomed to keep driving on this empty highway in the dark now, with no destination in sight, for the rest of his natural life. Also, he has this magical capacity to turn invisible at will, that dude driving in the dark, after drinking this secret potionlike admixture of his own invention. He would turn invisible and start punishing bad people in that state. Like an invisible, and therefore much more efficient, Batman. That's kind of a parallel story line. But his dog, his only true friend, an Afghan so beautiful, no one ever believes he actually is its owner, which constantly pisses him off a little—the dog doesn't have the same ability to turn invisible, and that leads to a whole bunch of serious complications in his life.

ME: Sounds interesting.

CBPO: Nah, it was stupid. But anyway . . . Actually, let me ask you, since I have an actual professor in front of me: How do you tell people that their stories, like, suck? Which I'm sure they often do. You know? . . . I guess what I'm actually asking is, how can you tell a good story from a bad one in the first place? How do you always know?

ME: I don't always know. But I'll tell you, it's much easier to say why a poorly written story is bad than why a really good story is good.

CBPO: Yeah, I suppose. Although, frankly, I didn't understand what you just said. But anyway . . . So, you live in Montreal?

ME: I do.

CBPO (lowering his voice): So . . . how is it up there?

ME (also lowering my voice): It's okay.

CBPO (lowering his voice even further): And you were born in Russia?

ME (practically whispering): I was.

CBPO: A strange choice of a place to be born. Well, anyway . . . Cool coincidence, wouldn't you say?

ME: Yeah. Really unusual. Shall we take a selfie together?

We both laugh. He hands me back my passport. I start walking away.

CPBO: Oh, by the way! You're not bringing in any illegal substances, are you?

ME (turning back mid-stride): No way.

CBPO: Didn't think so, but still thought I'd ask.

Publication Credits

The Night Andropov Died: newyorker.com,
June 17, 2014

Some of the World Transactions My Father Has Missed Due to His Death on September 14, 1999:
Land-Grant College Review, no. 1, June 1, 2003

Necessary Evil: *Guernica,* January 15, 2014

Klodt's Horses: *The Literarian,* no. 10, October 3, 2013

Why? Why?? Why???: newyorker.com,
December 12, 2012

Sentence: newyorker.com, September 4, 2014

A Soviet Twelve Days of Christmas: newyorker.com,
December 20, 2013

The Night We Were Told Brezhnev Was Dead: *Apofenie,*
July 5, 2020

Moscow Windows: *Guernica,* May 2, 2016

Our Entire Nation: *Fourteen Hills,* vol. 10, no. 1,
Winter/Spring 2004 (in a slightly different form)

Flying Cranes: *Boulevard,* nos. 34 & 35, December 1997
(in a slightly different form)

April 1st, Sunset Hour: *Cosmonauts Avenue,* Winter 2015

First Death: *Inertia Magazine,* no. 14, April 2016

The Beginning of a Long Road: *Witness,* vol. 25, no. 3, Fall 2012

Almost Nine: *Manoa,* vol. 5, no. 1, Summer 1993 (in a slightly different form)

Life: How Was It?: newyorker.com, March 13, 2013

BELLEVUE LITERARY PRESS is devoted to publishing
literary fiction and nonfiction at the intersection of
the arts and sciences because we believe that science and the
humanities are natural companions for understanding the
human experience. We feature exceptional literature that
explores the nature of perception and the underpinnings of
the social contract. With each book we publish, our goal is
to foster a rich, interdisciplinary dialogue that will forge new
tools for thinking and engaging with the world.

To support our press and its mission, and for our full catalogue
of published titles, please visit us at blpress.org.

BELLEVUE LITERARY PRESS
New York